A Certain Magical Index

6

KAZUMA KAMACHI

ILLUSTRATION BY
KIYOTAKA HAIMURA

"H-Hey, wait. Miss Komoe, what is…?"

Academy City high school student **Touma Kamijou**

"W-Wow! That must be that *high-tech* thing Touma was talking about!"

Nun managing the Index of Prohibited Books **Index**

".........Umm..."

Transfer student
Hyouka Kazakiri

"Wh-What's the matter with crying?! Every single year, the tears just come out on their own! I can't help it!"

Touma Kamijou's homeroom teacher **Komoe Tsukuyomi**

"Oh, come on, don't cry. If that's all it takes to make you cry, then you'll be bawling your eyes out during graduation!"

Gym teacher **Aiho Yomikawa**

"…Oh, oh my. At a time like this, too. How very bold of you."

Mikoto's roommate **Kuroko Shirai**

"What exactly are you doing here with a girl on top of you?"

Tokiwadai Middle School student **Mikoto Misaka**

"I'm starting a war, and I need a trigger for it…right, Ellis?"

English Puritan sorcerer **Sherry Cromwell**

contents

A Certain Magical Index

VOLUME 6

KAZUMA KAMACHI

ILLUSTRATION BY: KIYOTAKA HAIMURA

YEN ON

NEW YORK

A CERTAIN MAGICAL INDEX, Volume 6
KAZUMA KAMACHI

Translation by Andrew Prowse

TOARU MAJYUTSU NO INDEX
©KAZUMA KAMACHI 2005
All rights reserved.
Edited by ASCII MEDIA WORKS
First published in Japan in 2005 by KADOKAWA CORPORATION, Tokyo.
English translation rights arranged with KADOKAWA CORPORATION, Tokyo,
through Tuttle-Mori Agency, Inc., Tokyo.

English translation © 2016 Hachette Book Group, Inc.

Yen On
Hachette Book Group
1290 Avenue of the Americas
New York, NY 10104

www.hachettebookgroup.com
www.yenpress.com

Yen On is an imprint of Hachette Book Group, Inc.
The Yen On name and logo are trademarks of Hachette Book Group, Inc.

The publisher is not responsible for websites (or their content) that are not owned by the publisher.

First Yen On edition: February 2016

ISBN: 978-0-316-34060-1

10 9 8 7 6 5 4 3 2 1

RRD-C

Printed in the United States of America

PROLOGUE
In Front of the Backstage

In Academy City, there was a windowless building.

It had no doors, windows, hallways, or stairs—it was a building that served no function. Without using teleportation—a Level Four ability—you couldn't even get into it. At the center of one of its secret rooms was enshrined a giant, cylindrical container.

This cylinder, made from reinforced glass, was four meters in diameter and ten meters tall. Each of the room's four walls was completely covered in a variety of machines and devices. Tens of thousands of cords and tubes extended from them. They crawled about and mingled on the floor, finally connecting to the glass tube in the middle.

This windowless room was always in pitch darkness—save for the lights given off by the machines' lamps and monitors. These lights created a wide circle around the tube, twinkling and sparkling like a starry night sky.

A person in a green surgical gown floated upside down in the red fluid filling the tube.

This person was the Academy City general board chairman, Aleister.

The figure looked both male and female, both old and young, both saintly and sinful. It had given all of its biological functions over to machines, and in doing so, had acquired an estimated lifespan of 1,700 years. The entire body, including the brain, was in a nearly comatose state. Most of its thought processes were assisted by machines.

...Now then, let's begin.

As if on cue, the very moment Aleister thought those words, two figures suddenly appeared before the cylinder. One was a petite girl—a user of teleportation. Holding her hand was a tall man, whom she had escorted here.

The teleporter silently gave a slight bow, then disappeared once again into thin air.

Only the tall man was left in the darkness.

He was a young adult who hid his eyes behind blue sunglasses. His short, blond hair was spiked up. He wore a Hawaiian shirt and shorts, an outfit wholly inappropriate for the place he was in.

He was Motoharu Tsuchimikado, one of Academy City's pawns. He leaked information to them regarding the English Puritan Church.

"Security's more lax than ever. Are you fooling around or something?" he asked irritably of his employer. He was a spy but far from some submissive toady.

His brisk tone would have caused his acquaintances to recoil in surprise. Aleister smiled faintly at his clear dissatisfaction.

He replied, "It matters not. We are in pursuit of the intruder as well. We have plenty of options. Simply by changing the route a bit, I can reduce plan 2082 to 2377—"

"Let me tell you something," Tsuchimikado interrupted, slamming a report against the glass cylinder. Clipped to it was a candid photograph showing the visage of the female intruder.

She appeared to be in her late twenties. Her blond hair and distinctive brown skin clearly placed her homeland elsewhere. Her hair, though, was mussed and messy like a cheap theater wig. It looked like she didn't care for it properly. From the back, her silhouette evoked the image of a lion. She wore a jet-black dress decorated end-to-end with white lace in the classic gothic lolita fashion. Its fabric, however, had been worn through, and the lace was frayed and faded. She obviously wore the extravagant clothing on a daily basis.

"Sherry Cromwell. She's no wandering sorcerer—she's a member of the English Church's Necessarius. This isn't like the problem we had with Aureolus." Tsuchimikado's expression was irritated, as though he'd been forced to quit smoking. He continued. "The English Puritan Church is like any other human organization. It's not monolithic. In fact, in terms of its composition, it's the most complicated state religion in the world. You understand all this, of course!"

"Beloved neighbors quarreling amongst themselves. What a delightful workplace, is it not?"

"You got that right." Tsuchimikado sighed. "But it means it has as many different ideals as it has factions, and not all of them are so keen on cooperating with Academy City. Some of them even want to colonize the entire world under the British flag. You may have an arrangement with our princess, but we don't know how far that's going to go."

There were those among the many factions who went so far as to be suspicious of the agreement between the leaders of English Puritanism and Academy City. After all, Index, a treasure trove of knowledge, now resided in the city. There wasn't a doubt in their minds that she presented a very real danger of the Church's secrets being leaked. Of course, these people probably had no idea that the Knights, an organization separate from Necessarius, were actually absent from their assigned duty of maintaining Index's security.

But it got even worse than that. Even within the Knights, there was a faction that, even after all this time, had inherited the conquering mindset from the age of the Crusades. They viewed Academy City as so dangerous that if Tsuchimikado hadn't been manipulating the information as well as he was, they might have already made moves to subjugate it.

"I can plant ideas in *some* minds when I infiltrate the Church, but only to a certain extent. I can't touch the differences between their groups and factions. And even if I did, the information we've been controlling would end up getting altered somewhere along the line."

He paused there for a moment, then continued.

"And besides, I had my hands full just dealing with the Aureolus situation! Sorcerers must be the ones to judge sorcerers—you would understand that rule far better than I do. Academy City has its science, and the Church its mysteries. We both gain an advantage by having sole possession over our respective technology. Just try to get someone from Academy City to destroy a sorcerer. We defend our technology to the death—just the fact that monopoly could *possibly* leak would cause enormous political issues."

A young man named Touma Kamijou had fought against a number of sorcerers in the month or so prior. However, the city had made a deal with the Church beforehand in the cases of Stiyl and Kanzaki, and Aureolus and Yamisaka were wandering sorcerers not attached to the Church at all. Discord on those fronts had been mostly avoided.

This situation, though, required far more caution. The sorcerer intruding on Academy City possessed many original techniques and spells from English Puritanism. There was no deal this time, either. They couldn't be sure whether a certain faction had put Sherry up to this or if she was acting on her own. Even if responsibility did fall squarely on her shoulders, however, they couldn't take her down carelessly.

Among her peers at the Royal Academy of Arts, Sherry was the most accomplished decoder of symbolic artwork. *Symbolic artwork* referred to pictures into which the contents of grimoires were encrypted. Imagine, for example, a painting of a boat floating on the sea, seen from above. The sun is setting over the horizon, bathing the entire image in the golden glow of evening.

Normal people would think of it as nothing more than a landscape. However, the seawater represented *salt* and the sunlight *gold*—and if you put those two facts together, you could figure out that the painting was describing a magical method of using gold and salt to gain fishlike swimming abilities.

In addition, the color and thickness of the paint, the time being evening, the perspective above the boat...Every single part of the painting, down to its most minute details, had some sort of encoded meaning. Oftentimes, hundreds of years would go by before someone realized that a piece of symbolic artwork had been read incorrectly. Becoming a true specialist in this field was incredibly difficult.

If Index's task was the collection and storage of knowledge, then Sherry was an expert at using cipher techniques to seal and unseal that knowledge. If she fell into the hands of another group, then the complex, mysterious decoding arts so long protected by the English Puritan Church would be laid bare to the world.

If they took her down without due caution, it would cause relations between the Church and Academy City to begin cracking apart. If the faction that sent her here held ill will toward the city, those cracks would be all the larger.

Tsuchimikado didn't dare say any more than that aloud, though.

Rather, he *could* not. The sentence caught in his throat, then decided instead to speak itself in his chest.

The worst-case scenario would be a war of the worlds—a war between science and the Church.

He continued, glaring at Aleister. "Well, as long as we don't make any stupid choices, we won't fan the flames at all, but someone might drown under the water we use to put them out. Secret machinations always come with collateral damage. What are you thinking, exactly? You could have easily shored up security and prevented far worse breaches than this," he spat. "Anyway, I'll defeat her. If a sorcerer does it, it will make the shock waves a little smaller, at least. And I quit being a spy after this, too. It'll be more than enough for them to call my loyalties into question. For God's sake...I may be good at worming my way into psychological blind spots, but even I wouldn't be able to do shit as a spy if I was being monitored around the—"

"You needn't do a thing," Aleister cut in. Tsuchimikado froze for a moment.

He didn't understand what Aleister was trying to say.

"I said, you needn't do a thing."

"...Are you serious?" he responded, sounding very much like he doubted Aleister's sanity. "The probability's not zero, that's for sure. Covert ops is like getting from one skyscraper to another on a tightrope. Slip up one time and *bam*, we're at war!"

When blueprints of weapons of mass destruction get leaked to other countries, that's justification enough to wage war. Arresting a sorcerer within Academy City would carry the same weight.

As long as nothing major happened, it wouldn't end in all-out war. But if something *did*, then it *would*. It wouldn't be a war between nations—it would transcend borders. It would truly be a world war.

There wasn't a major power gap between Academy City's science and the Church's occult practices. If a conflict actually started, it would be a protracted one.

"Aleister, what are you thinking? Is the prospect of throwing Touma Kamijou at sorcerers that attractive to you? His right hand may be your anti-magic trump card, but it can't take down the entire Church by itself!"

"I can reduce Plan 2082 to 2377. That is my only reason. Why do you ask?"

Tsuchimikado caught his breath at that.

Plan, Aleister had said—but the nuance was closer to a *procedure*.

Whenever Aleister used that word, it only referred to one thing.

"A method for controlling the ith School District...the Five Elements Society," murmured Tsuchimikado hatefully. The ith School District—with i being the symbol for an imaginary number—was said to be the laboratory that started Academy City itself, but nobody knew where it was now or even if it existed at all. It was treated as an illusion. An urban myth. The rumors went that it had imaginary technology that even current engineering couldn't reproduce. Some even thought that it secretly held complete sway over the city's matters.

The Church and the sorcerers on the "outside" seemed to think it referred to this very building, but *they were wrong*. This place wasn't anything like that. And the truth would never be told to them.

There was no way they could tell them. They couldn't possibly reveal that something with such an immense effect on the city was, in fact, something *nobody could control* and *no one knew the reason for.*

As the ruler of Academy City, Aleister needed to use any means necessary to gain an understanding of how to control the Five Elements Society. Actually, in all likelihood, he already *knew* the way to control it. However, they didn't have the resources necessary to carry it out—they didn't have the *key.*

It was more of a procedure, similar to how the Level Six Shift experiment with Accelerator was carried out. The key needed to be created in the same way—through a specific sequence of incidents and problems occurring.

At the center of that *procedure* was a single boy:

Touma Kamijou.

Aleister had planned to involve him in the process from the beginning, but Tsuchimikado suspected that they hadn't counted on the magical battles with Index and the alchemist. Every time something out of the ordinary happened, Aleister would rearrange the plans. Not only would they correct their mistakes, but they'd use them to their advantage, thus reducing the enormous procedure little by little.

So even Sherry Cromwell is factored into it.

Aleister's procedure would end at some point, even if they didn't meddle here.

"All…for that?"

"Given this city's military power and influence, its significance cannot be understated. It is like a runaway horse that could tear the world apart, after all. The safest thing to do is to grab the reins as soon as possible."

Aleister smiled thinly. Tsuchimikado couldn't sense any one emotion from the gesture. It looked happy, it looked mocking, it looked sad, and it looked pleased, all at the same time. Every feeling he could think of was contained within it.

This is insane, he thought with a *tsk.* He would just ignore Aleister's orders and deal with Sherry himself if he could, but that wouldn't happen, either.

He had no way of getting out of this building in the first place. It had no exit. No doors, no windows, no hallways, and no stairs. There wasn't even ventilation—even the necessary air around them was manufactured by on-site facilities. On top of all that, the building was strong enough to withstand the blast wave from a nuclear bomb.

Depending on the situation, it was even nastier than being confined in a bank vault or a nuclear shelter. It inspired levels of despair akin to being trapped without a space suit in a shuttle blasting out of the atmosphere.

"And I can't contact anyone outside it, either. Hey, Aleister, use that connection of yours and call that teleporter back. Otherwise, I'll pull every single cord out of that damn thing of yours."

"I don't mind. If you wish to relieve stress, then please do as much as you'd like."

Tsuchimikado made a sour face. He had dimly suspected this before, but all the tubes, cords, and machines in this room were probably dummies. If this room alone was enough to cover Aleister's life support, the building wouldn't need to be this giant. The cylindrical tube itself was probably one big lie, too. Maybe it was actually a huge hologram projector.

He turned his back to the floating Aleister and asked once to be sure.

"You're *positive* you can avoid war before it happens, right?"

"I should be asking you that—it *is* your job to scuttle around behind the scenes. You must be the one to have confidence. What? Depending on how well you do, these *secret machinations* of mine may avoid collateral damage entirely."

Shit, he spat.

This is what it always came down to—always doing jobs like this.

CHAPTER 1

Entrance Ceremony

Baby_Queen.

1

September 1st, early morning.

Academy City, which encompassed one-third of the Tokyo metropolitan area, was suffused with cool air despite the sunlight pouring down on it. People were few and far between, too—only middle school students walking their dogs and college students out for a jog were around. The propellers of the wind turbines here and there spun slowly, churning the cool, forestlike air.

And…

Touma Kamijou limped through this clear, cool scene, completely exhausted.

"I-I'm beat…This was definitely *not* a normal day in the life of a high school student…"

The high school boy's T-shirt and pants were sopping wet, as though he'd just run a marathon. His body felt twice as heavy thanks to his clothing absorbing all the moisture.

When you got right down to it, the previous day, August 31st, had been the root cause of everything.

That night, Kamijou met a man named Ouma Yamisaka. And then they both left Academy City in order to save a woman the man knew.

"Left"—as in "broke through by force." Academy City was encircled by a wall, and a police-like force guarded it. They didn't allow anyone out without permission. If Yamisaka hadn't helped, it would have actually been difficult. The sorcerer had a convenient spell called "Beguiling Bowstring" that made the capturing forces *think* Kamijou and Yamisaka had permission to leave. Mental defenses varied from person to person, though, so the technique itself was somewhat capricious. Sometimes they had to take a more forceful approach.

"...It doesn't even make sense. He risked his life to get through that security net, but then what? Do all sorcerers mercilessly beat the shit out of amateurs? Damn, if I had a journal, yesterday would take up an entire *book*. I just know it."

And after everything was over and done with, he'd broken back *into* Academy City with Yamisaka's help. And that was just a little while ago.

...Ah, I can finally see the dorm. Yes, I've made it back to the normal world at last!

In reality, it hadn't even been a day since he left, but he felt like he was returning home after a months-long vacation. Of course, he was an amnesiac with no memory of what happened before August, so he didn't exactly know what doing something for the first time in months felt like.

Kamijou's body sagged with exhaustion and sleep deprivation. He dragged it back to the dorm and took the tiny elevator up to his room.

Ugh...I'm so sleepy.

He fought back a yawn. All he wanted to do was leap into bed and sleep like the dead for two or three days straight. Unfortunately, today was September 1st, the day of his entrance ceremony.

He had lost his memories during the summer break, though, so he didn't really know anyone in his class aside from one or two people. It would just be a normal day for the other students, but for him, it would be like he'd just transferred in. As a transfer student, he couldn't afford to skip out on his first day just because he was a little sleepy.

And of course...I definitely don't want anyone to know that I lost my memories. There're no classes today, so I need to use it to relearn how I lived my school life and figure out my relationships with people, he thought, feeling rather sophisticated. He breathed a sigh of sleepiness and opened the front door.

As soon as he did, he heard the shrill yell of the girl inside.

"Tooouuummmaaa!!"

Her voice was mad, but that was all. She didn't come running over to the front door.

He made a dubious face for a moment...then finally remembered.

As he worked his tired brain, the voice's owner finally appeared. It was a foreign girl, with fair skin and silver hair that went down to her waist. She wore an extravagant nun's habit made of pure white fabric, decorated with golden embroidery, which for some reason had a handful of safety pins stuck into it along the seams.

The girl, for whom the term *girl* was still apt, was named Index.

...And at the moment, she was bound hand and foot with slender rope. Unable to move her limbs, she had wriggled out of the room like an inchworm. Incidentally, the calico sat nimbly atop her head, yawning without a care in the world. The term *inverted social order* was quite intuitive and fitting.

"Ack, I totally forgot! Were you tied up this entire time?!"

"Touma! You left me behind and the first thing out of your mouth is *that*?!" Index shouted, baring her teeth.

As explained before, Kamijou had met a man named Ouma Yamisaka last night, then fought his way in and out of the city to save an acquaintance of his. Of course, there was no way they could bring the **weakling** Index with them. As soon as he explained that, though, she started to rage at him, throwing punches and kicks. He had no choice but to have Yamisaka tie her up using his rope-binding skills and have her mind the dorm in his absence.

"Every time, every single time, you go out there alone...Touma, just take these ropes off! It's just a small barrier created with a *shimenawa*! Your right hand should be able to break it!"

His right hand.

In it rested a power called Imagine Breaker. It could nullify any abnormal power, whether it was magic or supernatural abilities, without question. Its flaw, though, was that it only worked from his right wrist to his fingertips.

"But, I mean...When I undo the rope, you look like you'll just throw a huge fit..."

Index had this terrible habit where when she was mad, she'd bite his head. He couldn't let down his guard when she was infuriated like this. It would be like letting a hungry, savage dog off its leash. He really didn't want to go to the first day of the new semester with a girl's bite marks all over him...

Then, her expression softly changed.

To put it in simple terms—into the kind of face a mother might give to a scared, lost child.

"Touma, if you untie me now, I won't get angry with you. So would you please just undo these ropes?"

"...Really? You're really not going to get angry?"

"I won't."

"You won't start to chomp on me the moment I undo the ropes?"

"Don't worry, I won't," she said, with a smile as soft as the Holy Mother herself.

Kamijou stooped down to her, lying on the floor, and touched his index finger to the ropes binding her body. Like a magic trick, the knots in the dozens of ropes all came undone at once.

A moment later, Index, now freed from restraint, immediately attacked him.

"Eh?"

She bit into his head like a caveman tearing into a huge piece of meat.

"Touma, you idiot! Idiot idiot idiot!"

"Gyaaaahh?!"

By the time he cried out, it was too late. He writhed as the pain violently shot through him. Not even his Imagine Breaker, which could wipe out any magic or supernatural ability, could stand up to this girl's brute savagery.

"Y-you're a liar! You said you wouldn't get angry—owww?!"

"Of course I got angry! I can't believe you'd just leave me here even though you knew you were gonna go fight with a sorcerer! No matter what strange powers you may have, you're still an amateur when it comes to magic, Touma! What would you have done if something happened?!"

When he looked at her, her entire face was warped in anger, and yet her eyes looked about to burst into tears.

Index stroked his head, embracing the object of her memories.

"...Seriously, what would you have done?"

Kamijou heard the voice come down on him like rain.

A faint, sweet smell wafted from her long silver hair.

He realized she was trembling a little.

She had probably been worrying all night about him until he got home.

"I'm sorry."

That was all he said.

No other words would come out.

I can't cause any more pain for someone who has been sick with worry over me, he thought. It was an honest, earnest wish that came from the bottom of his heart—he didn't want to hurt her.

As it happened...

...she didn't know that he had lost his memories.

He hadn't told her, because he knew that if she found out, it would hurt her for sure.

2

Kamijou shook his head from side to side to drive off the sleepiness as he made breakfast for two. It was toast, bacon, eggs, and a steamed salad, with milk—a super-simple four-piece set.

As soon as Index saw the food, she—and the cat—ran over to the table. He, however, walked about the room with a piece of toast in his mouth, throwing everything he'd need for the entrance ceremony into his bag.

"...indoor slippers, stuff to write with...Homework was due... today, wasn't it? Yeah, it was today. I never finished it, did I? What should I do...? And a...report card? They should've just sent it in an email."

Maybe it's to prevent hacking, he figured idly as he tossed the pasteboard report card in.

Index, sitting by herself at the table, gave him a displeased look. "Touma, do you really have to go to school?"

"Hmm?" He put his now-loaded bag down, wolfed down the rest of his breakfast, and brought his dish into the kitchen. "Ahh, right. Now that the semester is starting, you'll be all alone here by yourself."

"Mgh. T-Touma, I'm not worried about feeling lonely or anything, okay?"

Kamijou was actually under the impression it would be dangerous to leave her, but he decided to keep that to himself.

Of course, he couldn't tell her not to take a step out of the dorm. But the thought of letting a girl with no knowledge of Academy City loose seemed risky, too. In the month that she'd been here, she hadn't shown any signs of adjusting to the city life. That kind of sense wasn't something he was going to be able to simply explain to her, either.

Thinking on his past experiences, the quickest solution would be to have her come with him everywhere, but she obviously couldn't transfer into the same school as him.

Even Kamijou knew that sorcery and science didn't get along. If Index, one of the sorcery side's most important people, were made into a scientific esper with the same curriculum Kamijou had taken, it would be a problem.

"Gonna have to think about that, too. Sorry, Index, today you'll just have to mind the dorm while I'm gone. Just rinse off the dishes in the sink, all right?" he explained hurriedly, glancing at the clock.

He went into the bathroom—which he'd turned into a half bedroom—and washed his face, brushed his teeth, and changed into his summer uniform. He really wanted to take a shower, too, but there wasn't time.

Having finished getting ready, he opened the bathroom door again to find Index waiting there. She looked up at him questioningly.

"Touma, will you come back soon?"

"Hmm. I know—when I get back, let's go out and do something."

Index's face lit up.

Kamijou was happy to see her smile, but he also felt complicated. Most of her connections to the outside world relied on him. In fact, her interpersonal relations were all with friends of his, or friends of his friends.

Depending on how you looked at it, that seemed really lonely.

But it was hard for Kamijou to help with that problem, since the solution was for her to build a new relationship without involving him.

"All right, I'm off."

He wasn't able to do anything about it, so he left the issue aside.

"Okay. Come back soon," Index said, smiling to him.

Five minutes after he left the room, she was completely bored.

She had held down the fort a few times before, but that didn't mean she liked it very much. She was a very active girl. It was easy to imagine how unsuited to sitting and waiting by herself she was.

The television was still on, but she didn't look at it—she was lying flat on the floor, playing with the cat. Before too long, she stopped abruptly.

I'm bored. I want to go outside. I want to follow Touma.

Her impulses raced, but she immediately shook her head. She couldn't let her desires get in the way of others. All she needed to do was imagine their positions reversed. If Index had received a summons from St. George's Cathedral, and Kamijou had followed her because *he* was bored...

She'd be sort of happy, but he'd be bothering her.

Index was far from a beginner when it came to sorcery, and she didn't want him to see too much of that side of her—when she was at work. It was embarrassing to be seen in a different way by somebody you know.

In the same way, if Index chased Touma, it might bother him. When she thought of it that way, she knew he would feel ashamed if she naïvely sought him out.

And he said he'd take me to play somewhere when he got back, too.

Index began playing around with the calico cat, rolling around on the floor. *I'm bored, but I'll endure it,* she resolved.

But suddenly, it hit her.

"…Huh? Touma, what about lunch?"

Her face paled.

She had no cooking skills to speak of. There were no leftover snacks, either, since the cat had torn into the bag of them and devoured it all.

"Wh-what do I do? This is the crisis of the century…," she murmured in spite of herself, casting her gaze toward the front door.

Past it was the big, wide outside world where Touma Kamijou was.

3

Meanwhile, Kamijou was running down the road toward school.

The prankster city crows had left some pebbles on the tracks, which had been enough to bring the city trains to a halt.

The school he attended recommended taking excessively expensive school buses, so its rules forbade him from taking the train. On the surface this was to prevent misconduct and trouble with delinquents. In actuality, of course, the management would make more money that way, since they managed the buses.

But the real problem was that first, they rolled along at half the speed of trains, and second, they cost three times as much. Anyone would use the trains once they realized that. After taking a bus one time for his remedial classes during summer break, he had secretly decided to use the train from then on.

But because the school had such absurd rules, he couldn't get a delay certificate from the train company and use it to excuse his tardiness.

Damn it…I'm sleepy! I'm exhausted! I swear, my rotten luck wakes up before I do. I mean, I guess I'm not the only one unlucky this morning. But that doesn't make me any happier!

His brain managed to pump out a few sentences in a row, but just then, someone whipped past him from behind.

It was a girl with shoulder-length brown hair. She wore the uniform of the elite Tokiwadai Middle School, complete with its short-sleeve blouse, a summer sweater, and a gray pleat skirt. Her fierce, all-out sprint told him she was wearing short pants under her skirt so she didn't have to worry about it flipping up. The way she presented herself was totally removed from the traditional "proper young lady" image he'd expect out of a student from such a school.

"...Oh, hey, it's Biri Biri." Kamijou's sleepy brain finally churned out the answer for him.

He ran on, blinking his tired, dispirited eyes, and called out,

"...Heeyy. You young people sure are energetic in the morning!"

Biri Biri, or Mikoto Misaka as she was normally referred to, reluctantly slowed her pace and let him come alongside her. She turned to look at him with a face that said, *Hello. I'm not in a good mood right now.*

She glared at him.

"Why exactly can you address me so casually? You totally, completely, utterly, entirely ignored me last night! Don't you have any sense of shame?"

Kamijou rubbed his half-open eyes and processed what she had just said.

Now that she mentioned it, on August 31st—well, last night—when Index had been kidnapped by Yamisaka, he thought he remembered running into her. He also thought he remembered leaving her there, given the situation and everything.

Continuing a fairly quick run down the road, he responded, "Wait, what? Did you actually need something from me?"

"W-well, not really. I mean, I didn't *need* anything, but..."

"???" Kamijou blinked hard, trying to get the sleep out of his eyes. "There's something I want to ask. If you didn't need anything, then why did you stop me?"

"Sh-shut up! It doesn't matter, I'm changing the subject! Did you always use this way to school?!"

Don't outright declare that you're changing the subject, he thought. He didn't say it, though. "...No, the trains are stopped, that's why. I mean, it's just two stations away, so I should make it if I run."

"By the way, you seem pretty low on energy. Are you not a morning person?" Mikoto gave him a mystified look, but his own face turned to one of exasperation.

"A lot of stuff happened yesterday, and I'm really tired. Wait, how are you *not* tired at all, anyway? Is this the power of youth at work?"

Mikoto had gotten herself into a spot of trouble yesterday, too. Of course, Kamijou had been the one who had to pay the price for that, plus tax...

"Wh-what? Did pretending to be my...my b-boyfriend yesterday tire you out that much?"

"Huh? Oh, it wasn't just that. There were plenty of other things happening!"

"I see," she replied, giving a little sigh.

She seemed to be relieved to be able to push aside the guilt over having gotten him wrapped up in annoying events yet again, but then...

"Hmm? Other things...? You weren't doing the same thing with some other girl...were you?"

"Idiot. You're the only one who would ever come up to someone with a humiliating request like that so calmly."

"Wha...?!"

Kamijou's voice was composed, purely because of sleep deprivation. His composure made Mikoto's face go bright red immediately.

"I-I wasn't calm at all! I-I was...I was totally out of options and really distressed, so I swallowed my pride and asked you!!"

"...Ah, right, right. I see, is that so? I get the picture."

"You're not actually listening to me, are you?! Don't start using your low energy level as an excuse to ignore me again!"

At opposite ends of the energy spectrum, they fought and bickered about this and that as they each ran toward school.

4

After Kamijou parted ways with Mikoto, he continued to run until his destination came into view.

Somehow...it looks like I won't be late. Man, it's a good thing I went to those summer classes.

The remedial classes he'd had to take had gotten him familiar with the way to school and its general layout. It was thanks to that he didn't have to wander around with a map in one hand, looking suspicious.

There are two school buildings. The one in front is a newer building, and the one in back is older. My classroom is on the third floor of the new building, second room on the right. The shoe racks are to the right of the entryway. I got this!

He organized all the information in his head so that he'd be able to pretend he hadn't lost his memories. Without slowing his run, he passed through the school gates with the other students.

Schools in the city didn't generally have a schoolyard, but this one did. The plot of ground wasn't all that big. There were two school buildings—one in the front and one in the rear—connected by a roofed passage in the middle. It looked like a big capital *I* when seen from above. To the left was a D-shaped gymnasium, and to the right was the pool.

Irregular school building construction wasn't a rare sight in the city with 2.3 million students. Some had pools on the rooftops, and others had big warehouses below the gymnasiums.

This high school, though, was a paragon of normality. It was bland; it was without character. The students he'd passed on his way here all wore standard uniforms that didn't stand out at all.

I guess it would just be a pain if it were too unique, though. Like how crazy Tokiwadai seems to be.

As he turned that over in his mind, he ran toward the entryway. There wasn't very much time left, but most students seemed to come to school around now. As he was passing by the employee parking lot, he suddenly heard a shrill warning sound. He looked over to see a car trying to back into a parking space. It stopped midway through the process and honked its horn a few times. A white cat, yawning away without a care right smack in the middle of the parking spot, leaped up in surprise and ran away. The car was a bright green subcompact with a rounded design. But it was small even for a subcompact car—there wasn't even a passenger's seat. It had been designed for a single occupant.

Whoa, what's with that car? It looks as handy as a scooter. Except you wouldn't get wet if it rained. Must be nice. I can't get a car, but maybe I could buy a bike...No, that's a bad idea. It would definitely get stolen if I parked it at a train station. The thief would go straight for mine and ignore all the other ones.

Kamijou could see it all too clearly in his head, as used to rotten luck as he was. He sighed...

...then suddenly noticed...

...that his teacher, who looked like an elementary school girl, was sitting at the wheel.

"—Hey! Do your feet even reach the brakes?!"

"Th-they don't, but I can still drive!" Miss Komoe shouted back, opening up the door.

A closer inspection revealed that the mini-car's steering wheel was different from normal ones: It had buttons on the left and right. It looked kind of like the controllers used for racing games. It was probably equipment meant for handicapped people so that they could control the car's acceleration and braking by pressing the buttons.

She parked the car unexpectedly smoothly, as though well used to driving it. Then she got out, holding a thick, clear folder in one hand that she must have needed for work.

"You couldn't think of anything better to say our first day back from summer vacation? That's not the Kami I raised."

"(...*Anyone* would fear for your safety if they saw that, I think...)" Kamijou said to himself, averting his eyes.

"Did you say something, Kami?! You're not thinking of sneaking up behind me and holding me way up in the air again, are you?!"

"Of course not! Don't be so paranoid!"

As they shouted between themselves, Kamijou and Miss Komoe walked along the path to the school building. She was trotting along, since she probably had things to do before the entrance ceremony—but every time a student greeted her, she'd stop and say good morning to them. Kamijou, with his broad stride, had no problem catching back up to her.

"What're all those papers in that folder? You're not gonna give us a pop quiz on the first day, are you?"

"Kami, your teacher would never do something she wouldn't have liked when she was a student. Now, come, don't lag behind. Hurry!" prompted Miss Komoe. "This isn't part of my school job. My friend from university asked me to collect some data for a paper, so I'm helping her."

"From university, huh?...Oh, right. You have a teaching license, don't you?"

"Kami?" Komoe looked at him askance as he muttered to himself.

He returned his gaze to the folder and asked, "What kind of a paper is it?"

"It's not really anything difficult! It's about involuntary diffusion fields—something you're very well-acquainted with."

So she said, but he'd never heard the term *involuntary diffusion field* before.

Evidently concerned about the time, she continued her quick pace. She brought her explanatory teaching mode to bear. "You'll study it when you get a little older, Kami. Involuntary motions are ones you do unconsciously, without thinking about them. These involuntary diffusion fields are just that—fields of energy emitted naturally from espers, kind of like body heat."

"Huh. Maybe that's like how Misaka's body generates a weak electric field..."

"Hmm, Misaka...? Wait, um, could you be referring to *the* Misaka?" She slowed down a little. "Anyway, the type of involuntary diffusion field an esper gives off depends on what power they have.

For pyrokinetics, that would be heat, while telekinetics exert pressure over their surroundings. Of course, they're all very minute, and you'd need to use precise equipment to measure them at all."

Kamijou overtook her, and she hurried to catch back up with him. "Huh. So if there was an esper who could detect those involuntary whatever things, they could act like they're in a manga and say stuff like, 'Hmm, I sense an esper nearby!'?"

"Ah-ha, that's right. Taking it further, they might even be able to measure the type and strength of the ability, too. Something like, 'Hmm! His power level is 70,000!' Anyway, there are a lot of curious people passionately studying the subject."

They broke out into a run toward the school building as they talked, but soon parted. The employees had a separate entrance.

After Miss Komoe went out of sight, he exhaled softly.

…Here we go.

Resolving himself, he went through the entryway.

The amnesiac Kamijou's falsehood-ridden school life was about to begin.

Having already taken some remedial classes, he had no trouble remembering where his shoe locker and classroom were. He tossed his shoes into his shoe locker like a totally normal student, put on his slippers, climbed the stairs, walked down the hallway, and came to the door of his classroom.

This was where the problems would start.

When he was taking remedial classes (well, *makeup* remedial classes, apparently), back around the time he had first met Little Misaka, he and Miss Komoe had been the only ones there. He sat at a desk in front of the lectern. That hadn't been his seat, though. The amnesiac Kamijou didn't know where his real seat was.

What to do now…

He was a bit worried, but it would be suspicious for him to stay standing here. Without coming to any good solutions, he opened the classroom door.

Oh, wow...

As soon as he entered, he cursed to himself. Not even half the students were here, and nobody was sitting at their seat.

If all of the students had been here and sitting already, he'd have been able to find his desk. It looked like things wouldn't be that easy.

As he stood in the entrance, unsure of what to do, he spotted Blue Hair, who must have come in mere moments before. The 180-centimeter-tall kid walked over to him, saying,

"Hmm? What's the matter, Kami? Don't tell me you came all this way and you forgot your summer homework at your house, bro? That sure would be unlucky of you, eh?"

At that, all of the kids in the classroom turned to look at Kamijou. They all began speaking separately.

"Wait, what? Kamijou, did you forget your homework?"

"Umm, Kamijou, did you really forget it?"

"Whooaaa, yeaaaah! It wasn't just us! We have an ally! He's on our side!"

"Hooray! And Kamijou has such rotten luck that the teacher will just get mad at him and cut the rest of us some slack! Hooray!!"

Kamijou made a sour face at his now-excited classmates.

Their fathers would probably seriously worry about *that* sort of treatment being shown to their sons, but for Kamijou, this was just his comedic life as usual.

"You mean none of you did your homework? You're all going to make Miss Komoe cry!"

He briefly wondered what all his effort was *for*. He'd tried so desperately to get all his homework done, even though he knew he wouldn't make it. He'd been the only one.

Blue Hair grinned at him. "What? It's okay, dude. You know she seems to like problem students better than smart kids, yeah? Bro, *two-thirds* of us were in remedial classes, and man, did she look happy about it."

"...You don't think she goes to bars afterward and cries to herself, do you?"

"Ah-ha-ha. What're ya sayin', Kami? Ya know, I did all my homework, but I left it at home just so she'd get mad at me!"

"The hell? She's gonna cry at that for sure!! You're like some five-year-old teasing the girl you like!" shouted Kamijou without thinking. The rest of the classroom didn't pay attention to him. They seemed to be treating it like business as usual. The cluster of students broke apart and they restarted their own conversations.

For his part, now liberated from the clutches of the throng of weirdos, he wanted to catch a little shut-eye at his desk before homeroom started. Unfortunately, he didn't know where he sat.

Let's see. It'd be weird if I just straight up asked where my seat was.

Kamijou thought for a moment, then turned to Blue Hair. "Hey, sorry, could you get the notebook out of my desk for me?"

"Hmm? Kami, didja forget something at the closing ceremony?"

Somewhat unexpectedly, Blue Hair obediently went to a seat in the back by the window.

I see, so I sit over there, he thought as Blue Hair took a look inside his desk.

"Hey, Kami, there're no notebooks in here, bro!"

"Huh? Wait, did I not put it there?" Kamijou gave the confused Blue Hair a vague answer, then finally went to his seat.

Blue Hair sat in the seat next to him, and they started to talk.

"So this so-called *well-informed* guy, right? He says that manga nerds are right up there with video game nerds. I think he's a moron. If manga altered your brain, ability development would be cake! It'd be totally sweet if we had a manga instead of a curriculum textbook, you know?"

"Yeah, but the kind of manga they'd use in place of a textbook would probably be really boring. Like, the color pages would be full of teaching stuff."

"You idiot! That's what the whole concept of *hidden moe* is all about, bro! Why don't you realize the destructive power unexpectedly included in children's anime and *tokusatsu*? My fist will tell you all about it!!"

"Why are you so mad about this? I don't know if I'd trust someone who got to Level Five like that!"

Kamijou felt himself blending in to his surroundings as he and Blue Hair made their ordinary, dumb conversation.

A month had already passed since he'd lost his memories. The current Kamijou wasn't a blank slate. He could almost feel his new self overwriting his old self.

He could already talk about things he remembered.

His amnesia handicap was already slipping away.

But that was only good for Kamijou.

It wouldn't be any comfort for that girl in white.

He didn't know how the two of them met. From what he'd heard, though, they hadn't known each other for years or anything. It seemed to be that they had just met recently. It was possible that they had spent more time together *after* his memory loss than before it.

But that didn't matter.

In that short period of time, Index had come to trust him. The memories she had of that slice of time had to be precious ones that she would never forget.

Index was friendly toward him right now, but that was because she didn't know the truth.

He had already lost all his memories. They didn't share those precious ones she had.

"…"

"Kami? Heeeey, Kami!"

Kamijou snapped out of his reverie at the sound of Blue Hair's voice.

"Oh, uh, sorry. I kind of spaced out. I didn't get any sleep yesterday."

He smoothed over the whole thing and returned to his life of lies.

5

"Okeydoke, everyone, homeroom is starting now! We're pressed for time because of the entrance ceremony, so let's get things wrapped up quickly, okay?"

By the time Miss Komoe entered the classroom, most of the students had taken their seats.

"Huh? Miss Komoe, where's Tsuchimikado?"

"He hasn't told me he was taking the day off, so maybe he overslept!" answered Miss Komoe to Kamijou's question, craning her neck. "So, before I take roll call, I have big news for everybody! We have a transfer student joining us starting today!"

That got everyone's full attention.

"And she's a girl, too! Congratulations, fellows! Better luck next time, kittens!"

The class began to buzz with excitement.

Kamijou, however, was suddenly overcome with dread.

It couldn't be. There was no way that his utterly unfortunate life would include a totally normal, attractive, female transfer student. It was impossible.

...I have...I have this really bad feeling this won't end well...

He immediately suspected Aisa Himegami due to her preestablished connection with Miss Komoe, but the world was a big place. It could be the likes of Mikoto Misaka or Kaori Kanzaki, having lied about their age. Or maybe Accelerator's real name was actually Yuriko Suzushina. Or perhaps the ten thousand Sisters were gonna barge in and immediately multiply the student population by ten. Or it could even be an angel hiding her wings about to descend on them.

"N-no, stop! I heard that, brain! You said it might be fun! Stop that right now!"

"Kami, why are you holding your head and muttering to yourself?" Miss Komoe seemed a bit flustered, but she continued. "Anyway, this is just a short intro! Please leave more in-depth introductions until after the entrance ceremony. Okay, Miss Transfer Student, come on in!"

After she said that, the classroom door clattered open.

He cast his gaze in that direction, wondering what kind of insanity awaited him.

And there was a nun dressed in white, holding a calico, unsure of what to do.

*   *   *

"Nbaghh…!!"

This was completely outside anything he could have predicted. His mind went white as a sheet.

His classmates seemed to be puzzled. After all, she clearly wasn't wearing a normal school uniform. *What kind of Catholic school does she come from?* was one of the questions he immediately heard being whispered around the room.

Index ignored all of it, and in the same way as always, said,

"Oh, it's Touma! Okay, so this means that this is definitely that school thing Touma goes to. I should thank Maika later for showing me where it is!"

Everyone in the class looked to Kamijou all at once after hearing what she said.

Their eyes spoke to him, saying, *Not you again.*

"…………………………………Um, what? What is this?"

For some reason, even Miss Komoe, who had introduced the "transfer student," froze in place when she saw her.

"H-hey, wait. Miss Komoe, what is…?" began Kamijou, but it seemed that she hadn't expected this to happen, either. She finally snapped out of it when she heard Kamijou's voice and said,

"Miss Nun! Where on earth did you come from?! You're not the transfer student! Come on, leave, leave, get out!"

"Ah, but, but I need to ask Touma about lunch and—" Index tried to complain, but Miss Komoe wasn't hearing any of it. She pushed on the nun's back and drove her out of the classroom.

He reflexively rose from his seat.

"Uh…H-hey, Inde—!!"

"Kami! Please don't make this any more difficult than it needs to be!"

"What?!"

He was about to run after Index, but Miss Komoe's shout stopped him dead. He was less scared of his teacher being cross with him and more afraid that she was about to cry—that's certainly how she looked at the moment. She pushed Index out of the classroom and left.

He stood there dumbly for a bit and watched them leave.

To replace them, a long-black-haired girl stepped into the room.

"In any case. I'm the real transfer student. My name is Aisa Himegami."

Relieved at the sight of a familiar face, Kamijou fell back down into his seat.

"O-oh jeez. I'm so glad it's just boring old Himegami. And she's not even in her shrine maiden outfit, either. She's just wearing a normal, boring school uniform. Thank God…"

"I can feel traces of spite in what you just said," replied boring old Himegami, a little bit irritated.

6

Index walked down the hallways in a huff after being chased out of the classroom.

She held a 2,000-yen note. Miss Komoe had pushed it into her hands, saying, "Jeez, why are you even here? Go home now! People we don't know aren't allowed to come here! Come on, now, go call a taxi!"

…*Touma looked really freaked out.*

She frowned as she recalled what she'd seen back there. She'd been with him for more than a month already, but this was the first time he had given her such a look of pain when he saw her—such a clear expression of *rejection*.

Without really knowing how to deal with her murky feelings, she realized that now she was hungry. *When it rains, it pours*, she thought, biting her lip.

Then, she passed by the cafeteria.

The cat in her arms began to mew at the sizzling sounds of things being fried and the lovely smells wafting over to them. Index stopped dead in her tracks.

"…I'm hungry."

Now that she thought about it, the breakfast Kamijou had made her seemed a little bit hastily thrown together, what with how busy he was. On a satisfaction scale of one to ten, she put it at maybe a four.

She shuffled into the cafeteria like a zombie.

It was a large room, but its furnishings were rather slapdash. Around one hundred sets consisting of a round table and four pipe chairs were installed here. One corner of a wall was a counter, and there seemed to be a kitchen behind it. The sounds of things frying were coming from that direction. Three food ticket machines were set up in another corner.

Hmm, I've read about those in manga. You just put the money in and press the button for the food you want, and you get a ticket you can trade in for it, right?

She came to that conclusion by comparing her albeit-*biased* knowledge with the scene in front of her. Stiyl would probably faint dead away if he knew that *shounen* manga were beginning to infiltrate her archive of famous grimoires such as the *Kin'u Gyoku-toshuu*, the *Sepher Yetzirah*, and *The Book of the Law*, but she still had them all properly recorded and stored. It wasn't really a big deal.

She walked up in front of the ticket machine.

She held the crumpled 2,000 yen up to it and fed it in.

See? I can do this just fine! Touma says I'm old-fashioned and antique, but this is nothing to get worried about. All I have to do now is press the button!

Having come into the possession of a handful of pride, she stuck her finger out to the machine to press the button...

...but then stopped.

There wasn't a single button on it.

Wait...what? What's...Huh? Where do I push? What do I do to make this work?

There was an electronic stand arm reaching out from the vending machine, and the LCD monitor attached to it displayed the prices of different items, but that was it. There was no button for her to actually make an order.

In reality, it was just a touchscreen, like the ticket machines in train stations, but Index didn't understand things like that.

Uh, eh, erm, umm...R-right. I'll just get my money back for now... Wait, how do you get change back? Where's the button???

There was indeed a button in the corner of the LCD that said "Cancel," but it was too far in a psychological blind spot at the moment. Index's cat would always helplessly whack the television screen with a paw whenever they watched cooking programs, so she was pretty sure it was impossible for anything to happen if you touched a screen.

Index grabbed the vending machine with both hands and jiggled it around, then peeked into the change dispenser. Nothing happened, of course.

She moaned. "Maybe I caught Touma's rotten luck..."

Tired out and at a loss, she crumpled to the floor. She wailed on her hands and knees like a high school baseball player who had lost the Koshien Championship. The cat, for its part, didn't understand what was happening. It gave a great yawn, looking bored indeed.

Then, she heard the *tip-tap* of footsteps behind her.

Before she could give it any consideration, someone clapped her shoulder.

The entrance ceremony would take place in the gymnasium.

The hallways were packed full of students coming out of their classrooms to head over there. It was as crowded as a train station on a holiday.

Meanwhile, Kamijou had left his classroom. His reason was simple—he was so worried about Index being left to her own devices that he had to find her.

"Damn...This may sound funny coming from me, but she sure manages to get involved in a lot of trouble herself..."

She had perfect recall, too. If she saw any of the workings of the ability development curricula, then it would put scientific secrets at risk of being leaked to the world of magic. He hadn't thought that far ahead, though.

I just need to go find Index, and fast, he thought, racking his exhausted brain as he ran down the hallway.

The one who had tapped Index's shoulder was a girl she'd never seen before.

She was taller than Index, but a little shorter than Kamijou. Her hair was black with a tinge of brown, but it was probably natural. It was straight and went all the way down to her thighs, and she had one bunch of hair tied up with elastic on the side of her head. She wore glasses with thin frames, but they were sliding down a little bit for some reason. Index looked at her chest, and after seeing the bulges in her summer uniform, she was forced to admit that the girl definitely had her beat there.

Who could this be?

Index was one to talk. The girl's clothing was slightly different from the outfit that students at Kamijou's school wore, though. The girls here wore a white, short-sleeve sailor uniform with a navy blue skirt. This girl, however, wore a short-sleeve blouse and a lighter blue skirt. A red men's necktie accented her white and blue outfit. That, too, was definitely different.

Their eyes met.

From behind her slipping glasses, the girl was giving her a look as though Index were some sort of small animal.

"Umm…You have to press a button."

"Huh?"

"Well, you need to press a button on the monitor…," she said in a low, quiet voice, pointing a finger at the ticket vending machine. Index finally caught on. She followed her fingertip right to the LCD monitor on its arm.

Index made a face like a child who was lost in a country she didn't know the language of. "Button? But there aren't any buttons on this machine."

"Err…," she muttered, worried. "You just have to touch the monitor with your finger…Didn't you know that? I-I mean, please, don't cry…"

"You're lying! I know all about this. Nothing happens to the people on TV when I touch it."

"…"

The girl silently went in front of the vending machine and pressed the cancel button at the corner of the monitor.

Vreeem. The motors inside groaned and the 2,000-yen note she thought was gone forever slid right back out. Index's eyes ballooned at the sight.

"Wh-what's going on?"

"Like I said…you just need to touch the monitor…"

"W-wow! This TV is connected on the inside!"

"Umm…This isn't a television…"

"Wow, cool! Again! Do it again!"

The cat began to cry out in protest at her sudden shouting. She was now having so much fun that she forgot how hungry she was. She pushed the bill back into the machine again. Then, she looked back at the girl expectantly, as though the girl were a magician.

The girl's face creased into a worried frown, but she pressed the cancel button again.

The bill came back once more. That was all Index needed to look at this girl with profound reverence.

"Th-then what about this one? What is this button? The one that says *exclude* or whatever?"

"Umm…If you type a word into there, it lists everything except for that…So if you're allergic to eggs, you can type in *egg*, and it will only show you things that don't have eggs in them…"

"What about this one that says *data search*?"

"It's just how it sounds…You can search for things like how much nutrition everything has, like vitamin C or iron. If you search for everything under one hundred and fifty calories…it shows only diet foods."

Index cheered like a child every time the girl finished one of her pointless explanations. She looked like a kindergartener with aspirations to be an astronaut being shown around the space shuttle. The girl, bearing the brunt of Index's praise, wondered in apprehension whether she should just be happy about it.

After quite a few more explanations, Index looked at the girl with a broad grin.

"Thank you! What's your name?"

"…Um. Hyouka Kazakiri."

*   *   *

Index and Kazakiri sat down at one of the tables without actually ordering anything and started to talk to each other. Actually, it was mostly Index complaining to Kazakiri. She was so absorbed in their conversation that the fact that she had an empty stomach had slipped right out of her mind.

"And then, and then even though I called his name, he didn't answer me. He actually looked away! Jeez! It's his fault he forgot about lunch in the first place…"

Kazakiri glanced between Index and the cat she held, then replied, "Uh, umm…Well, outsiders generally aren't allowed in schools…He probably got worried that you came in like that. If a teacher found you, you'd be in a lot of trouble…"

"But Hyouka, you came in, didn't you?"

"I…I'm different. I'm a transfer student, so I just don't have a uniform yet…"

"Then I'll be a transfer student, too!"

"…Umm…" Hyouka Kazakiri frowned, looking troubled.

"Anyway, I've got a thing or two to say to Touma. I don't want to just go home like this, and if I don't ask him about lunch, I might really die from starvation!"

"But…You stand out way too much wearing those clothes…"

"Hmm?" Index looked at herself.

Index never paid much attention to her clothing, since she wore it all the time. Her gold-embroidered, pure-white nun's habit stood out like a princess's dress.

"If you get caught…it'll cause him problems, too, won't it?"

"Then what should I do?"

If Kazakiri were the sort of person inclined to play the straight woman, she would have just said, "Go home already!" However, her gaze wandered uncertainly.

"…Umm, if you go to the nurse's office, there might be a spare uniform…Well, maybe not an *actual* uniform, but an all-sizes gym uniform…"

"What's a *gym uniform*? Will I not get caught if I wear it?"

Hyouka Kazakiri made a flustered face at the innocent question. She did admit that Index wouldn't stand out as she did while wearing her gaudy habit. But Hyouka was pretty sure that if Index wore a gym uniform to the entrance ceremony—there were no classes today—it would still stand out a lot. Plus, school rules prohibited students from bringing pets in anyway. She didn't have any better ideas, though…so Kazakiri finally gave a vague, uneasy answer.

"…Yes. I think so. Well, probably. Maybe? You'll be fine…I think."

Index and Kazakiri walked down the deserted hallway.

"Hmm. So what kind of clothing is this *gym uniform*?"

"Umm…Well, it's sort of…They're clothes meant for exercising. They're stretchy, so they feel comfortable, and they're made of fabric that lets you sweat easily…"

"W-wow! That must be that *high-tech* thing Touma was talking about!"

"………Umm…"

"Wow, that's so cool! Oh, you should come try it, too, Hyouka! It sounds really awesome!!"

"……………………Umm, well…"

The timid Kazakiri found herself unable to correct Index's overactive imagination. Index began to drag her along. Her eyes nearly began to well up with tears behind her big glasses.

Meanwhile, Kamijou was still searching for Index.

There were no more students around, despite the massive flood of them earlier. He heaved a gloomy sigh as he ran down the empty halls. The entrance ceremony would have already started by now.

…Shit. I'd finally managed to blend in with my class normally, too. Well, the entrance ceremony is just listening to the principal talk…but I don't know what the principal looks like. Anyway, I need to deal with Index right now.

He glanced back and forth as he ran.

Then, he suddenly heard a familiar voice fill his ears.

Huh? This voice…Enemy detected! Identified as a stupid nun!

He stopped and listened carefully to the sounds around him. It sounded like the voice of a girl having fun. He could hear her relatively well because there was no one else around. He looked in the direction it was coming from, then scowled. There was a door with a plate that had the words NURSE'S OFFICE written on it.

He grimaced.

D-damn it. Here I am, sleep-deprived and frantically searching for someone, and she's just sleeping the day away in a bed in the nurse's office? Is that it?

He put his hand on the sliding door to the office and called out, "Hey, Index! Why the hell are you in the nurse's office?! If you're sick at all, you're sick with apathy!!"

Slam!! went the door as Kamijou threw it open.

He was all set to stomp in and go into full-on lecture mode today, but…

What he saw were girls in the middle of changing their clothes, just like in a manga.

And there were two of them, too.

First was the nun he knew well. She wasn't wearing her habit, for some reason, but rather a short-sleeve shirt and the short pants of a gym uniform. *Except*…her short pants were only halfway on. She was bent over, with one hand holding either side of them, and she had completely frozen—save for the corners of her lips, which were turning up in an awkward way.

Second was a girl he did not know, wearing the summer uniform of a different school. She had straight hair, with a clump of it tied up with elastic at the side of her head. Her thin-framed glasses were sliding down her nose, though he couldn't tell if it was on purpose or if they just did that anyway. *Except*…all the buttons on her blouse were undone, and she held a short-sleeve gym shirt in her hands. She was also completely frozen, save for her eyes, wide like a small animal and dangerously close to watering.

They looked back at him. It seemed they hadn't yet fully grasped the reality of the situation.

The cat, who didn't care one way or the other, drowsily cleaned its face with its front paw.

Kamijou's danger sense went into overdrive.

"...............Err, sorry, wrong room!!"

The next moment, both girls' faces went bright red.

He wanted to believe it was because they were blushing or embarrassed—but no.

One moment later there came a shriek of anger and the roaring crash of something breaking.

7

Kamijou was extremely angry.

He was the one being subjected to this absurdity in the first place. He was very sorry that he had walked in on them changing, but he would not be satisfied with simply letting Index get angry at him and thereafter having her tooth marks imprinted in his head.

This led to them going to the cafeteria after the two of them had changed back into their normal clothes. Kamijou and Index glared at each other while the girl who he didn't know looked at them and fidgeted, as though wondering what to do. None of this was any concern of the cat's, though, who proceeded to make itself comfortable on the table.

In a low voice mixed with sleep deprivation and anger, Kamijou asked, "So, Index, who's this girl?"

For some reason, the unfamiliar girl's shoulders twitched in surprise. In contrast, Index morosely replied, "I don't know, but she's my friend."

"What do you mean you don't know? Don't go walking around with strangers!"

"I don't know, but I know Hyouka's my friend, okay?!"

The girl named Hyouka jolted like a frightened animal every time one of them shouted, but she finally took a deep breath and, very hesitantly, tried to settle them down.

"I-I'm...Hyouka Kazakiri...Who are you?"

"Hmm? Oh, I'm Kamijou." He said it casually, though her shoulders still gave a jerk.

Index saw that and said, "Touma, you mustn't scare Hyouka…It'll be okay, Hyouka. Touma is a rare species. He's a very vigorous male, and he's indecisive, and he wants to butt into girls' business all the time, but he's a good person."

"…U-umm…Am I supposed to be relieved…?"

Kamijou grimaced at how seriously Kazakiri asked that question.

However, she didn't look like she was coming out of her trembling, scared mood any time soon. Index tried to ease her nervousness.

"There, there, Hyouka. I'll let you hold Sphinx! If you pet him, it might loosen you up a little."

"Umm…Is Sphinx his…his name?"

Without a hint of hesitation, the cat rolled onto its back and showed its stomach, as if to say in a very gentlemanly voice, "Now, Miss, you can cry into my belly all you need." It began to spread its front paws wide.

Kazakiri's troubled face persisted as her hand hovered in the air, but she finally brought it down and stroked the cat's soft stomach.

"Oh…He's warm."

An unintentional smile crossed her face. The cat, on the other hand, started to twitch back and forth as if someone were tickling his feet. He looked like he was trying desperately to endure something, as if saying, *I-I'm just fine, Miss. You'll hear no complaints from me, this is nothi— Owhoa?!* Meanwhile, Kamijou moped a little at how he'd been eliminated from the conversation.

"Yep! You can try holding him if you want. He does shed a little bit, but I think it feels good to hug him."

"Um, okay…Like…like this?"

Doing the same as she saw Index do, she softly embraced the cat, holding him to her breast. The motion wasn't any different from what Index always did, but…

Sproing.

The cat's head got buried in Kazakiri's generous chest.

Kamijou snapped out of his foul mood and immediately went red in the face. He jerked his head and eyes far away from the defenseless Kazakiri. The cat squirmed about, as if to say, *Gwooh?! N-now, Miss, I appreciate the gesture, but I may suffocate— Agh!!* He slipped out of her hands, landed back on the round table, and shook himself off.

However, the girls in question didn't seem to realize why the cat had shown such rejection.

"Umm...Animals have sharper senses than humans...so maybe he can smell the difference between you and me..."

"Hyouka, don't look so sad! You just have to get to know each other a little better...Hey, Touma? Why are you looking over there?"

"No reason," Kamijou answered.

He locked eyes with the cat, both of them knowing the truth, but the cat meowed in exhaustion, as if telling him that there are some things in this world better left unsaid.

Kamijou, strangely self-conscious, wanted to change the topic. However, he was under the faint impression that Kazakiri might have androphobia, so he took aim at Index instead.

"So why did you come here, anyway?"

"Mgh. That's right. Lunch, what about lunch? You left without leaving any lunch for me. I could have died of starvation!"

"Today's the entrance ceremony, so I'd have been home by noon!"

"Y-you didn't say anything like that! How was I supposed to know?"

"Just know! It's common sense, okay?!"

"Okay, then, Touma, you know this, right? About how when you're casting a spell in a sanctuary to create an idol and fill it with Telesma from an English cross? You know how the time and cardinal directions are related to the caster's position, right?! You know about defensive magic circles to protect yourself from the main spell's aftereffects, and how you have to put it in a very precise location! And how if you're even a little bit off, the main spell will eat up the defense and it won't work properly! This is a golden rule, but you knew that already, didn't you? Come on, it's just common sense!"

"Now...now, stop..."

They continued to yell at each other like this, with Hyouka Kazakiri trying to mediate every twenty seconds or so.

They weren't the only ones angry. Miss Komoe was at the end of her rope.

Wheeere aaare youuu, Kamiii? How bold you are to blow off the entrance ceremony on the first day like this! Hee, hee-hee-hee, eee-heee-hee-hee…

When she'd realized Kamijou wasn't present in the gymnasium, she began to smile that dark, evil smile that no one should ever see and began to search for him.

Hmm. Well, he may have fallen ill, or been wounded, or had extenuating circumstances…Kami, you're okay, right?

Even though she was currently raging mad at a certain truant, she couldn't help but worry a little. She was a kind teacher at heart, after all.

However…

She heard the sounds of talking coming from the cafeteria. Every student and faculty member in this school should have currently been in the gymnasium.

Could it be? Miss Komoe headed that way, and sure enough, there was Kamijou.

Surrounded by a pair of girls, no less.

They were arguing with one another, somehow looking like they were enjoying themselves.

Ah…aha…

The needle on her anger gauge rose exactly as much as how worried she had been.

She took a deep breath, filling the very bottom of her lungs, and put every ounce of strength she had into her next words.

"K-K-Ka-Kami!! What in the world do you think you're doing?!!"

At the sound of her shout, the cat curled up on the table, yelped, and nearly fell off.

They stopped their conversation and turned around.

A female teacher barged into the cafeteria. She was 135 centimeters tall and looked like she was twelve. Her face was red all the way to her ears. Probably from intense anger.

"H-huh? Miss Komoe, what's wrong? Isn't the entrance ceremony happening—"

"You shouldn't be talking, Kami! I'll have you know that your teacher was so worried that you weren't in the gymnasium, she left and came all this way to look for you! And yet here you are, reveling in your school popularity! If you flirt with girls that much, you're going to fall victim to impure members of the opposite sex one day!"

"Well, no, I wasn't flirting…Miss Komoe, did our yelling at each other really look that way to you?"

"You both look so calm even though you're yelling at each other. That's basically what flirting is! I-in the first place, why do so many girls just gravitate toward you, anyway?! Are you giving off some kind of weird involuntary diffusion field or something?!"

"Th-that's got nothing to do with it! Why even bring that up at this point?"

And like that, Kamijou and Miss Komoe began a face-to-face quarrel…

…and five minutes later, the conversation started to get a little strange.

"Tsuchimikado never came to school, and a nun *did* come to school, and I was already busy! So no more weird questions out of you! I cannot leave you to your own devices when you're so…so *frivolous* with girls!"

"Tsuchimikado and Index have nothing to do with me, do they?! Besides, good old Kamijou is super hard-headed! Even if I happened to trip some flags, no events would happen! Only bad stuff would happen!"

"K-Kami? What about you is hard-headed, exactly?! Here you are, wallowing in your loud, flamboyant school life, and yet you say you're *hard-headed*?!"

…Ten minutes later, the conversation started to get *really* strange.

"Why do your mental and physical faculties suddenly increase whenever girls are involved, Kami?! You should use that enthusiasm for your studies instead!"

"W-wait a second, Miss Komoe! You're not just writing me off as some merrymaker who would risk his life just to make friends with a girl, are you?!"

"...Touma, don't you realize that risking your life is *why* you make friends with girls?"

"Damn it, not you, too, Index...?!"

...Fifteen minutes later, the conversation was in a completely different place altogether.

"A-anyway, you're coming with me, Kami! I'll give you a lecture you'll never forget!!"

"Touma, instead of listening to a lecture, I think you should give your confession to me."

"Agh, jeez! I'm running on no sleep and I have a terrible headache, so please stop yelling in such a high-pitched voice! Come on, Kazakiri, say something! You're the only good person around here— Huh? Wait, what?"

Kamijou looked over, stupefied. Index and Miss Komoe looked over as well.

Hyouka Kazakiri had been at their table, but at some point, she had disappeared. The only thing left was the empty folding chair sitting by itself where she had just been.

"...Oh man, did she get fed up and leave?" he wondered aloud, but there was, of course, no response.

8

Index, having been driven off of the school grounds, leaned against the chain fence next to the school gate. She had decided to wait for Kamijou. The cat in her arms seemed sleepy.

"...Umm...I just wanted to say, that was...well. I was a little surprised, I guess..."

She turned around at the hushed voice to see Hyouka Kazakiri, who they thought had left because she got tired of them.

"That stuff always happens. Hyouka, you should have said something, too!"

"Really...? That teacher seemed really mad, though..."

"Komoe wasn't angry. How come you're so bothered by it, Hyouka?"

"Well, I mean...She was making kind of a...well, a sad face..."

Index fell silent for a moment. Then, she said, "...Touma was mad."

"?"

"We fight with each other all the time, but this time it seemed different. He wouldn't listen to anything I said, and he was angry the whole time, and he never smiled..."

Index made a sour face at her own words.

She had looked pretty energetic while arguing with him, but it seemed she was a little depressed on the inside.

"I wonder if Touma hates me now..."

Her gaze fell.

Or maybe...

She hesitated to think the rest.

Maybe he just hated me from the start, and I only just realized it now.

She bit her lip.

The cat in her arms started to mew in protest as she tightened her grip unconsciously.

Kazakiri smiled a little at her. "...That's not...true. Really good friends...are friendly enough to fight with each other."

"Why? People get hurt when you fight. It hurts when someone says something rude to you. I wouldn't want to do that to someone I'm good friends with."

"Friends who are close enough to fight with each other...," began Kazakiri in a soft voice. "It means that when they fight...they can make up. So their friendship doesn't end. That person...He knows that even when you and he fight, you won't stop being friends...so I think that's why he can fight with you."

"Really?"

"It's true...Would you rather not argue at all? If you don't want to fight...then you would keep everything you want to do pent up inside you, and just smile even when you don't feel it...And if you have a fight anyway, you wouldn't even make up after it…You would leave that friend and make other friends. Would you rather be on thin ice like that…?"

Index made a grouchy face.

Kazakiri gave her a small smile.

"No, I don't want that. I want to be with Touma forever," said Index.

"Yes…I think you two will be fine…because you feel that way… At the very least, he would get angry on your behalf…so you'll be okay," responded Hyouka Kazakiri.

But under her breath, she added, "………But he does talk like nothing happened even though he saw us naked…"

At long last, Kamijou was freed from the clutches of Miss Komoe's lecturing.

There were no students left in either the hallways or the classrooms. Both the entrance ceremony and homeroom were over, and everyone had gone home by now. The only voices he heard were of people at after-school clubs. That must be why the cafeteria was open.

He never saw Tsuchimikado. Maybe they had missed each other, or maybe he really hadn't come in today.

…*B-blech*…

He drooped like a wilting vegetable under the weight of his exhaustion coupled with his lack of sleep.

It was already past noon. He idly reflected on how he was hungry as he returned to his deserted classroom, picked up his bag, and headed for the entryway. He traded his slippers for his shoes and exited the building. He plodded through the courtyard and past the soccer club, which was in the middle of its stretches, and discovered Index and Hyouka Kazakiri waiting for him at the gate.

"Heeey!" he called out to them as he ran outside.

"Oh, Touma's back…"

"Huh? Why the long face?"

"What? No, it's nothing."

"Huh? Whatever. You want to get something to eat? Somewhere cheap."

Index made a confused face and replied, "Touma, we're not eating at home today?"

"That's too much of a hassle. We were gonna go do something afterward anyway."

"…"

"What? I told you this morning, remember?"

"I-I remember…but…" Index's face flushed a bit and she tightened her grip on the cat, who started squirming about and mewing in annoyance.

Kazakiri, standing next to her, giggled.

"Oh, do you want to come, too, Hyouka?"

"Huh…? May I?"

"There's no reason not to! Touma, you're okay with that, right?"

"Right," he answered without skipping a beat. Kazakiri looked a little surprised.

"Umm…Th-thank you…," she replied in a hushed voice to Index.

"Hmm. If we're gonna be out all day, we're gonna need some money. I'll be right back. I'm just going to go withdraw some cash from the store, so wait here."

With that, he headed for the convenience store by the school and started using the ATM next to its entrance.

Every student in Academy City was included in its scholarship system. Each month they would receive money, sort of like a paycheck.

It sounds like a pretty convenient system, but you could also look at it as the contract fee for agreeing to be a human experiment for ability development. The better your school and the higher your Level, the bigger your scholarship was—meaning you were that much more important to their research.

Kamijou didn't get much money, because he was a Level Zero who attended an average school.

…*Well, it's not like they're treating us like lab rats or anything.*

He stuffed the money into his wallet and left the store.

Then a voice suddenly addressed him from the side.

"Hey, hey, you, young man! That's dangerous, y'know."

He turned to the female voice and saw a rather good-looking

woman in a green jersey standing there. Her long hair was tied back, but her somewhat sloppy impression only served to bolster her appeal. However, judging from the crest on her shoulder, she was a member of Anti-Skill.

He thought female Anti-Skill members were pretty rare. The reason was simple—despite Japan's equivalent pay laws, the gender ratio in its defense force was overwhelmingly one-sided.

She looked at him and said in exasperation, "Don't go flaunting your wallet next to an ATM like that. It's almost like you're asking people to steal it!"

"Huh? Oh, um, I'm sorry."

He didn't really know what to do but apologize, but that seemed to satisfy the woman in the jersey.

"Right, right! Be more careful next time, young man."

Grinning, she left Kamijou and went elsewhere.

He scratched his head. Professional Anti-Skill officers had a lot of training under their belts, but their real job was teaching. Normally, side jobs were forbidden to government employees, but that rule didn't apply here. It wasn't a specific exception, though—it was because they weren't paid for it. Their job was essentially like a neighborhood watch that volunteers to keep an eye on things at night. The only thing they got for doing such a dangerous job was special jurisdiction as members of Anti-Skill. He heard it was still pretty popular to do, though. From an educational guidance standpoint, it seemed to make their jobs easier in a few different ways— not the least of which was to keep your students in line when you told them you were an official member.

But why was she hanging around here? Is she actually a teacher at our school?...Argh, I was talking to her like we'd just met, too! Well, I guess she wasn't talking like she knew me, though...

Someone tugged on his clothes, breaking his train of thought. *What is it?* He turned around and saw Aisa Himegami there.

"Huh? What're you doing, Himegami? You haven't gone home yet?"

"...I just transferred into your school. And yet you give such an indifferent response."

"Uhh…"

Now that she mentioned it…The events of today were still pretty hazy for him thanks to Index bursting into the classroom. The big event of the day had been Himegami's first day at her new school, hadn't it?

"I see. I really am. An easy girl to miss."

"No, well…Don't get so down on yourself! It's just that the sun doesn't quite shine as much near you, or something…"

The *gong* sound effect was nearly audible as Himegami got more depressed. Eventually, though, she lifted her head up.

"More importantly."

More importantly…? Man, she doesn't really understand conversation, either…

"I recently heard something. That girl wearing the glasses. Is her name Hyouka Kazakiri?"

"Huh?" Kamijou shifted his gaze.

Index and Kazakiri were standing a little ways off. He couldn't hear them from here, but they looked like they were enjoying their conversation.

He looked back at Himegami and replied, "Oh, yeah, that's right. Hyouka Kazakiri. Wait, is she a friend of yours?"

"…" After hearing his words, she looked at Kazakiri from afar.

It wasn't a very favorable stare. It was more like an observational glare or something.

"Hey, what's the matter with you?"

"Just to be sure. Her name. It's really Hyouka Kazakiri?"

"Well…I mean, she and Index both say so. It's not like she showed us her ID or anything, but does she really need to?"

"Hyouka…Kazakiri." She said the name to herself again. "Do you know? The name of my school. The one I used to go to."

"Well…no."

"Kirigaoka Girls' Academy. It's an elite school like Tokiwadai. If we're talking purely about ability development. Tokiwadai specializes in helping espers with regular abilities. And excellent all-around academic skills. Kirigaoka deals with weirder ones. Strange ones. Irregular espers with abilities that are difficult to reproduce."

"Hmm," mumbled Kamijou to let her know he was still listening.

Now that she mentioned it, her own power, Deep Blood, didn't seem very useful for any scientific pursuits. Put in those terms, he wouldn't be surprised if they would treat his right hand as a treasure. Of course, he hadn't the slightest intent of going to a girls' high school.

"I have seen Hyouka Kazakiri's name. At Kirigaoka," she asserted, placing emphasis on the word *name*.

"Wait, so did you two transfer in together, then?"

"..." For some reason, she didn't answer. She was acting a little odd.

"Since she went to Kirigaoka, that must mean she has an unusual skill like you, right?" he asked, not really surprised. He knew a top-class electric user, and he had a unique ability himself.

However...

"I don't know."

"Huh?"

"Nobody knows. Hyouka Kazakiri's power." She paused. "But her name. It always shows up on the test grade bulletin boards at the top."

"Hmm. So she's smart, then?"

"No. It has nothing to do with her intelligence. Kirigaoka gives ranks based on rarity of ability. It is simply that. Her power is the most unusual. Whether or not it's useful. Is a different story. However..."

She paused again there.

"But nobody knows. What class or year she's in. In the first place. Everyone at Kirigaoka knows. The name Hyouka Kazakiri. But there is nobody. Who has actually seen her. And yet she appears at the top of the test rankings."

"...That's kinda weird."

"Yes. We don't know anything. I once asked a teacher at Kirigaoka about it. And she told me in secret. That Hyouka Kazakiri is called *Identity Unknown*."

That wasn't all she had to say.

"But. That isn't the most important part. The most important thing the teacher told me. Was not about that Identity Unknown. It was something else."

She continued.

"She told me. That Hyouka Kazakiri. Is the key to discovering the identity of the *i*th School District—the Five Elements Society."

Kamijou frowned.

The *i*th School District was also known as the Five Elements Society and got its moniker from the symbol used to designate an imaginary number. Some called it the imaginary school district. It was said to be the first-ever research institution in Academy City, and that it possessed all sorts of sci-fi technology that modern science couldn't reproduce. If the rumors were true, then the entire city was being managed from within it. It was the dark spot of this city.

It was a mysterious facility that should certainly exist, and yet nobody knew where it was.

This was starting to sound like a certain girl.

"From what the teacher said. Hyouka Kazakiri had her own special class. Though it was more like a laboratory. So they could research it. People almost never create a laboratory for just one person. But it was not actually for Identity Unknown. It was to uncover the truth behind the Five Elements Society." She, too, seemed lost in thought. "But. The teacher said that she hadn't ever seen Hyouka Kazakiri, either. Even though there was a lab for her. Even though she showed up on test results. Very few teachers know her identity."

"But...but that's..."

"Yes. I don't know how much of it is true. And that's why. I thought I would warn you about her. So be careful."

And then, as if to say that her job here was finished, she turned to leave.

"Hey, wait a minute. We're going to go and hang out. Do you want to come?"

"—"

She turned back around. Her impassive face held the slightest tinge of surprise.

"...Stupid...Komoe."

"Huh?"

"Nothing. I have been asked to do something. So I can't go," she explained calmly, turning her back to Kamijou again. He stared after her for a few moments, noting that she looked crestfallen, but suddenly she remembered something and turned back to face him.

"By the way. Hyouka Kazakiri. How did she enter the school?"

"Huh? If I recall...Well, Index said she's a transfer student."

"I see," she replied succinctly. "But. As far as I remember. I am the only transfer student."

Kamijou wasn't sure what to say. Himegami told him once again to be careful, then left for real this time. He looked away from her and back to the girls next to the school gate.

Hyouka Kazakiri stood next to Index, smiling along with her. She didn't look like anything but a normal person.

She looked like she had nothing to do with any of that weird imaginary school district stuff.

Man, I don't get it. Are they just rumors? Or are they real?

He scratched his head and then walked over to them.

Index and Kazakiri smiled at him to welcome him back.

The cat mewed.

There was nothing strange about this.

At least, not at the moment.

INTERLUDE ONE

The road in front of the station was packed with swarms of high school students.

All schools had their entrance ceremonies today, so every student had been released into the afternoon city at once. People were particularly crowding around one corner of the train station, where all the big department stores were.

Kuroko Shirai made her way through the chaos.

She was shorter than your average female middle school student, and she wore her brown hair in two long pigtails. She was best described as *cute* rather than *pretty*. She was fully dressed in Tokiwadai Middle School's summer uniform, but she had a brassard on her right arm.

On it was written the word JUDGMENT.

Judgment was the name of an anti-esper peacekeeping force—essentially the city's version of the riot police. In contrast to Anti-Skill, which was comprised of school faculty wielding next-generation weapons, Judgment was made up entirely of espers.

The reason there were two separate peacekeeping organizations was so that they could each keep an eye on the other's internal affairs to prevent corruption. Unique though they may be, they were just students and teachers. There was no discarding the possibility of a renegade cop showing up and abusing his or her position of power.

...Goodness. They should have split up the recreational facilities in this city a little more. I wonder if the developers are short on traffic and environmental psychologists? grumbled Shirai—one of those students—completely ignoring things like property values and consumer attraction methodology.

Like most people, she hated crowds. But there was a reason she had braved the combination of the blazing, late summer heat and the sweaty, crowded atmosphere to come to this station.

There she is...

Shirai saw a figure ten meters away and compared it to the photograph on her cell phone screen. The woman looked foreign. She hadn't noticed Shirai's presence. She was walking boldly through the throngs of people, seemingly uncaring of the fact that she was on the run.

Two people had broken through Academy City's walls at approximately the same time, right before seven this morning.

One of them was under Anti-Skill's jurisdiction, not Judgment's, so Shirai didn't know the details. From what she'd heard, though, it was a student registered in the city's databanks—a corporate spy, perhaps?

She was on the tail of the other suspect.

Her cell phone screen showed an enlarged image from a security camera. The blond-haired woman depicted had actually attacked the city gates head-on. After causing fifteen casualties, including three with major wounds, she had forced her way past security and entered the city.

The anti-terrorism security level "Code Red" was currently in effect. Entry and exit were being completely blocked, and the members of Judgment had been excused from class and ordered to search for the intruder.

Thus, Kuroko Shirai had skipped her entrance ceremony and had been walking around the city for a while now, but...

In a normal situation, I would call for support, have the civilians disperse, and confirm that she's the one we're after...but if I take very long, I'll lose my chance, won't I? she whispered to herself, making her way through the crowd, still glaring at her target in front of her.

Though the city's security forces were split into two, Anti-Skill was usually the one on the front lines, not Judgment—the latter was made up of students, after all. Shirai's orders were only to capture the criminal—everything else was in Anti-Skill's ballpark. Unfortunately...

I can't just leave this in Anti-Skill's hands, either. People have already been wounded at the gates. I shall ask all powerless individuals to please evacuate, then.

This decision was based on her confidence as a Level Four esper. The teachers, who surrounded themselves with armor and next-gen weaponry, seemed extremely fragile from her point of view.

She didn't want to give Anti-Skill a job they wouldn't be able to handle. She'd have trouble sleeping at night if the Anti-Skill officers she handed off the baton to got hurt. She'd feel more at ease if she were the one who did the fighting.

She reached a hand into her skirt pocket and came out holding what looked like a small handgun. However, its muzzle was more than three centimeters wide. It was a device for firing signal flares.

I don't want to write the report I'll have to make after firing this, but...!

Shirai pointed the barrel into the sky and immediately pulled the trigger.

Pop! With something of a comical noise, a metallic cylinder the size of a tube of lipstick flew about seven meters into the air.

Right after that came a *boom* and a brilliant flash of light as the contents of the cylinder scattered everywhere. Those in the area put up a hand to shield their faces from the sudden and extreme brightness.

A moment later, they all took swift action. Everyone scrambled into nearby buildings, screaming and shouting. The university students and teachers who were driving at the time stopped their cars right away and also dashed indoors.

Everyone in this city knew what this meant.

It was the evacuation order used by the security forces. It said that a battle was about to start, and it urged bystanders to find shelter somewhere stray bullets wouldn't hit them.

It didn't even take thirty seconds for the bustling street in front of the station to completely empty out.

Now, only Kuroko Shirai and the aforementioned target remained.

The woman neither fled nor caused a stir; she simply stood, relaxed, within the center of the explosion of light.

There was a bit more than ten meters between them.

Shirai cast her gaze over the woman.

She was an odd person to look at. It seemed fair to call her a gothic lolita—she was wearing a long black dress with white lace and ribbon decorating its ends. Nothing a blond-haired, blue-eyed girl wore would look bad.

Despite her long blond hair, her skin appeared weathered and brittle.

She was in her late twenties, and strands of hair stuck out like a wild animal. She must not have taken proper care of it. Her skin was brown, but not the shade that went well with sunlight. Her dress, too, seemed fairly old and worn-through, its fabric damaged and the white lace beginning to fade into a dingy tone. She was certainly pretty, but she looked somehow crazy at the same time. Looking at her would destroy the illusion of gothic lolitas being neat and trim.

"Please, it would be better for both of us if you stayed where you were. I am Kuroko Shirai, and I am a member of this city's security force. I don't believe there is any need for me to explain why I'm arresting you, is there?"

The woman with the wild blond hair didn't show much reaction to her voice.

Was she effete or just emotionless? She turned her neck slightly and took a look around. She seemed more interested in the people who had all disappeared than in Shirai.

After five seconds, the woman finally looked toward her.

"Suspending search." She paused. "...Make things harder for me, will you?" she said with clear disdain. Then, without waiting for a reply, she stuck a hand into one of the ripped sleeves of her worn dress faster than Shirai could move an eyebrow, and was about to bring something back out—

*　　*　　*

—but at that point, Kuroko Shirai was already standing right in front of her.

They had been ten meters apart just a moment ago. In less than a heartbeat, Shirai had reduced that distance to zero.

The woman's relaxed expression took on just a hint of doubt.

Shirai wasn't about to explain, though. The woman didn't need a lesson on how she used her Level Four teleportation ability to cross through space.

She reached out her hand and grabbed the lace-covered woman's wrist.

The next thing the woman knew, she was on her back on the ground. There was no pain or shock, nor did she even remember when she fell. Shirai had actually just used her teleportation ability to move her to the ground as she touched her. To the woman, however, ignorant of her abilities, it probably looked like a martial arts throwing technique she'd never seen before.

Irritated, she took evasive action anyway, and tried to get herself up off the ground, but…

"I said…"

Kachink-kachink-kachink!! A sound like a sewing machine split through the air.

When the woman looked back down, there were two metal arrows piercing through the loose parts of her dress sleeve and skirt fabric, pinning her to the asphalt.

"…not to move. Do you not understand Japanese?" Kuroko Shirai demanded quietly.

This, too, was an attack that used teleportation. She had instantly moved the arrows hidden in her skirt into specific points. It was both as strong and fast as a machine gun. It couldn't be blocked with anything, since the arrows instantaneously warped from one place to another. There also wasn't any chance of collateral damage. It was a truly unbelievable attack.

However...

Even presented with that, the expression on the woman's brown face didn't change.

Except...

...for the corners of her mouth. Her face was like a steel mask, but her lips began to stretch across it, thinly, long, and silently, into a smile.

"Wha..."

On the other hand, Kuroko Shirai frowned in surprise...

...and suddenly, the ground just behind her exploded violently.

"...at...was that...?!"

She was surprised, but she had no time to turn and look. Her body flew into the air, flung by the bulging in the asphalt. Once she slammed on her back down on the cold, hard ground, she finally glanced behind her.

It was a giant arm.

There was a two-meter-long arm sprouting from the road like a sea serpent stretching its head above the surface of a lake. It was *shaped* like a human arm, but it was made up of asphalt, bicycles, guardrails—from all sorts of things nearby—that had been kneaded together like clay. It vaguely resembled the metal arms that were attached to heavy machinery for building deconstruction.

Shirai quickly tried to get away, but her ankle caught on something.

The road around where the arm was sticking out had bulged, and the broken asphalt plates were coming back together like mismatched jigsaw puzzle pieces. Her ankle had gotten caught in between two of them.

...Agh...She's just an outsider...Could she be an...esper...?

The pressure slowly increased around her ankle, causing her face to distort with pain.

She looked back to the woman and saw her pinned hand holding something resembling white chalk. She was using it to draw symbols on the road.

They weren't any scientific symbols she'd ever seen. In fact, they looked like occult, magical letters.

She may be controlling her ability by using some kind of patterns for self suggestion, like the compressed memory in a cell phone, she speculated, ignorant of magic and going purely off what she knew.

Th-this is...really bad. I need to...get back up...!

She made a valiant effort to calm herself, but then she noticed something.

The giant arm was sticking out of the ground, causing the surrounding areas to bulge upward. Her ankle was caught between pieces of road from that bulge, but the swelling itself looked somehow...round. Almost like a human face.

It was as if her foot *were being bitten by asphalt teeth.*

Oh...no...

Shirai possessed the ability to teleport. This power let her cross freely through empty space, unbound by three-dimensional limitations.

But it had a weakness. She couldn't just warp around however she wanted. It went beyond three dimensions—the ability required her to derive her current spatial coordinates in *eleven* dimensions, then calculate her movement vector from there. The commands she needed to give were on a completely different level than those of normal espers, who could just think phrases like "create fire" or "make lightning."

Because of that, if anything were to rob her of the calculation abilities she normally possessed—something like pain, exhaustion, or confusion—she would no longer be able to use it.

Creeeak. The road fragments only closed a few millimeters, but her ankle spasmed in agony nonetheless.

Ah...gh...gah...?!

She could flee immediately if she teleported, but her fear was overriding rational thought.

She saw the woman on the ground smiling to herself as she moved the chalk around with a few snaps of her wrist. As if being controlled by it, the arm's elbow gradually bent and slowly changed the direction it was facing...as if it were about to crush a bug crawling on the ground.

Shirai understood all that, but she still couldn't move.

Her calculations were in disarray because of the pain and her fear of death. She had an escape route right in her hands, and yet she couldn't make use of it.

It was like losing the key to the door of a nuclear shelter.

The woman swung the chalk into the air in an arc, and the arm clenched its five fingers into a fist. At the same time, the pavement dug into her ankles even tighter. Shirai slammed her eyes shut at the incredible pain.

Bkk-bkk-gkk-bkk!

Then she heard a loud, strange noise ring out from somewhere in her self-induced blindness.

Was that the sound of her anklebones shattering? No, it wasn't.

The sound of the giant arm made of countless pieces of scrap coming down to strike her? *No, not that, either.*

It was the sound of somebody severing the arm.

Wha...Eh...?

She opened her eyes, surprised at the sudden strike.

The arm had been cleanly cut in two at the wrist. Before she could give it a closer look, the "teeth" holding her ankle in place were mowed down. Suddenly freed from her shackles, she toppled over backward. As soon as the hand was severed, all the materials composing it reverted to their normal state and flew off in all directions.

Bzzzzzzzzz...! A strange sound hundreds of times louder than the buzzing of bees assaulted her ears.

When she looked, she saw something floating in the air. It was like a black whip or like a rapier many meters long. That's where the sound was coming from. Closer inspection revealed that it was iron sand. An enormous clump of iron was being controlled by someone, possibly with magnetism, and it was *vibrating.*

In other words, it was a supersonic chainsaw.

Bshh-bang!! came a piercing sound as the iron whip returned to its owner.

Wa...wait...Controlled by magnetism...? Could...could it be...?!
Taken with a fit of coughing, still trying to get oxygen, she looked over there.
And there...there was...

Mikoto Misaka.

There was a small *chink* of metal.
It was the sound of her bouncing a coin on her thumb. It danced slowly, slowly, slowly over her head.
She spoke.
"I don't know what all this fuss is about..."
The arm, its hand gone, had transformed into essentially a mountain of trash sticking out of the ground. As if collapsing under its own weight, the garbage tower fell toward Kuroko Shirai in an attempt to hit her as hard as it could.
Before that happened, though, the coin landed back on Mikoto's thumb.
"...but don't lay another one of your dirty fingers on her, you pig!!"
A moment later...
...she fired the attack that had given her the name Railgun. The coin flew forward at triple the speed of sound. It heated up as it rubbed against the air and became an orange beam as it lanced straight through the "tower," which shattered instantly at the extreme impact. It and the "head" attached to it all blew into a million pieces.
Grashh!! came the roar an instant later.
A dust cloud rose up like a screen, but a sudden gale drove it away—the trailing shock wave from the Railgun attack.
A-amazing...
Shirai continued to keep an eye on her surroundings, but most of her mind had been stolen by something else.
She could match normal wind users just with the gusts coming from her shock waves. Big Sister! Just how much more invincible are you planning on getting?

On the other hand, Mikoto was walking toward her, relaxed, as if to say that the crisis had already been defused.

"Uhh, Kuroko, you can loosen up now. I think that giant hand was a decoy. It blew up on its own, not because of my Railgun's power. See? That jerk of a woman used the smoke to get away," Mikoto said, pointing and sticking out her tongue a little in spite.

Shirai looked. She'd pinned the woman's dress to the ground, but she was nowhere in sight. The only things still there were a few pieces from the end of her dress's black fabric, sticking around like a stubborn stain.

"So who was that? Someone related to Judgment? You were the one following her, after all."

"Y-yes, that's correct. She seemed to be the illegal intruder, but... Oh, Big Sister!"

Then she lunged toward Mikoto as if her legs had given out.

"Hey, would you quit it?! This isn't the time for your crazy fantasies—"

She reacted a second too late, though. She finally tried to peel Shirai off her chest but didn't put any strength to it, because...

Shirai was weakly clinging to the chest of her summer sweater.

With just that one point of contact, Mikoto realized that she was trembling.

"Jeez." She sighed, thinking.

What would that boy have said to her if she had been the one like this?

"Kuroko, you try to do way too much by yourself. It was stupid to go up against someone like that. There's no rule that says you have to fight by yourself, you know."

She thought about it. Words themselves didn't have any meaning. The feeling she put into them as she spoke was what gave them meaning.

"Rely on me more, all right? Not just if something really bad happens, either. Even if things only kind of look bad, contact me. It won't cause me any trouble, so stop thinking like that. If you rely on me in hopeless situations, then that just means you trust me more, right? I'd never refuse that."

Pat pat. Mikoto lightly stroked Shirai's head.

Then, her underclassman, still trembling, said, "...Heh-heh-heh. This is a once-in-a-lifetime chance. This close to Big Sister, I have full access to her cleavage...heh-heh. Heh-heh-heh-heh!!"

"Wh...Hey...What? Wait! I-I'm seriously trying to make you feel better here! You were trembling with excitement, Kuroko?!" Mikoto shouted as her face turned red, but it was too late.

Shirai brought her hands around Mikoto's back, locked her in, and started rubbing her cheek all over her "big sister's" chest.

CHAPTER 2

After School
Break_Time.

1

"Wow! So this is that underground world I heard so much about!"

"It's an underground mall, not a world," retorted Kamijou in his low-gear, sleep-deprived state to the effervescent Index.

There were many underground malls in Academy City. Department stores, centered around train stations, would connect to one another underground, forming a labyrinthine structure. A lot of students were coming and going down here, but not quite as many as there were on the main road above them.

Like the security robots and wind turbine system, these underground malls were an experimental feature of Academy City. Japan, both strapped for space and renowned for its earthquakes, demanded world-class earthquake-resistant construction technology. Many places throughout the city had been dug up to assist with practical tests for such technology.

Kamijou had no particular reason for choosing this place to hang out, save for the simple fact that Index had never seen it before.

"Let's go get something to eat first. Index, any requests? Oh, err, nowhere expensive. Or with big lines."

"We don't have to go to a place like that. We should go to a restaurant with cheap, delicious food and lots of it, and where people don't go often."

"...That's gonna be hard to find. Kazakiri, what about you?" he asked, turning to look at her over his shoulder. For some reason, her shoulders twitched, and she began to tremble. She tried to hide herself behind Index.

"Uhh..." *Did I do something?* he thought to himself.

"...Oh, no...I'm...sorry. I'm not...scared or anything...," she answered, peeking out from Index's shadow. "...I mean...you saw me...naked...so..."

"Huh?" He couldn't hear the last part.

"Um, err...no, it's...it's nothing. But...you saw me...and your reaction was so...well, calm, and...umm..."

She was essentially mumbling to herself at this point, so Kamijou didn't catch any of it. *Well, she's hanging out with us already, so she's probably not scared, right? She's probably okay with this, but why the polite sense of caution?*

Then, Index gave him a rather cold look, as if she understood what Kazakiri hadn't said. "Touma, you're scary!"

"Heh? How's that?"

"It's those beastly eyes of yours. It's like they're eagerly watching for womenfolk. Your lips say you're totally harmless, but your eyes say that they won't let a single good-looking scrap get by them! It's scary!"

"Spouting nonsense like that is just gonna make her even more scared!" shouted Kamijou, causing Kazakiri's shoulders to jerk once again.

Then, very hesitantly, still hidden behind Index, she began, "...Um, well..."

"See, Touma? Your yelling is scaring her!"

"Uh, yeah, okay! I see, whatever! Fine, I guess I'm just a beast then! But once I accept it, I really will become an animal! You will behold the true form of Evil Kamijou and tremble!!"

"...Umm...You're not...scary or anything...but...lunch..."

Kazakiri's barely audible voice stopped the argument between the two of them, fighting half desperately. They turned toward her at the same time.

She was pointing somewhere.

They followed her gesture to a restaurant.

2

"Cafe-ter-ia restaurant?"

"Yeah, a cafeteria restaurant," Kamijou replied.

Index's face said she didn't really understand what that meant. It was the same face she had when they'd entered the underground mall.

The three of them had gone into a totally normal family restaurant. Kamijou and Index sat facing each other at a table for four, and Kazakiri sat next to Index.

The cat was on Index's lap, too. He thought a dining establishment would have refused them because of the animal, but apparently cats were fine. Apparently it was owned by the same company that owned the usual joint they frequented, which was also totally okay with pets.

"Academy City is filled with schools, big and small. So some places bring all the delicious parts of school cafeteria menus into one place. Anyway, they have school food here, too. This way people don't have to miss out on what kind of food people eat in other schools."

"Mgh. Touma, what do you mean by 'cafeteria meals' and 'school food' in the first place?" asked Index, giving the giant canvas of a menu a challenging stare.

Kamijou, being an amnesiac, didn't have any recollection of the school meals of his compulsory education. But he still had the knowledge of it, so he was pretty sure he knew basically what they were.

"Well, putting it broadly, they're both food that you can only eat at schools."

"W-wow, so they're like limited editions!"

"...Uhh, yeah, sure, let's go with that. They're rare."

"Umm...I don't think you should leave the explanation at that...

just because you think it's a drag…" Kazakiri offered a nervous word in edgewise in place of Kamijou, who was sleep-deprived and thus fresh out of witty retorts. Index didn't seem to hear her, though. She had her face buried in the needlessly large menu like a father reading a newspaper. She looked past it with her eyes on him.

"Touma, can I get anything on here?"

"Umm, nothing expensive," he warned vaguely, but he wasn't too worried. This restaurant specialized in school lunches and school store food. There wouldn't be anything that expensive.

Then, Index slammed the menu down onto the table and pointed at one part of a photographed meal so that even he could understand.

"I think I want this."

"Hmm? Which one?" He looked at what her pale, slender finger was pointing at. There, he saw the words…

Tokiwadai Middle School Lunch Set—40,000 Yen

"…"

Kamijou silently closed the menu, then hit Index's head with the corner of it.

"Oww!! What did you go and do that for?!"

"I told you, you're not allowed to get anything expensive! Wait, I thought you were *asking* for that one!"

Just what kind of life is that Biri Biri living, anyway? he thought to himself, speechless. He fearfully opened up the menu again. The photo of the meal sparkled and shined. It looked like someone dressed up in formal attire trying to attract customers.

"…U-umm…I think I'll have…this…"

Beside the arguing pair, Hyouka Kazakiri pointed to a meal on the same page of the menu.

It was a picture of a completely and totally normal school lunch, including a peculiarly simple bread roll and a milk carton.

He couldn't help but feel a little bit moved. Maybe it was because Index had just picked the most expensive thing on the menu.

"Do you see this, Index? This is what a true honor student picks."

"What? Hyouka, you have kinda boring tastes. I want to eat something flashier! More colorful!"

He heaved a heavy sigh at the girl's griping and said, "You need to choose foods based on their taste, not their appearance, Index. Also, don't start recommending the Tokiwadai set to her by taking advantage of her confusion, stupid! If you call her boring, it might actually hurt her feelings and then she'll rethink her choice! So knock it off!" he shouted. Kazakiri twitched and hid her face behind her giant menu. It seemed that her favor gauge had bottomed out. Raising any further flags appeared hopeless.

After a little while had passed, their food was brought out.

It consisted of a milk carton, a bread roll with margarine, a bowl of meat-and-potato stew, a salad, some fried chicken, and cups of yogurt for dessert. The waitress looked like an expert on school lunches. From what she told them, their selling point was the fact that they transcended national borders. Their food was slightly more expensive than normal school lunches because though they used the same recipes, they had to use different ingredients, thus they couldn't reduce production costs as much.

"All right, then. Let's eat before it gets cold. By the way, Kazakiri, how come you chose to eat from this menu? Is yogurt a favorite food?"

This shop's menu was divided among schools, creating an additional choice beyond just what kind of food you were in the mood for. You might, for example, want to try the menu of a school you really wanted to go to but didn't pass the exam to enter.

But Kazakiri didn't appear to have put that much thought into it. She shook her head.

"...Um, well...I...I've never eaten somewhere like...this...before..."

"Hmm. You've never eaten a school lunch?"

"Well...no." She made an apologetic face for some reason, and Kamijou thought to himself,

No relation to school lunch, maybe that means she eats a bento every day, maybe she makes it for herself, or maybe her dorm has a

bento service or something, man, that sounds great, you could stare at the line warfare in the cafeteria without it concerning you, that would be a much more civilized mealtime, ah, I wish my dorm would offer a bento service like that so I didn't have to do anything in the morning— but wait, there's a freeloading girl living with me, maybe Index could work for them…no, that would never work, ah, no way, she can't even use a microwave, I can't expect her to know how to cook, what was I thinking?

"Eheh-heh-heh…" He chuckled as a dark smile came over his face and a negative aura emanated from his body.

"…Um, er, well…your eyes…they're kind of…scaring me…"

"Hyouka, Touma has a disease where he does this sometimes, so just smile and nod at him, okay?"

3

A woman in a black dress was walking through the city streets.

Her name was Sherry Cromwell. She was a member of the English Puritan anti-sorcerer group Necessarius and used Kabbalah statues for her work. She weaved through the crowds of people, her mouth stretching into a smile.

She had thought that her odd outfit, a lacy dress that was torn here and there, would draw curious stares, but it wasn't evoking much of a reaction from these students. In fact, they seemed more interested in her age than her clothing. Students made up 80 percent of the city's population, so the fact that she was in her late twenties was standing out more than her gothic lolita look.

"—In the beginning, there was the earth," she declared theatrically as she walked.

She removed something, a white, chalk-like object, from a torn dress sleeve. It was actually an oil pastel meant for constructing magic circles, made from consecrated salt hardened by holy oil.

"—God created His image from the earth and breathed into it life, and He named His creation 'Man.'"

As she recited, she twirled her oil pastel along the surface of a vending machine nearby with the speed of a master. On the machine appeared things that were somewhere between characters and patterns.

"—God's secrets were at last revealed to Man by the fallen angel."

Then onto the guardrail, and the trees lining the road, then onto a cleaning robot, and the support beam of a wind turbine…Sherry's oil pastel danced over everything in her path.

"—However, the works of God cannot be achieved by the hands of Man, and the fallen angel could not speak of it in the proper way."

At last, seventy-two inscriptions later, she brought her pastel into the air.

"—Thus was the life created by the hands of Man mere rotting dolls made of mud…Now, Ellis, my muddy golem. Smile and allow me to use you to your fullest, for my sake."

Finally, she brought her hands together with a *clap*.

A moment later…

The *squish* of a pus-filled wound being broken echoed throughout her surroundings. Not just once or twice, either, but dozens of times. The sound was faint, so it did not reach the ears of the conversing students walking among the throng.

Change, however, was certainly happening.

The vending machine, the guardrail, the trees lining the street, the cleaning robot, the wind turbine's support beam—out from everything that Sherry had drawn on appeared mud-like bubbles about the size of a ping-pong ball. Her brand of magic worked regardless of what materials she used. Every single thing in this place became her weapon.

A crack appeared on the face of each of the ping-pong balls, slicing across the surface in a line.

From out of that, as though they were grapes being peeled, appeared white, muddled eyeballs.

Sherry removed a black piece of paper about the size of a postcard.

"Automatic Clerk, is this my target? 'Kaze,' 'kaza'…What is this? Is this country's writing system *hieroglyphics*?"

Her white oil pastel flashed across the black paper and scrawled characters on it. She couldn't read kanji very well, but her brain processed them as pictures rather than meaningful characters. She scribbled them as one would the likeness of a person from memory.

Sherry then gave a flick of her fingers, sending the postcard-size piece of black paper out of her hand. It flew through the air, spinning like a Frisbee, and gently landed on the ground.

The name *Hyouka Kazakiri* was written on it.

It was like characters written in a notebook in pencil had been stamped in photonegative onto the black paper. Dozens of the muddy eyeballs crowded in tight to it. The scrap was torn apart, ripped to shreds, and incorporated into their filth-bodies. Within seconds, the black paper had disappeared without a trace.

Then, after they had absorbed all the thin paper fragments, the many eyeballs scattered in every direction, stiffly, like fleeing cockroaches. Some swam along the surface of the ground, while others sunk below the concrete, every one of them restlessly moving their big eyes around.

"Don't make me wait too long, Ellis."

Sherry smiled and disappeared back into the crowds.

4

After they finished their meals, Kamijou and the others left the store.

Index looked a bit perplexed as she recalled the taste of her first school lunch.

"It wasn't bad, but it wasn't that good, either. Hmm. I wonder why that is? I don't quite feel satisfied for some reason."

"That's because school lunches are made to be eaten every day. Instead of trying to make it really good, they specifically make them so you won't get tired of eating them. If you ate these grand full-course meals every day, you'd start throwing up within a week."

She put her index finger to her chin, then looked up to the ceiling and reflected on that. Then, she said, "No, I think I'd be okay with eating so many full-course meals that I threw up."

"…Right, well, maybe *you* would," he responded, not really caring. It was now past one in the afternoon. Above ground, the roads had surely transformed into a veritable hell under the blazing heat of the sun. The room temperature down here in the underground mall was somewhat cooler because of the air-conditioning, but that also made one shy away from going back above ground until the harsh sunlight eased up a little.

Hyouka Kazakiri looked at the two of them, both lost in their own thoughts, and said, "…U-umm…Where should we go now…?" She clearly seemed to be speaking to Index and not Kamijou.

"I dunno. Touma, what do you do in *underground malls*, anyway?"

Considering Index's situation, she was probably fully satisfied just by standing here in the path. She ceded the decision-making to Kamijou, not unhappy with anything in particular.

"Hmm. Well, it's the underground mall…so I guess arcades?"

There was a profuse number of arcades underneath Academy City, partly to reduce noise.

Right as he was thinking about it, they happened to pass by one.

Index's eyes widened at the flood of electronic noises drifting to them from inside. "Whoa, whoa, what's that? There's, like, a ton of televisions in there!"

"Ah, they're not televisions, but…well, whatever. If I sweat the small stuff I'll be done for. Yeah, they're televisions. TVs."

"…Umm…Like I said, you're not trying hard enough…"

Arcades were generally split into two different types.

One was the "outside type," and the other was the "inside type."

The first was the variety of shop with games imported from outside of Academy City, and the second referred to arcades featuring games developed within the city.

In terms of civilization and technology, Academy City was twenty or thirty years ahead of the rest of the world. That applied to video games, too. Most game companies in the outside world weren't up to that level of technology (or the technology hadn't been released publicly), so even if they developed a brand-new game cabinet, they would probably be lacking in the software department.

What they had found was one of those "inside" varieties. It looked more like an indoor amusement park than an arcade. Large, immersive cabinets made with all the latest tech lined the shop, giving it the additional impression of a futuristic exhibition corner at a science convention.

Most of these sorts of games had been developed independently by university research teams with no thought for making a profit. To sum it up simply, the city had a system where laboratories that had made popular games would receive more in the way of development funds. This resulted in many works with a strangely high level of effort put into them. Of course, there were plenty of stupid games that took that effort in the completely wrong direction, too.

"A-amazing! Everything is all sparkly, and glittery, and crackly! T-Touma, I want to go there! I want to experience all those bleep bloops!"

The three of them went inside, prompted by Index's insistence. As soon as they passed through the automatic glass doors, they were slammed by a flood of sounds that was double, even triple the intensity it had been outside.

There were a lot of unique, large game cabinets in this arcade. There were some high-def virtual reality games using 3D goggles, of course, but there were also a handful of irregular games, like shooters on rails that would measure your heartbeat and brain waves to display how scared you were at any given time.

"Index, is there any game you want to play?" he asked casually.

He got no answer. Dubious, he peered into her face, but she had completely stopped. Her eyes were quite possibly the happiest things he had ever seen. They were positively sparkling.

"Uhh, shoot...," he muttered to himself.

She had taken the bait—hook, line, and sinker. He hadn't seen her like this since she first met the cat.

She turned back to him energetically and responded, "All of them! I wanna play all of them!! Touma, Touma! I wanna start with that one first, I think!!"

No longer able to restrain herself, Index pulled his arm along.

Their destination appeared to be a kart-style game where you would ride walking, two-legged robots like a chair in a circular arena.

She was done for. No words of his would sway her at this point.

He breathed a heavy sigh, worried about his wallet. He looked beside him to see Hyouka Kazakiri smiling at him sympathetically.

5

"Ah-ha-ha! I see, Kamijou, is it? Man, Ms. Tsukuyomi, you're so fortunate to have a whole class filled with little brats, you know that? My entire class is just honors students, so it all gets so boring!"

It was after school in the empty teachers' lounge as Aiho Yomikawa opened her mouth wide and laughed heartily.

She was an attractive adult woman with long black hair tied back into a ponytail. If she were to put on a stiff gray suit or something, she'd immediately turn into the classic sexy English teacher. Unfortunately, she was a gym teacher, so she wore a green jersey all year round. Everything was just wasted on her—in more meanings than one.

Yomikawa put her hands to her hips then stuck out her chest; just one of her breasts was probably larger than Komoe's head. "Wow. So he met with an outsider and they were having a secret tea party, huh? Sounds fun! None of the little squirts in my class would ever dare to do something that bold. I'd be so affectionate to any of them if they were like that, too! I'd basically treat them like a pet!"

Incidentally, as a member of Anti-Skill, her definition of *affection* had some of that old-fashioned, sporting violence sense. She was proud of the fact that she would never point a weapon at a student, even if it were a Level Four pyrokinetic who had gone crazy. Aside from that, though, she would gladly take any *other* equipment that riot police normally used, like a specially constructed helmet or transparent, polycarbonate shield (since, by her logic, they were only for defense!) and beat the berserk esper over the head with it. Her peers had taken to calling her "the woman who makes the serious comical."

Miss Komoe, however, was more pacifistic. She glared at the violent teacher, though without very much force.

"Jeez! Anti-Skill is partly to blame for an outsider getting into the school in the first place! What would you have done if someone more dangerous than her had gotten in?! And don't go laying a hand on Kami! If you hit him on the head any more, he'll turn into such an idiot that I won't be able to change him back!"

"Ah, right, I'm just joking, just kidding, 'kay? Even I can tell the difference between a good idiot and a bad one! Man, you still have that habit of falling in love with all your students. Haven't grown out of it yet, have you?"

"Huh?! D-d-d-don't put it in those terms! Y-you see, I, well, each and every child is precious to their guardians, and I've been entrusted with them!"

"Oh, come on, don't cry. If that's all it takes to make you cry, then you'll be bawling your eyes out during graduation!"

"Grr...rrrrrrrr!! Wh-what's the matter with crying?! Every single year, the tears just come out on their own! I can't help it!"

"Ah-ha-ha, there, there." Yomikawa soothed her, rubbing a hand through her hair. Miss Komoe flailed her arms around and pushed it away.

"By the way, Teach. About the outsider—I heard there were two of them, but..."

Miss Komoe gave a start.

In recent years, many schools had been outfitted with security cameras around the premises. Any suspicious persons couldn't complain about their backgrounds being investigated.

Incidentally, Miss Komoe had announced to the teachers' lounge that nobody needed to look into Index personally. She was acquainted with the sister in white, so the nun wasn't technically an outsider. Miss Komoe also suspected she was the victim of certain circumstances that she couldn't tell anyone about.

"What about it?"

"Yeah. I just wanted to confirm one thing—**were there really two people there?**"

"Hmm?" Miss Komoe tilted her head for a moment. She didn't understand the question. Then, they heard an even knock at the teachers' lounge door, and it opened. Yomikawa blinked one eye closed.

"Anyway, this problem could be a wee bit messy, so don't mention it to the kids. Right, I'll get a report from you later. I'm busy with my own stuff, after all."

"Hmm? Do you have something to do?"

"Well…This is a secret to the students, too, but oh well. It's my *other* job. We've got a big fish to reel in this time. Some of this, some of that. You know how it is. I'm gonna go take a stroll through an underground mall. Okay, see ya later!♪" Yomikawa finished, then walked by the female student who was entering the room and left.

Miss Komoe's face retained its mystified expression, until finally she directed her attention to the student.

"I've brought you. The thing you asked me for."

"Oh, Himegami! Thanks for your hard work."

Miss Komoe stayed in her chair in the now-deserted teachers' lounge and waved her arms happily.

Today was a half day because of the entrance ceremony, so the only people still here were students with club activities and those clubs' advisers. Miss Komoe was an exception—she was working after-hours to help her friend write her report.

You can only find rank B terminals for faculty at school, after all. If only you could register terminals at your house! I'd be able to make a lot more progress that way.

Academy City's network-enabled devices were each given a ranking, which determined what information it had access to. It wasn't very convenient for those who preferred working at home.

"Sorry for asking you about it. I know I shouldn't really get students to do things for me, but I just couldn't take my hands off of this."

"It's okay. Is this the technical book you needed? There are so many books at your apartment. They all look the same. I was a little worried."

"Yep, yep! It's this one. You got it right!" answered Miss Komoe, taking the thick, leather-bound book from Himegami and rubbing her cheek on it. The cover was hot-stamped with the title *Involuntary Diffusion Fields And Their Possibilities* in gold characters.

"Involuntary diffusion fields. What is that?"

"Ah-ha-ha, Kami asked the same question!" Miss Komoe laughed brightly. "*Involuntary diffusion field* is the term for the weak power that espers unconsciously emit from their bodies."

"..." Himegami fell silent.

A power given off unconsciously. For Himegami, that almost certainly corresponded to the smell of death that lured vampires to her.

Miss Komoe overlooked the quiet Himegami's queer expression and sat back in her chair. "Oh, also, Himegami, I apologize for today. I had to leave homeroom to another teacher so I could punish Kami for skipping out on the entrance ceremony. I was worried about you being suddenly thrown into a room filled with people you didn't know."

"I was fine. There were no problems. But that aside. Did Kamijou do something bad?"

"Oh, right! That's right! Listen to this, Himegami! Miss Komoe could still forgive him if that nun followed him to school. And yet, can you believe that he took her and another girl into the cafeteria and was chatting the day away with them?!"

Himegami's eyes narrowed at her usage of the words *another girl*.

The image of the girl standing with Index at the front gate crossed her mind.

"That other girl. How was she dressed?"

"Are you interested? Mu-hu-hu."

"..." Himegami's silence spoke volumes, and Komoe's smile strained a bit.

"Um, hmm. She stood out quite a bit. She had crooked glasses and hair coming out the side of her head. And she wasn't wearing our school uniform, either—it was a short-sleeve blouse, a red tie, and a blue skirt. She was kind of like...well, she seemed sort of weak-willed, or like she was really worried about other people, or something like that."

Himegami averted her gaze and thought about her.

What had her name been?

"Miss Komoe."

"Y-yes?"

"Is there a student. Named Hyouka Kazakiri. In this school?"

6

They had used 8,000 yen in just one quick go-around in the arcade.

Index exhaled. "Wow, that was a lot of fun! I think I'm totally satisfied and content now, Touma."

"…Aye. Mr. Kamijou is also worn out and exhausted, you know. Hey, cat. It looks like starting today we'll only be eating bread crusts. You okay with that?" asked Kamijou, exhausted. The cat hissed like an angry snake, stubbornly refusing that idea.

"Touma, Touma! What should we play next?"

"…Why don't we play the *let Kamijou take a break* game?"

"Touma, you want to go around again?"

"No, please, anything but that! I'll go completely bankrupt if we do!" he cried.

Then, as if timed, his cell phone began to play his ringtone, though it was pretty crackly. It wasn't a bad phone, it was just that it had been treated so roughly that its speakers were out of whack. Of course, anyone who knew about his fantastic summer break would think it amazing that it was still working at all.

He looked at its screen. It wasn't a text message—it was a call. He didn't know whose number it was. He turned away from Index and Kazakiri and began to manipulate the phone. The latter noticed him.

"…Do you want…to go drink some juice?"

"Huh? Well, Touma should come with—"

"We'll buy one for him, too, okay?"

She took Index's hand and walked away from him. He gestured with his empty hand in apology, deftly took some coins from his wallet with the other, and tossed them to Kazakiri. This startled her, but she managed to catch them.

After watching them leave, he concentrated on his phone.

Unfortunately, despite finally getting away from Index for a minute, the only thing he heard from the speakers was static and the fragments of a voice.

"...zzz...hello...zzzzzzz...this...can you hear...zzz...meg...mi..."

The flood of sounds from the arcade was making it even harder to hear.

".........is...kaz...ri...zzzzzzz...you? *Zz, zzz...this...tant...can you...zzzzzzzzZZzzZzzZzz*!!"

Suddenly, the connection cut off with a *click*.

He thought he'd just barely made out a girl's voice, but that was it. He also thought he had heard the voice before, but he couldn't put his finger on it because of all the static and noise.

"Well, this is the underground mall, I guess..."

There were cell phone antennas set up underground, too, but it didn't take very much distance between one of them and the phone to render it essentially unusable.

"I wonder what that was about," he wondered, folding his phone up and sticking it back into his pocket.

"Touma's not a scary person, okay?" said Index, in the back of the arcade where the vending machines and café were. Hyouka Kazakiri looked at her from behind her glasses.

"...Huh?"

"I mean, you seem really afraid of him, but Touma is actually a nice person, okay?"

"Oh...yes." She looked down slightly. "...That's...not it. It's not that...he's scary, or I don't like him, or anything..."

"???"

"...I don't really get it, either...It's like...he has a lot of static electricity...It's like trying to touch a sweater, kind of..."

"Hmm." Index nodded along with her. She didn't know what *static electricity* was in the first place. Kazakiri saw her worried expression and said,

"...Maybe it's because...this is my first time...talking to a boy..."

Their conversation ended for a moment.

After a while, she changed the subject.

"Anyway...that game before was really fun...You were having such a good time..."

"You looked like you were having fun, too! Do you come to this kind of place a lot?"

"No...today's my first time." Kazakiri gave a forced smile, took out her wallet, and removed a few hundred-yen coins from it. "What... what would you like to drink?"

"Urk. I don't want to ask vending machines for things anymore, I think. They're impossible for me to use." She pouted. "Hyouka, you do it!"

Kazakiri smiled painfully again. Index's total defeat to the ticket machine in the cafeteria still seemed to be weighing on her. "...This is...my first time...so I don't really know what kinds are good...I'll push the button, so you choose."

"Hyouka, you've never had juice before?" Index asked casually. Her lack of modern sense and knowledge was probably why she didn't think Hyouka's words strange in the slightest.

In response, Hyouka Kazakiri said, once again, in a normal tone of voice,

"...No, *today's my first time.*"

7

Kamijou racked his brain trying to figure out who had called him. Suddenly, though, he stopped thinking when he noticed that Index and Kazakiri seemed to be taking their sweet time coming back here.

Lost?...Nah, couldn't be.

His common sense rejected that possibility. However, as he thought about it sensibly, he remembered that *common sense* didn't necessarily apply to either of them. He decided to search for them just to be sure.

"Heeeey, Index! Kazakiri?"

He made his way toward the back of the arcade, looking to and fro as he walked. The "inside type" of arcade had many large games, some the size of passenger cars, so there were blind spots in his vision here and there. As he continued to search for the two of them, he made sure to peek into the game cabinets' shadows, drawing hostile stares from the students waiting in line for their turns.

It brought him to the rest area, where there were three vending machines set up.

Hmm? I thought Kazakiri said they were going to buy juice...Did I miss them?

Kamijou looked around again, a shade of worry crossing his face.

Suddenly, a group of five high school girls walked past him wearing bunny suits.

"Huh?" His shoulders jerked at the shocking sight, but the girls walked through the shop with an air of nonchalance. They arrived at an old, somewhat beat-up sticker-printing booth, gathered around, and began smiling and taking pictures of themselves.

Wh-what? Is this place lending out clothes like that or something?

Upon closer inspection, he saw various ornaments on the bunny suits, like small ribbons and shoulder pieces. They must have been the outfits of some kind of characters, though he didn't know whom. Their designs all had clear, easy-to-understand motifs. Judging by that, and despite how much bare skin was involved, they might have actually been female characters from an anime targeted at children.

They seemed to be having fun, so he decided to let them be and looked away. Index and Kazakiri didn't seem to be anywhere around here, so he turned on his heel, ready to return to the entrance or the front counter...

...when suddenly he heard a couple of familiar female voices.

"...Umm, well...Again, are we...really going to do this...?"

"Yeah, we are! Come on! Wow, this is amazing! They have Magical Powered Kanamin's dress here!"

"Umm...are you going to...wear that?"

They were, without a doubt, the voices of Index and Hyouka Kazakiri. *Where, where, where are they?* He looked around. They seemed to be on the other side of the three vending machines.

?

He frowned and went around behind them. There, hidden in the shadows, he found what appeared to be a changing room, cordoned off by a curtain. It was bent diagonally, as if it hadn't been treated with the utmost care. Its fabric also looked a bit dirty.

Their voices were coming from there.

"But this is too small. I don't think I can wear it. All the clothing here seems like it was made for babies."

"Mmm. Well, there's…Around your waist, there's a dial…that you turn. It should change the size."

"Huh? Ah, whoa! What is this? The clothes got big all of a sudden?!"

"Umm…it's not quite…shape memory…I think it's using air. The threads in the fabric…are like pipes, and you can push air through them to get them to expand and make the clothing size whatever you want…At least, I think that's how it works, anyway…"

Wait. Haven't I been in this situation before?

Kamijou instinctively began to dig through his memories. Yeah, it was the same. Index was gone, he was looking for her, then he found her, and when he opened the door, he came face-to-face with the two of them fully naked. It had just happened back at school, in the nurse's office.

He walked up to the front of the changing room and stopped before the curtain. He was pretty sure it was the two of them in there, but he didn't want to mistake them for someone else.

"Index, are you there?"

Instantly, he heard two short yelps from the other side. It sounded like someone had just dumped ice into their clothes.

"T-T-T-T-T-Touma! What? Are you there?!"

"Umm, er…don't open that right now…I mean, really!"

Their voices sounded terrified, despite the fact that they were both behind a curtain. Having a man talk to them from the other side while they were changing must have been causing them to panic. Even Kazakiri's voice, usually soft as a fly, was loud this time. She was probably in a state of complete defenselessness, or something close, at the moment.

"Okay. Don't worry, Mr. Kamijou won't come into the nurse's office a second time. Opening the curtain right now would be awful. Accidentally falling into the curtain would be even more awful. I got it, I got it. Mr. Kamijou is going to withdraw from the combat zone."

"Ah, right. Okay, Touma. See you later!"

"…Umm…I would rather…you not see me in this outfit, either…"

As he heard their voices, he slowly, quietly stepped back about three meters. No problems. The changing room curtain was guarding the two of them like an iron wall. *Thank God nothing happened,* Kamijou thought, putting a hand to his chest. He was about to turn away, when…

Swish.

Without any warning, the curtain fell straight down.

"Huh…?"

The curtain was already pretty beaten up in the first place, but the rail holding it up had come off. The changing room was now fully open, like a cloth being pulled off a fabulous prize.

His mind went completely and utterly blank.

The two girls stood frozen in place.

Index was wearing floppy clothing based on the white outfit of Magical Powered Kanamin, which they had seen the rebroadcast of the day before. However, the clasps on the skirt were still undone. Parts of her that couldn't be expressed in writing were now in and now out of sight.

He had to give most of his condolences to Hyouka Kazakiri, though. She had chosen the outfit of the female villain from Kanamin (who, midway through the story, joined the main character's party)…except Index had probably chosen it *for* her. It was one of those sexy suits of armor with zero defense—basically just a black bikini. (It came with a long pareo, but it was fully open in the front, so the pareo was really just decoration.) In terms of

revealed skin…Well, it was the kind of clothing you apparently needed to remove your underwear to put on, but the front hooks on her chest armor (read, a pseudo-bra) were undone. She was bent over, and her hands were on each side of her waist armor (read, false panties), paused in an awkward spot between being pulled up all the way and being not quite there yet.

The next few seconds of silence felt like an eternity, but finally, time began to move again.

Index bared her teeth in rage and her eyes flared up. Kazakiri went red all the way to her ears and began trembling. Tears began to form in the corners of her eyes.

"Hey, wait. Just wait. This isn't fair. Let's consider this calmly, all right? I am three meters away from the changing room. My hands can't reach that far, and I don't have an ability that lets me drop curtains without using my hands. See? This isn't…my fault…I think…"

"Touma, why were you looking this way when the curtain fell, then? Isn't *that* your fault?"

"I-if you had been turned away…I-it wouldn't have been… this bad…"

Kazakiri was teary-eyed and looking guilty, but she was mad at the same time. Kamijou briefly reflected that it was a new expression for her in a vain attempt to escape reality.

"Umm, so…you're gonna do *that*, huh, Miss Index?"

"Yup," Index replied, firmly locking the clasps on her skirt.

"There's no use in arguing, Touma."

In the far reaches of his mind, he heard the reveling of girls.

"Photo stickers…Hyouka, Hyouka! How do you take these pictures? What do you do?"

"Umm…You put money in here…Then you push the button, and five seconds after…"

"Hmm. Hyouka, you look kinda bothered. Are you worried about something?"

"Um, well…Do we really have to take pictures? I'm, err…Ah, wait! Don't push the button! I-I decided I don't want to—"

"Come on, I'm taking it, okay, Hyouka? If you struggle too much, your face will come out weird."

"Ah, urgh…You're not…listening…"

Meanwhile, Kamijou was on the floor in the shadows three meters away from them, reduced to a ruined pile of human garbage.

8

Index and Kazakiri changed into their regular clothes. They looked like complete opposites. Index was in very high spirits as she gazed at the photo stickers they had made, but you could almost hear the depressed, bell-like *gong* sound effect behind Kazakiri. Her mind was in tatters, having suffered the double shock of being seen naked and having terrible pictures taken of her.

"Okay, Hyouka, here's half!"

Index paid no mind to any of that, though. She split the block of sixteen photo stickers along the perforation lines into two halves, each with eight, and handed one to Kazakiri. She was probably deathly embarrassed about what she looked like in them, but she still wanted to treat them as a treasured memory of her time with a friend. She was making a pretty complex facial expression.

"Wow, it feels like the whole day has already gone by, huh?" remarked Index, looking at both of the split sheets. "So this is school life! Yeah, it's really cool."

"Actually, no, in reality you have to take boring classes and suffer through these horrible tests and stuff. It's nothing like this."

Kamijou, the amnesiac, had never experienced either of those things, but he still carried on the conversation acting like he knew.

She grinned at him. "If you can call it boring, then that probably means you're happy."

He thought for a moment. "…Yeah, maybe." He nodded.

Index was, of course, not a resident of his world. He didn't know whether they had mandatory public education in her world. At the very least, the whole "go to a good school and get employed at a good company" pre-charted future probably wasn't part of it.

Maybe she saw his insignificant school life as a treasure she could never reach—a peaceful world, without war...and comfortable times they could call boring.

It was a law of nature that the longer you stay in an arcade, the more money disappears from your wallet, so Kamijou and the others decided to leave.

Hours had passed since then, but the activity in the underground mall was showing no signs of waning. However, the school uniforms in the crowd were steadily changing to personal attire. The students who had gone home to change were coming back at this point. No sunlight got down here. The brightness was kept constant by fluorescent lights, so cues like these were all that gave you a sense of the passage of time.

As he was talking to Index and Kazakiri along one of the walls, conscious of the flow of traffic, a female high school student ran past them. She wore the Judgment brassard on her arm.

"...Hmm?"

He casually tried to look away again, but then suddenly realized the Judgment girl had stopped and was glaring at them. She walked straight toward the dazed Kamijou without hesitation, looking quite mad about something.

She drew herself up to her full height before them and said, "Hey, you there! Everyone else is paying attention, so why are you just hanging around? Run away, quickly!!"

Not only Kamijou, but Index and Kazakiri as well were surprised by suddenly being yelled at.

Um, but did...did she say something earlier? He was confused. He was pretty sure she hadn't said anything to him yet.

The Judgment girl scowled.

"My telepathy! Don't you hear it? How about now?"

The girl's face went red with strain. Then, Index and Kazakiri cried out at the same time and looked around.

"H-huh...? Where did that voice...?"

"Mgh. I think we heard it come directly into our heads."

Beside the flustered pair of girls, Kamijou still stood there with a blank face.

"Oh, right, telepathy, huh? That power that lets you talk to people from a distance. And there're a bunch of different transmission types, too. I remember Miss Komoe talking about this stuff during my remedial classes. Reading and writing bioelectric fields, using low-frequency sounds beyond the range of human hearing...but no, I think this is the string telephone one. See, watch."

Kamijou stuck a hand in front of Index's face, and another look of surprise came over her face. He had probably intercepted the telepath's power and silenced the voice in her head.

The string telephone.

As its name implied, it was a type of telepathy that created an invisible string by changing the transmission rate of the vibrations in the air. This string worked like a speaking tube. The voice would be conveyed through the pipelike cord of air vibrations and only come out of the very end of it. Kamijou couldn't see what path the strings were taking—since they were invisible—but his right hand had probably touched the string linking him and the telepath girl, which is why it couldn't reach him.

"Although, telepathy is still under active R&D. I heard that it was disappearing with the popularity of cell phones now, kind of like pagers..."

"...*You*..." The Judgment girl's temples twitched and convulsed, but she continued. "I wonder why my voice isn't reaching you? Well, whatever. I'll explain orally."

Slide. She took one step closer to Kamijou.

"Huh?"

"There's a terrorist somewhere in this mall right now. Code Red is in effect. They're going to seal off the gates to the underground mall so they can begin a capture operation in...umm, nine hundred and two seconds. It's going to turn into a shoot-out, so I'm going around asking everyone to get out of here quickly. Understand?"

Kamijou flinched.

Index didn't know what Code Red meant. Even though Kazakiri

would have known, the reality of such a rare occurrence probably hadn't set in just yet. She returned the Judgment officer's words with a blank stare.

"If the terrorist knew about the operation, they might flee. That's why they requested I use telepathy, since it doesn't rely on sound. Don't cause a stir. Please evacuate as casually as possible."

"Hmm. So you're telling everyone except the terrorist. Huh? Wait, so does that mean you already know what they look like?"

"There's no need for a civilian like you to worry about that. We've all gotten search instructions, complete with mug shots, so there's no problem."

The Judgment girl flipped open her cell phone. On its screen was a picture of somebody's face. *Is it the terrorist?* thought Kamijou as he tried to look, but she closed the phone again with one hand.

"Okay, now, if you understand, please evacuate. Less than eight hundred seconds remain before they close up."

With that, the Judgment officer left.

He looked around him again. The students now all seemed slightly worried, as if they had heard her voice. They were heading for the exits as naturally as they could manage, just as she had told them. From a distance, though, it still had that strained, tense feeling like during an evacuation drill.

"Hey, this is pretty bad…Let's get out of here, Index."

He didn't need to get involved in any kind of unfortunate trouble. It was dangerous here. He figured he should take Index and Kazakiri and get out immediately.

However…

…Huh? Wait a minute, wouldn't that be bad?

He stood there without moving, at the side of the department store staircase. The two girls looked at him questioningly.

There were four or five armed Anti-Skill men near the exit. They were clad from head to toe in black body armor with helmets and goggles adorning their heads. They looked sort of like robots, gripping rifles he'd never seen before.

Index didn't live in this city. She did have a temporary guest ID, but he didn't know who had issued it, and it didn't change the fact that she was here illegally.

If they investigated her more thoroughly…couldn't she be arrested?

If this had been a normal situation, it wouldn't be worth thinking about. Index was probably fine walking around the city anyway. But this was an emergency, and inspections were commonplace. They would closely examine anyone they found even a little suspicious. They might end up discovering that she was an outsider.

In reality, the tighter security for events like the Olympics or the World Cup was done to round up large numbers of drunks and others who weren't obstructing the actual events at all. The relationship between the current security setup and Index was close to that.

He didn't know who this terrorist was, but he wanted to give them a piece of his mind. If Kamijou and Index approached the exit carelessly, they could be caught by Anti-Skill, but if they stayed here, they might be caught in the crossfire.

But I guess we don't have any choice. I'd rather be inspected by Anti-Skill than stuck in a gunfight any day. Damn it, I hate lose-lose situations!

Kamijou decided to leave, risky though it might be.

However, something put an end to those thoughts right then and there.

The hands of something *strange* had wormed their way into his reality.

"—I've fooound youuu."

It was a woman's voice.

But he heard it from the wall; there shouldn't have been anything there.

When he looked over, his whole body stiffened in shock. On the wall, at about eye level, was a clump of brown mud about the size of his palm. It kind of looked like chewed gum someone had stuck on there.

But in the middle of that mud, there was a human eyeball.

It darted back and forth, looking around, rolling, restlessly moving like a camera lens.

Kazakiri just looked at it blankly. It didn't seem real to her. It might have just been a fake eye made of glass. Kamijou was in a similar spot. Something in the back of his head was tingling, and his mind couldn't quite process the visual information being sent to it.

Index, however, looked at the eyeball calmly, without being surprised.

The surface of the mud rippled subtly, and those vibrations created a voice.

"Hee. Hee-hee. Hee-hee-hee-hee. The Index of Forbidden Books, and Imagine Breaker, and the key to the Imaginary Number District...Which one should I choose? Can I have any of them? Tee-hee-hee. I don't know! So many options to choose from!"

Her voice was both bewitching and husky at the same time.

The decadent voice was reminiscent of a songstress who had ruined her throat with tobacco—but then it became something altogether different, harsh and crude, a voice that you would be hardpressed to find even in the dingiest of pubs:

"—*Guess it'd be fastest just to kill 'em all, eh?*"

Kamijou couldn't figure out what this strange voice intruding on them was. Was the strange mud the product of some supernatural ability, or was it sorcery? He couldn't tell.

However, Index cut the question down without waiting a second.

"A false human image created from the earth—the arrangement on this Kabbalah technique is pretty similar to *ours*. Especially the part where it substitutes the golem, guardian of Judea, for England's guardian angels."

He couldn't keep up with Index's abrupt attitude shift. He tried to parse what she had just said, but it didn't help.

So he decided to venture a question for now. "A golem? You mean that eyeball?" he asked, pointing out the mud and the eyeball stuck to the wall. It was so disgusting he thought he might throw up, but he didn't feel any threat to his life from it. And besides, the golems he knew about were these giant, clumsy puppets made of giant boulders. They were in all sorts of video games.

Index kept her gaze on the muddy eyeball, however, and replied,

"There is an oral tradition, passed down through the ages, that says that God created man from the earth. Golems are a subspecies of that concept. I think this sorcerer made just the eyeball part so she could have it specialize in searching and observation. Creating even a single golem is quite a feat, so I guess only making the eyeball reduced the cost and let her control a lot of them like pawns."

At Index's explanation, the eyeball sent ripples through the surface of the mud again, and the voluptuous voice gave a laugh.

Kamijou didn't know how this worked, but he understood, at least, that this mud and the eyeball were like a radio-controlled car. Somebody was controlling them.

"So that means...that this sorcerer is the terrorist, then?"

"Hee-hee," laughed the mud. "A terrorist? A terrorist! Heh-hh. Does the word *terrorist* refer to people who do things like *this*, I wonder?"

There was a *splash* as the mud and the eyeball burst open, then melted into the wall and disappeared.

Then, a moment later...

A loud *ga-thunk* shook the entire underground mall.

"What...?!"

The tremors shook the structure like a small boat in a storm. Kamijou nearly toppled over. Out of the corner of his eye, he saw Kazakiri catch Index in her arms before she fell.

Then, another quake rocked the mall like a pirate ship hit by a cannonball. The point of impact was far from them, but its shock waves immediately spread throughout the whole underground.

Dust sprinkled down from the ceiling.

The fluorescent lights flickered twice, three times—and then suddenly all light sources went out at once. A few seconds later, dim red emergency lights began to illuminate their surroundings.

The once-orderly wave of evacuating people erupted into a panic. Kamijou's eardrums were overcome with the loud, stamping footsteps of a stampede of enraged bulls.

The next sound he heard was a low, heavy one.

The Anti-Skill officers had begun lowering the partition at the entrance ahead of schedule. It was thick as a steel castle gate—maybe it was for preventing the underground from being flooded, or maybe it was designed to be a tight shelter door. In any case, it descended from the ceiling to block the exit. It crashed down to the ground as if to bite the tails of the crowd. The students at the front were very nearly crushed under its weight. Now, having failed to flee, they started banging on the steel wall in a state of complete panic. Even a few of the Anti-Skill officers who had been doing inspections nearby began to try and draw near to it.

They were trapped.

People were packed like sardines into the narrow exit, forming a wall that prevented Kamijou and the others from getting close. He didn't want to think it, but if the enemy had anticipated this, then they'd immediately know where everyone had gone. She may have known where they were, as well as the overall layout and state of construction. She might have figured it all out from those muddy eyeballs she'd dispatched.

"Now, let us begin the party…"

They heard the woman's voice from the squashed mud. The already destroyed eyeball, in its final moments, acted as a broken speaker.

"…Scream all you want from your fetid grave in the earth!"

Then, once again, an even stronger tremor shook the underground mall.

9

Kamijou looked around for other exits just to be sure, but his efforts were in vain. All the staircases and elevators were sealed off by partitions, and the ventilation ducts weren't big enough for anyone to fit through in the first place.

The temperature underground was rapidly increasing, perhaps because the air-conditioning had been shut off. With the red emergency lights, it felt like they'd been thrown into an oven. He even started to feel like the air was getting thinner, though he knew that was impossible. He felt sick; it was like they'd been buried alive in a giant coffin.

As he looked around the dimly lit hallways, he spoke in an annoyed tone. "...They attacked when they saw us, so I have to go looking for her first. Index, take Kazakiri and hide somewhere."

The enemy knew where they were. However expansive this closed-off space might have been, if she searched thoroughly enough, she would eventually find them.

The enemy was after their lives. Now that they couldn't flee, they had only one option.

I'll go out and take her down before she lays a hand on Index or Kazakiri. Damn it. If only I knew how many of them there were, I'd be able to come up with a plan...

Kamijou racked his brain thinking about it. Index, holding the cat, puffed up her cheeks in annoyance.

"No, Touma, you go hide with Hyouka. The enemy is a sorcerer, so this is my job."

"Are you dumb? You can't fight with noodles for arms! Go ahead, hit someone with your fist. You'd just hurt your own wrist. Go with Kazakiri and hide somewhere!"

"Mgh. Touma, I think you're getting a couple of lucky breaks confused for actual abilities. It doesn't matter how crazy a power you have if you're just an amateur when it comes to magic! So do as an amateur should and go hide somewhere with Hyouka!"

"Hah! What sayest thou? I am the gentle Kamijou, the very personification of rotten luck. I've never gotten a *lucky break* in my life...Urgh, that stung, and I'm the one who said it..."

He began to sink into self-hatred. Hyouka Kazakiri was flustered.

"...U-umm...I don't know what's going on, but...Isn't there...anything I can...um, help with?"

""No!"" said Kamijou and Index at the same time. Kazakiri hung her head, dejected.

The very next moment, they heard footsteps approaching from around the corner.

"?!"

Kamijou tried to put himself in front of Index and Kazakiri, and Index tried to put herself in front of Kamijou and Kazakiri—as a result, they ran into each other, and the two of them crashed down to the floor in a tangle. Kazakiri remained unharmed, but she was frozen, having drawn her hands to her chest. The *click-clack* of footsteps was getting closer. The cat, close to being crushed in Index's arms, cried out and frantically waved its front legs.

The *click-clack-click-clack* of footsteps sounded like an antique grandfather clock.

They heard girls' voices from around the corner.

"Oh, my. I believe I hear a cat crying out for help!"

"Kuroko, I thought you didn't have any interest in animals."

"Yes, but I know that you do, Big Sister."

"I-I don't…"

"Oh, my. I know all about it. You feed the stray cats behind the dorm on a daily basis. But the weak electromagnetic waves your body gives off always make them all flee, and you end up just standing there alone with a can of cat food in your hand!"

"Why do you…?! Wait, Kuroko, have you been stalking me again…?!"

The two girls turned the corner and stopped when they found Kamijou and Index there on the floor. It went without saying, but Mikoto Misaka and Kuroko Shirai were not the enemy.

I got all nervous for nothing…, thought Kamijou, his body loosening up. Mikoto looked at him strangely.

"What exactly are you doing here with a girl on top of you?"

"…Oh, oh my. At a time like this, too. How very bold of you."

For some reason, there were little sparks crackling out of Mikoto's bangs, and Shirai spoke in an oddly icy voice.

However, Index made no move to get off of him.

"Touma, just who are these unrefined girls? Do you know them? What are they to you? That one with the short hair looks like the *cool beauty* from before, but she's a different person, right?"

"Wha…" Shirai caught her breath in surprise, and Mikoto began

to give a smile—a dangerous one, which *almost* looked peaceable—
to Index, who was clearly raring for a fight.

Oh, right. Index and Little Misaka met before, didn't they?
Thought Kamijou, trying to escape from reality.

But, wait. Why does the air around them feel so...strained?
A few moments later, he came back to reality.

Index and Mikoto exchanged stares.

"So you and Touma know each other, huh?"

"Touma...? Wait, so you know him, too, then?"

"...Umm. Well, I guess he saved my life and stuff?"

"Oh...Did he come running to save you, too? Even though you
didn't ask for it?"

"".......""

The two of them stayed silent for a moment, then they both sighed.
Ah! It looks like the tension resolved, he thought optimistically.

""Hey! I want an explanation! What have you been doing while I
wasn't looking?!""

No, they'd simply changed their targets. To him.

Eek! Kamijou slammed shut the door to his mind that was just
beginning to open.

Kazakiri watched him get scolded in stereo and, hands at her
mouth, started to wobble around uncertainly. She looked like she
felt bad for him, but she didn't have the guts to stand on the front
lines in this battle. She looked to and fro, quite worried, then finally
noticed that Shirai was standing a couple of steps away from her.
Kazakiri considered pleading for Shirai, the lone neutral party, to
intervene and make peace, but...

"(...My goodness, I see, she owes him her life, I knew it was suspicious the whole time, when that man came to Big Sister's room,
something happened that day, didn't it, and she didn't say a word
about it to me, and yet she revealed everything to this...urchin...is
that it, is that how I should read into this, heh-heh-heh. Oh, my, how
strange, heh-heh-heh-heh.)"

Kazakiri's glasses slid down on one side after hearing the girl's all-
too-calm muttering.

It seemed the girl with twin pigtails was not a neutral party, but a separate faction altogether. Kazakiri, now all alone, was frozen in place, unable to do much of anything. She knew that it would be impossible for her to get in the middle of such a complex map of political fissures.

Kamijou, when he was finally released from their protracted stereo lecture, managed to crawl out from beneath Index. Then he explained in simple terms their situation to Mikoto and Shirai. Of course, he spared the details regarding the sorcerer, since he knew they wouldn't believe him.

"Hmm. I don't really get it, but what this really is…is that you got wrapped up in trouble again, huh? But a terrorist this time, huh? A terrorist…Kuroko, think it has anything to do with that goth lolita from earlier?"

Mikoto looked at Shirai cheerlessly.

"It may be. Would it not be appropriate to consider it related just based on the characteristics of the voice you claim to have heard? Still, I cannot believe that an esper has attacked Academy City from the outside. It would not be strange were a natural esper to exist, but…"

"Maybe they do ability development in other places than Academy City. Though I suppose rumors of outsiders having supernatural abilities are about as trustworthy as government UFO conspiracy theories."

Neither Shirai nor Mikoto knew about sorcery, so they seemed to be basing their speculation about the recent happenings firmly within the concept of extra-normal abilities. Kamijou glanced over at Index to see her looking agitated, but he held up a hand to keep her in check. They didn't need to complicate the discussion any further.

The Judgment brassard on Shirai's arm rustled as she heaved a sigh.

"For goodness' sake. To think we'd allow a terrorist in…I think I need to refocus as well. I heard that two people broke in, and yet just one of them is causing this much of a problem. I'm worried about the other one now, too."

Hmm? Kamijou couldn't help but be drawn by what Kuroko Shirai was saying.

"What, Kuroko? There's still more trouble than this?"

"Yes. According to the information we received from Anti-Skill, there are two intruders. They entered through different places and using different methods, so they were believed to be separate incidents, but we cannot be sure."

Hmmm...? Kamijou broke out in a profuse, cold sweat.

Index seemed to have noticed it first. She tugged on his shirt with both hands and asked, "Touma, you look like you're trembling. What's the matter?"

Mikoto smirked at her. "Heh-heh...Maybe it's because you're so stuffy and annoying."

"I'm not annoying!!" Index shouted back to her. Kamijou took no notice of her.

"Excuse me, er, please, don't get angry at what I'm about to say. I think that other intruder was, er, probably me."

"Huh?" Everyone present looked at him.

Kamijou began his clever ruse to escape from all the stares. "Well...I met this clumsy man named Yamisaka last night. And we absolutely had to leave Academy City in order to help his friend, and then we finally settled that problem, and I just returned this morning, so...umm...what is it? Mikoto, Shirai, why are the two of you sighing like you totally understand and this is just a disease I have or something?"

He instinctively knew that he needed to change the topic to something else. He revved his brain motors to full. "Wait, so, what are you two doing here, anyway?"

"I am a member of Judgment, so I have come to evacuate the people who got locked in here. I *am* a teleporter, after all."

"Huh. Then what about you, Mikoto?"

"Oh, er, I didn't really..."

"?"

"Wh-what?! It doesn't really matter, does it?!"

Mikoto shouted, her face turning all red for some reason, confusing Kamijou. Shirai shut one eye, making no attempt to hide her displeasure.

"(...Well, I can't say that she was tagging along with me while I was working, then saw you come up on the Code Red security cameras in the office, and then ran here because she was worried about you. It's not something one could say normally.)"

Kamijou looked over at her, whereupon she snorted a *hmph!* and turned away.

Unaware of what was transpiring beneath the surface, he considered her teleportation ability. It would probably be pretty easy to get out of the locked-up underground mall if she used it.

"I am still a member of Judgment, so I can't overlook this terrorist, or whatever she is," she remarked, shooting a glance down the dark hallway. "But human lives come first. If it's true that they shut the partitions ahead of schedule, then we don't have any time left. If a large battle is going to happen here, then I must complete the evacuation before it does."

Even now, there were dozens of students who hadn't quite been able to escape gathered around the gate. They were all still struggling in vain to somehow get the steel wall open, when there was no way they'd be able to.

"All right. I'll buy you time while you get the trapped people out, so could you take *them* outside?"

The moment Kamijou said that, Shirai, Mikoto, and Index all angrily pointed at him at once. Mikoto exchanged pained glances with Index, as if saying that they seemed to get along at the stupidest times. Kazakiri, the only one left, couldn't muster the courage to retort and could only wave her hand uselessly in the air.

Mikoto spoke for the group.

"You need to get out of here first. I mean, you're all being directly targeted! You think we'd leave the most dangerous person on the battlefield?!"

"...Well, no, but..." Kamijou scratched his head. "My right hand nullifies all abilities, Shirai's included."

"Now that you mention it...I did fail that time you came to the girls' dorm, didn't I?"

She noted, suddenly remembering it. Mikoto's eyes immediately sharpened. He gulped and took a step back. For various reasons, he had forced his way into Mikoto's room without warning one time.

"A-anyway, I can't get outside with Shirai's power, so the only thing I can do is go fight her."

When Index heard that, she latched on to his arm.

"Then I'll stay here, too!"

This time, Index was set upon by four people—by Kamijou, Mikoto, Shirai, and Kazakiri, all at once. Even the timid Kazakiri seemed to have rallied her bravery. Her eyes were shut tight, but she definitely got in a chop to the back of Index's head.

Shirai put her hands on her hips. "My power has its limitations, though…I can probably only take two people with me at once. Though if this little brat is heavier than I expected, it may not be so easy."

"Hmph! That's funny, you calling *me* a brat! You're the most childish one here!!"

"Wh-what was that? You're flat as a board but you're telling *me* that…?!"

Mikoto gave a sigh at the enraged Kuroko Shirai. "Now, now. It doesn't matter. From a step back you're both children."

"…" From one *more* step back, and from a high school student's point of view, Mikoto looked like a child as well. Kamijou decided to smile vaguely and keep his mouth shut. After all, he was 50 percent composed of pure, distilled kindness.

On the other hand, Kazakiri was another step away, looking at them in much the same way a kindergarten teacher watches over her children. Nobody noticed her, though.

"But you can only carry two, huh…Okay, then take out Index and Kazakiri first."

"Touma, are you saying you'll stay down here with Short-Hair?" said Index in an oddly cool tone. Her canines glittered in the dark as if to say that her attack preparations were complete, and that she could bite his head at any moment.

"…Uhh. Okay, then just take Mikoto and Kazakiri."

"Oh-ho. You want to stay here with that little runt, don't you?

Hmm." This time, static electricity began to flutter about Mikoto's brown hair. The bluish-white sparks snapped and crackled sporadically, lighting up the darkness.

"Aagh, shit! Just bring Index and Mikoto, then!!" yelled Kamijou, practically tearing his hair out at this point. Shirai sighed.

"Then I'll take Big Sister and this brat, but I'll be jumping out there, too."

"Huh? Isn't it a pain to keep going between the surface and underground? I feel like it would be faster to just send one person at a time up there."

"I can control where we go much more finely if I go with them. If I send them away willy-nilly, then in the worst case, I'd be off by a bit and warp them straight into a building. I do not want to be responsible for creating any strange human pillars. Now then, if you will, both of you."

Shirai put either hand on Mikoto and Index as they glared at each other, as if to mediate.

The next moment...

There was a *poof* as Index, Mikoto, and Shirai all disappeared into thin air. Kamijou thought he heard Mikoto saying something like, "Huh? Wait, Kuroko! I'm staying here!!" but he figured she was worried about her underclassman staying here at the battlefield by herself.

He and Kazakiri naturally looked at the ceiling. Had they gotten up there safely?

"So those two first...Sorry about leaving you here."

"...N-no, don't be. I'm fine...with being last...but what...about you—"

Her words were cut off in the middle as...*gr-grash!!* The entire underground mall was rattled again by a huge tremor.

However, unlike the previous times, this blast seemed to be closer to them. The explosions of guns along with angry shouts and yells began to drift over to them from down the dim passageways.

The main event's here?...Wait, this is too soon!!

Their opponent had already scanned the underground mall with those eyeballs, so it wasn't surprising that she was heading straight for them.

The students gathered by the wall heard the sounds of fighting from afar and burst into panic once again. However unique their own powers may have been, they were just simple students at heart. They all began to run to get away, to put even a few more feet between them and the danger, but thanks to the meager red emergency lights, they stumbled over one another and started falling like dominoes.

Kamijou stared intently down the passage.

There was no time to be lost in thought about this.

If a battle were to happen here, where there were dozens of others, there would surely be sacrifices. His right hand could cancel out any strange powers, but he didn't have much confidence that he could completely protect that many people.

If I can't avoid battle one way or the other, then...

His decision was swift.

"Sorry, Kazakiri. You wait here for Shirai to come back."

"Huh...what about you...?"

As she spoke, another loud *gonk* shook the underground mall. This time it was close. A warm breeze blew up the hallway and pushed past them.

The sporadic gunshots and shouting were gradually becoming clearer and more vivid. They weren't very far from the enemy anymore.

He directed his gaze into the darkness before him, without glancing at her.

"I'm...gonna go stop it."

That's all he said. Without waiting for a reply, he ran into the dark.

He had no idea who the enemy was or how strong they were, but the sounds reaching him were enough to make him shudder. If whatever it was came this far, dozens of lives would doubtlessly be lost. And Hyouka Kazakiri would be among them.

That was something he couldn't let happen.

He ran into the darkness, tightening his right hand into a fist.

CHAPTER 3

Blockaded

Battle_Cry.

1

Sherry Cromwell retained her grace and elegance even as she walked through the gunshots and whirling dust clouds on the battlefield.

A stone statue stood in front of her like a giant shield. Its form had been created from floor tiles, sign boards, and pillars—anything that it could find here in the underground mall, rolled up like clay. It was easily four meters tall, but that made its head hit the ceiling, so it was constantly hunched over.

She sliced her white oil pastel through the air. That action became an order, and the giant statue advanced.

There were Anti-Skill officers clad in jet-black armor before her. They had brought tables and couches from a nearby café out into the passage to create a barricade. They were laying down heavy fire from behind them. They were separated into groups of three, so that when one group had to reload, another one would begin to shoot, thereby eliminating the potential opening—just like the firearm squads of Oda Nobunaga.

They have some skill, but they lack style, Sherry judged, disappointed.

The halls of the underground mall were narrow to begin with, but the statue—the golem, Ellis—was like a moving bulwark. Not even one bullet made it past the golem to where she was.

Hundreds of them impacted Ellis, but none made a decisive hit. The bullets could open holes in its limbs, but it would automatically repair all damage by tearing off wall tiles nearby, sucking them in like a giant magnet.

Ker-click, came a metal noise.

One Anti-Skill had lost his temper and pulled the pin from a hand grenade. He tried to hurl it under the statue's legs and past it in order to deal damage directly to Sherry.

"Ellis."

A second before he could, Sherry swiped her oil pastel across the air.

The statue stomped on the ground. *Grrunch!!* The floor of the underground mall shook badly like a boat being tossed around by large waves. It took less than a second, and that was the very moment the grenade left the Anti-Skill officer's hand. It stole his sense of timing, and the pin-less grenade rolled right back to his own feet.

A shout.

Then an explosion.

Blood spattered. It was a shrapnel grenade rather than a firebomb, so it didn't blow away the barricade, but she still smelled blood from just across the thin separation. Even those who managed to avoid the storm of shards were forced to dive behind the barricade to escape the explosion.

Many of the officers had dropped their rifles from the impact.

Bwshing!! The oil pastel cut through the air like a sword being drawn from its sheath.

A shadow appeared above their heads. Ellis brought down its arm like an industrial construction machine.

They reached for their spare sidearms, but it was too late.

They were far too weak to stop this enemy.

2

It was a battlefield.

The very moment Kamijou turned the corner, he wanted to cover his mouth with his hands.

It was a real-life battlefield.

In the scene that lay before him, there was no fighting, no gunshots, and no shouting. Wounded people, broken people, and people whose bodies were torn limb from limb were leaning against pillars and walls. These weren't the front lines. It was a field hospital, the place to which the defeated could temporarily retreat and tend to their wounds.

They were Anti-Skill officers.

Twenty of them, he estimated.

Their wounds were not normal ones. Just how strong had their opponent been? Their injuries demanded more than simple bandages and dressings. It was like their bodies were ripped fabric, and they needed to be repaired with a needle and thread.

How crazy is this enemy? You're telling me a sorcerer can do this much against this many Anti-Skills?

He was speechless. Even an amateur like him, with no knowledge of the inner workings of their respective organizations, knew that there was a science-based faction and a magic-based one. Yet he'd always vaguely assumed that the power levels of each faction were roughly balanced.

But look at this.

Kamijou had crossed paths with a number of extraordinary sorcerers, so he thought he understood how strong they were. It came as no small shock to see the reality before him—of the science faction getting crushed like this.

These people were supposed to protect the peace in Academy City, but they were no better than the cannon fodder in a Godzilla film.

In spite of all that, they had no intent to withdraw.

Anyone who could move, even the slightest bit, was taking chairs and tables out of the nearby stores and trying to build a barricade. Actually, it had nothing to do with whether or not they could move. They were beyond the stage where they could even care about that.

They weren't doing this under the assumption that they'd die.

Kamijou felt their absolute resolve—to complete their mission even if it cost them their lives.

But why...?

He didn't know what to say to that.

They may have had plenty of training as professionals, but...they were really just schoolteachers. Nobody was forcing them to do any of this, and they weren't getting paid for it. There was simply no reason for them to risk their lives fighting like this. They weren't real police officers; they hadn't passed civil service examinations. Who would blame them for running away under threat of death? And yet...

Then, an Anti-Skill officer leaning against the wall found him standing there in the corner in a daze. Surprisingly, it was a woman. She stopped what she was doing—wrapping an injured comrade's arm in a tourniquet—and shouted.

"You, the kid over there! What on earth are you doing here, huh?!"

All of the Anti-Skill members present turned to look at him when they heard her shout. Kamijou stood there, unable to answer. The woman who had shouted began to look really angry.

"Damn, it's one of Ms. Tsukuyomi's brats. Were you locked in here? That's why I told them not to rush to close up the walls! Young man, you need to run in the *other* direction, got that?! There are Judgment reinforcements at Gate A03, so if you can't get out, then evacuate there first! And here, take this helmet! You're better off than without it, got it?!"

Tsukuyomi—that was Miss Komoe's last name. That meant that she might have heard about Kamijou from her.

The Anti-Skill woman removed her own helmet while shouting and heaved it at him. Flustered, it bounced about in his hands like a basketball before he finally stopped it.

......He looked around again.

And then he realized the reason why they wouldn't retreat.

He took another step farther in.

"Where are you going, young man?! Shit, I can't even move! Somebody, *anybody*, hold that civilian back!"

The Anti-Skill officer shouted and held out her hand, but she couldn't reach him.

A few people answered her call and tried to stop him, but they could barely do that much with their injuries. They didn't even have the strength to stop a single high school student with no training of his own.

But they still weren't running away.

They weren't official police officers. No matter how much professional training they got, they were just teachers. This was really nothing more than an extension of patrolling the streets in the evening so that nothing bad befell the children.

Perhaps that's exactly why they understood.

Nobody was forcing them to do this—so they understood how easily they'd fall if they let their own weakness conquer them. And they knew *precisely* who would suffer the consequences if that happened.

Anti-Skill and Judgment members were never recommended or enlisted. They were always built from those who volunteered as candidates.

It was simple.

None of them were asked to do so; they were just here because they dearly wished to protect the children.

Goddamn it…, Kamijou swore to himself.

He brushed off the Anti-Skill members trying to stop him and proceeded forward. There was still a load of these idiots farther into the darkness—and from the looks of things, they were in a desperate situation.

He tightened his right hand into a fist.

He simply ran, gaze fixed ahead of him.

If conventional attacks stood no chance…well, the opponent was a sorcerer. If he used his trump card, his right hand, they might be able to turn the tables.

He headed deeper into the passageway, then noticed something strange.

I don't…hear anything?

There should have been a gunfight raging down here, but it was too quiet. He couldn't hear anything—not gunfire, not footsteps, not shouting. No floor-shaking tremors were happening, either.

He got a bad feeling in the pit of his stomach.

The feeling began to slip and slither through the rest of his body like a fungus.

Could this be...?

He ran forward, through the passages bathed in dim red light.

What was waiting for him?

"Heh. Hello. Hee-hee. Hee-hee-hee-hee."

A husky female voice echoed through the darkness.

A woman wearing a pitch-black dress with mussed blond hair and skin the color of chocolate stood in the center of the passage. Her skirt was long enough to conceal even her ankles. Its ends were frayed, damaged, and some of its seams were torn, perhaps because it had been dragged along the ground for such a long time.

A statue stood there, shielding her. It was a giant puppet, made of iron pipes, chairs, tiles, dirt, lamps, and everything else in the area all balled and mixed together by force.

And around them...

What had once been a barricade was now a mess on the floor, scattered everywhere. It looked as though it had been directly hit with a cannonball. Covered in those fragments were seven or eight Anti-Skill officers lying defeated on the floor. Their limbs twitched—they must still have been alive.

"Heh. Interesting. They're wearing shock-absorbent armor. That must be how they survived a direct hit from Ellis...Well, I had a pretty good time because of it."

Her smile was a cruel one.

Kamijou didn't know what she meant by "direct hit from Ellis," but he got the idea. An attack from that stone statue. He could imagine its power just by looking at what was left of the barricade.

"How..."

...can you do this? he finished mentally.

On the other hand, the blond woman wasn't especially interested.

"Oh, my. You're Imagine Breaker. I see the key to the Imaginary

Number District isn't with you. Hmm...What was she called again? Kaze, or wait, Kaza...something-or-other. Damn, why are Japanese names so complicated?"

She played with her hair, as if all of this was a lot of trouble for her. "It doesn't matter! Nothing matters. I don't absolutely *need* to kill that brat. No, not that one."

"What?" He doubted his ears.

He had guessed already that this woman was after Kazakiri and him. Why did she seem so uninterested?

"What do you mean *what*? It means I can kill you instead!!"

The woman whipped her oil pastel to the side.

As if connected to that movement, the stone statue stomped one foot into the ground. There was an enormous *crash*, and Kamijou lost his balance. Then, the statue brought its foot down again. Unable to withstand the second pound, he fell to the floor.

The woman, however, stood calmly in place—was she using some sort of trick? It was like she'd been cut out of the background. She was taking no damage from the quakes.

"The earth is my power. Before Ellis, none can stand atop it. Come on, start crawling. Think you can bite me like that, you dog?" she said pridefully, glaring down at him.

It was clear that this ground-pounding tactic could turn situations one-sided pretty quickly. The Anti-Skill officers with their guns wouldn't have been able to do much, either. Actually, if they accidentally let their aim wander, they could even end up hitting allies.

Kamijou tried to get back to his feet, but the woman preemptively flashed her oil pastel once more. The stone statue's foot came down again and rattled the earth. If he could touch it with but a finger, the Imagine Breaker would destroy the preternatural power, but he couldn't even take a step.

"Y-you...!"

"I'm not *you*, I'm Sherry Cromwell. Remember this...well, actually, never mind. You're going to die here anyway, so I shouldn't even bother naming myself as a member of English Puritanism."

"What?" He scowled.

English Puritanism was the group Index belonged to.

Sherry grinned thinly at him.

"I'm starting a war, and I need a trigger for it. I need as many people as possible to know that I'm a pawn of the English Puritan Church...right, Ellis?"

Sherry swung the oil pastel around with a flick of her wrist. Guided by her movements, the giant statue put its foot down on the ground, then swung its gigantic fist way up into the air. This had crushed the barricade in one shot, hastily constructed though it may have been. Kamijou tried to avoid it, but he found it difficult to move due to all the shaking. He desperately swung his right hand up and—

"Get away, boy!"

Suddenly, he heard a shout from beside him.

One of the injured Anti-Skill officers, still on the ground, was gripping his rifle.

Before Kamijou could do anything, fire erupted from its small barrel. The dim passage was filled with the sound and flash of a gunshot. Bullets ripped through the air one after another, impacting the golem's legs in an attempt to stagger it.

However...

"Agh?!" He felt a blast of hot air graze his cheek and cried out unintentionally.

Ellis's body, blocking the passage, was a conglomeration of metal and concrete. Its weight must have measured in the tons, so bullets were obviously going to ricochet off it like a pinball.

The Anti-Skill was trying to defend Kamijou from Ellis, and to his credit, the golem had stopped. Because he was aiming for the legs, it also couldn't stomp its feet. If it tried to, the bullets could hit Sherry, who was standing behind it.

But at the same time, the bullets were reflecting off of Ellis's body in every direction. As a result, he couldn't get up from taking cover on the ground.

The officer single-mindedly continued his barrage. Though Kamijou was afraid that at some point one of the bullets would hit him, all he could do was cover his head with his hands.

Shit, if only I could just get my hand on that giant bastard...!!

There were less than three meters between Kamijou and Ellis, but he couldn't carelessly make physical contact with it. Obviously he'd be at a higher risk of a stray bullet hitting him the closer he got.

If he had one chance, it was when the officer reloaded.

There was no way in hell the Anti-Skill's rifle would be able to take down that statue. It didn't have infinite bullets. He'd run out before long. In those few seconds he would spend replacing the magazine, the curtain of bullets would lift. He needed to rush Ellis during that time.

Kamijou readied his body, filling it with strength so that he could leap out at any time...

Pit-pat.

Suddenly, he heard quiet footfalls behind him.

Somehow, the weak footsteps left a clear imprint on his eardrums even as the sound of consecutive gunshots slammed against them.

He looked behind him, moving only his neck in order to avoid the bouncing bullets.

The red emergency lighting wasn't useful, and it couldn't light up the entire underground mall. It only illuminated a couple of feet. Darkness dominated the hallways beyond that.

The footsteps were coming from that darkness.

They didn't sound like trained steps. They weren't the fearless steps of a new enemy approaching, either. They were the steps of someone tiptoeing through a haunted house. The steps of a child who had come back to school at night to retrieve something he'd lost. Helpless, quivering footsteps.

A terrible premonition rose in Kamijou's chest.

Then, as if to answer his unease...

"...U-umm..."

...he heard a girl's voice.

The silhouette of the voice's owner appeared, coming out of the darkness and stepping under the red emergency light. He knew this girl. Straight, long hair that went down to her thighs, one bunch of hair sticking out the side tied up with a rubber band, thin-framed glasses on her nose—it was Hyouka Kazakiri, standing right in the middle of the hallway.

"You idiot!! Why didn't you wait for Shirai?!"

His shout was loud enough to resound in the mall, even within the vortex of gunfire.

She was just standing there defenselessly. He wanted to get up and run to her, but he couldn't, because of the bouncing bullets.

Kazakiri, however, didn't seem to understand the situation.

"...Oh. But, well..."

"Just get down!!"

"...Huh?" Kazakiri said, taken aback by Kamijou's yell, but right then...

Boom!! Her head flung backward.

"Huh?" Kamijou muttered stupidly.

Human eyes were, of course, not good enough to keep up with a speeding bullet. But anyone could still guess what had just happened.

One of the rifle rounds had bounced off Ellis's body and stricken Kazakiri directly in the face.

Something skin-colored came flying off. Her glasses frames were ripped up and flew apart.

But even though he knew all that, he couldn't wrap his head around it. He didn't want to. His brain reached critical capacity and blanked out. The gunfire had stopped at some point. The Anti-Skill officer was looking at the shot girl, looking quite dazed. Sherry frowned somewhat at the sudden development—her own target had suddenly self-destructed before her eyes in such an unexpected way.

Amidst it all...

Kazakiri leaned backward like a bridge...

...and collapsed to the floor, limp, like a puppet.

He heard the parts making up her face breaking.

They crumbled. What looked like a piece of her head fell to the floor separately, long hair still attached to it. The bullet had hit the right side of her face, but this destruction…it was like her very skull had been distorted. The broken glasses frames fell to the floor. One of the severed earpieces on the end of the frame was still attached.

"Ka…za…kiiriiiiii!!"

Kamijou panicked and stood, then ran over to her. His posture and gait made him look drunk.

When he reached her, his feet stopped abruptly.

His face was covered with an expression of surprise.

But not at the terrible sight.

Her wound was severe, to be sure. After all, the right half of her head had been totally blown away. It was a chaotic, terrible injury that looked more like something inside her body had exploded rather than a bullet hitting her. It was completely outside the realm of everyday violence. Maybe that's why it didn't feel real. The destruction was so complete, so *overwhelming*, that it very nearly appeared comical.

But that wasn't the issue.

There was a much bigger issue, a giant problem, and it made all that seem insignificant in comparison.

Kamijou looked at Kazakiri's wound again.

The insane wound. Half of her head was blown off—but inside it was **nothing but emptiness**.

There was no flesh. No bones. No brain. Nothing.

Not a single drop of blood flowed from her wound.

It was like papier-mâché or a 3D model made of polygons. From the outside, it looked like the elaborate skin of a human, but on the inside, it was like a smooth, light purple sheet of plastic.

A small object floated in the middle of her head cavity as if held there by magnetism. It was a tan-colored triangular prism. Its bottom was a triangle approximately two centimeters square, and it was a little less than five centimeters tall. It sat there in a fixed location, rotating around and around. Its sides were tiled with rectangles that were around one millimeter high and two across. It almost looked like a tiny keyboard. As if invisible fingers were clacking away on it, the rectangular keys on the side of the prism were rapidly moving in and out.

What...is this...?

Kamijou was bewildered. What he was seeing was completely unrealistic. He couldn't connect this to simple words like *that looks painful* or *that must hurt.*

Was this another esper ability? Was her Identity Unknown power responsible for all this strangeness?

Kazakiri looked nothing like a simple esper, though. Even the seven Level Five espers in Academy City, people like Railgun and Accelerator, had the same physical makeup and structure as a normal person. But Kazakiri seemed fundamentally different from a human.

"Ugh..."

As he struggled to think of what to do, she groaned softly.

Perhaps in reaction to her awakening, the keys on the keyboard on the spinning triangular prism in her head began to oscillate more quickly. They were going as fast as a sewing machine.

No...

Finally, Kamijou got a very realistic chill.

Isn't that...backward...?

Was the prism not reacting to Kazakiri's movements? Were Kazakiri's actions and expressions instead being created by the *prism's* movements?

He forgot all about Sherry's attack. He watched the sight that confronted him, baffled, unable to move.

The sounds of the prism's keys going *clack-clack-clack-clack* whispered like falling rain. The prism began to spin as fast as the wheel of a trackball. How was that being converted into action? Missing part of her face, she slowly brought her head up.

She stared blankly at Kamijou with her one eye.

She looked like she was waking up from a nap. She didn't seem to be feeling any pain.

With slow movements, she sat up on the ground.

"Huh...?...My glasses. Where are...where are my glasses?"

Her fingers searched across the part of her face where they should have been...and then she appeared to realize something. She jerked her hand back like she had touched hot water. Then, this time with much trepidation, she brought her fingers to her face again.

"Wha...what is...this?"

Her fingers went slowly into the edge of the cavity.

"N-no..."

She caught a glance of her side in the café window right next to her.

She realized it was her own face being reflected. The blood drained from the half of her face still remaining. Her one eye shot back and forth hurriedly, betraying the panic and disquiet she felt within her.

"No...!...What...what...what's this?! Nooo!!"

Kazakiri shook her head violently and screamed at the top of her lungs, as if something she'd been holding back had just exploded. Kamijou caught his breath. She rose to her feet clumsily, like she had lost her sense of balance, and then ran away from her own reflection in the glass. She was so confused that she actually ran straight toward the giant statue—straight toward Ellis.

Sherry snapped out of her thoughts at this and flashed her oil pastel across the air.

The statue's concrete arm howled.

Its fist swatted Kazakiri away with the back of its hand like a fly, hitting her arm and side. Her forward momentum was completely transferred upward and she went flying. Three meters in the air, her delicate body slammed against a support beam. Then, as if that wasn't enough, her body bounced off of it like a pinball, right back to where Sherry was standing behind Ellis.

There was a sickening *plop*.

Kamijou looked and saw that Ellis's attack had snapped Kazakiri's left arm at the elbow. Her side was a different shape now, too—it reminded him of a box of candy that somebody had stepped on.

"Ah..."

But still.

Despite that, Hyouka Kazakiri's body writhed on the floor.

"Ah, agh, ag, ah, aaaaaaaaaaaaaaaaaaaaaaaaaaaaaaaaaaaaaaaaaaa
aaaaaaaaaaaaaaaaaaaaaaaaaaaaaaaaaaaaaaaaaaaaaaaaaaaaaaaaaaaaaaa
aaaaaaaaaaaaaaaaaaahhhhhhhhhhhhhhhhhhhhhhhhhhhhhhh???!!!"

The scream unleashed from her broken, slender body seemed to surprise even Sherry. She leveled her pastel, paying close attention to her for the first time.

However, Kazakiri saw none of that. Such luxury was not afforded to her. When she realized that inside her torn arm was an empty void, she began to swing her arms and legs around like she was trying to get a spider off of them. She ran away into the darkness farther down the passage.

"Ellis." Sherry lightly tapped her fingertips on the surface of the oil pastel, and Ellis threw a punch at a nearby support beam. *Gr-krash!!* The entire underground mall shook, and the ceiling began to creak.

The next thing they knew, the building material right above the rifle-wielding Anti-Skill officer's head began to crash down upon him.

"Hmph. Interesting. Let's be off, Ellis. Such an absurd, unsightly fox we'll be hunting…"

Without sparing a glance at Kamijou or the Anti-Skill officer, now buried alive, Sherry swung around the oil pastel in her hand and, as she manipulated Ellis, disappeared into the blackness—most likely to follow Kazakiri.

Kaza…kiri…

He couldn't do much but stand there dumbfounded for a while.

What he had just seen had been burned into his eyes forever.

3

Kuroko Shirai wasn't sure what to do.

She had brought that stupid nun and Big Sister up to the surface, but when she got back…Touma Kamijou and that easy-to-miss girl were nowhere to be found.

How worrying...I could search the area, but...

Fortunately, she couldn't hear the sounds of battle, but she didn't know when one would start up again. Plus, there were still dozens of civilians here.

In terms of threat level, the terrorist was going straight for Kamijou and the girl, of course, but she still couldn't totally ignore these people, either—they could always be hit by a stray bullet.

She didn't even know whether she'd find them if she looked, and these people who had nothing to do with this were right here in front of her.

She briefly considered this and decided to evacuate the people before her eyes first.

One cannot put value on lives, can they? I'm worried about Big Sister and really want to go look for her, but I feel that leaving these people here would be wrong.

She sighed and walked up to the scared, trapped students.

The construction materials that had fallen from the ceiling were unexpectedly light, and the buried Anti-Skill officer hadn't been particularly hurt by them. Though the downed officers nearby were also wounded, nobody was dead, and they were busy wrapping their injuries and stitching them together with needles and thread.

Kamijou helped the officer move the debris from atop him. Then, while shrugging off his urges to stop, he began to run down the passage after Kazakiri and Sherry. There seemed to be a lot of department stores in this area, and they were connected underground by a complex maze of hallways. The passages before now had been little more than straight lines, but this was a labyrinth—a veritable spiderweb.

Damn it, what the hell is going on...?

Sherry calling herself a member of the English Puritan Church bothered him, but Hyouka Kazakiri blew all that away.

It didn't seem like she had been aware of how strange her own body was.

She'd looked at her own image in the mirror and screamed as if it were a monster.

As far as he could tell, she had just learned the truth today, at that moment—and it caused her to panic.

...And that means...that wasn't *Kazakiri's ability? Or was she one of those espers who didn't even know she was one? Shit, I don't understand anything. Is she going to be all right like that? How...how would you even heal her?*

Having thought that far, Kamijou stopped.

The strange scene came back to mind. Even if he were to save her, how would he do that? It only raised more questions.

Should I stop Sherry or meet up with Kazakiri first? Damn, what do I do?

He worried, then worried some more, and finally took out his cell phone.

There were too many unanswered questions about Hyouka Kazakiri. And if he needed someone on the science side of things who had far more knowledge than he did, there was only one person to call.

Komoe Tsukuyomi.

Maybe she'll know something, he thought. Unfortunately, he was out of cell range. Someone had called him when they were at the arcade, and they couldn't actually talk then, either.

First I need to get close to one of the underground mall antennae.

He walked along and looked around until he spotted a sporting goods store. Something that looked suspiciously like an antenna was attached to its wall.

He went right up under it and finally started to use his cell phone.

After two rings, Miss Komoe picked up.

"Ah! Kami, is that you?! Yay, yay! We finally got through! Kami, where have you been this whole time?"

"Huh? Miss Komoe, were you looking for me?"

"Himegami said she called you, but there was a lot of static."

Kamijou wondered. That meant the call at the arcade was from Himegami?

"Kami, Kami! I have something a little bit important to tell you. You see—"

"Sorry, Miss Komoe, but I've got my hands full. Could you listen to what I have to say first?"

"Huh?...This really is important, but all right. What is it?"

He was profusely thankful that she backed off so easily.

He summarized what he knew about Kazakiri. Of course, he hid her name and the fact that they were in combat at all, and basically just asked, "Yeah, this is what was happening, is there an ability like that?"

However, Miss Komoe thought for a moment, then replied,

"...Kami, are you talking about Hyouka Kazakiri, by any chance?"

Bull's-eye.

He didn't know what to say, and she continued, sounding less nervous.

"Hmm, well. Actually, the important thing I had to tell you was about her."

"Huh? Why are you investigating her?"

"You see, Kami...There's something called *security* at school. We have to protect all the secret information regarding ability development, too, and nasty crimes are on the rise on top of that. Why *wouldn't* we look into a non-transfer student outsider who came onto school grounds without permission?"

She also remarked that she knew the nun, so they didn't look into her too much.

Suddenly, he remembered Himegami's words from this afternoon by the school gate.

—But. As far as I remember. I am the only transfer student.

"And, to answer your question, Kami...There are certainly espers like that. For example, ones with metamorphosis. They can change their body into whatever they want!"

"Then is Kazakiri a..."

"No. Metamorphosis is an extremely rare ability that only three people in Academy City have. Hyouka Kazakiri isn't one of them." Her voice hardened. "And even if she were just a metamorphosis esper, it wouldn't make sense."

"What's that supposed to mean?" Kamijou got an instinctive bad feeling.

He couldn't determine whether that feeling was correct, though.

"Kami, as I said before, the school has a security system. There are cameras set up on the premises. However…"

She paused.

"Hyouka Kazakiri didn't show up on any cameras. We contacted Anti-Skill and asked for the satellite images, but there still wasn't anything suspicious on them…You and she were having such a *pleasant* conversation, so where did she come in from?"

"Wha…"

"When she disappeared from the cafeteria, did you notice it? I didn't notice it. It was like **she just suddenly disappeared into thin air!**"

"H-hang on a second! Then what, are you saying that she can use both metamorphosis *and* teleportation?!"

"Kami, double espers have been judged realistically impossible. There would be too much load on the person's brain! Of course, my explanation for this is even more unrealistic."

For some reason, he was hesitant to hear the rest.

But he couldn't get started if he didn't go ahead with it. He gulped, then asked,

"…What do you think, Miss Komoe?"

"Well, you see…," she began in a slow, relaxed voice.

"Involuntary diffusion fields—I think they're deeply related to all this."

Kamijou didn't immediately understand what she meant.

"You mean that power that espers give off unconsciously or whatever?"

"That's the one! Adding to that, the fields are so weak that you need instruments to measure them, and the type of power each esper gives off is different."

"So how is that related to Kazakiri? Is the power she's giving off unconsciously, like, crazy strong or something?"

Komoe didn't answer his question.

"I said this morning that I was helping a friend from college with research on involuntary diffusion fields." He heard the sound of paper rustling from the other end. "Leaking someone's thesis information is strictly forbidden, but I have faith that you'll keep your lips zipped…The research itself is investigating the waves that are created when multiple involuntary diffusion fields collide with one another."

He was getting further and further away from understanding what she was trying to say. Did any of this really have to do with her? Was she just complaining? Or gossiping?

"Kami, you know how you can get all sorts of data by measuring people with machines?"

"Huh?"

"Generation, emission, and absorption of heat…Reflection, refraction, and absorption of light…The creation of bioelectricity and the formation of magnetic fields that go along with it…Oxygen consumption and carbon dioxide expulsion…Mass and weight are two of the more simple data points you can collect. I could go on all day giving examples! We can gather thousands, if not millions, of data points with different varieties of machines."

"What about it?" Kamijou urged, still attentive to the darkness around him.

"This is purely speculation…" Miss Komoe paused for a moment. "If, instead, **all these humanlike data points were collected and put into one place**, would that mean there was a human there?"

"Wha…?" He broke off.

"There are many kinds of espers in Academy City. And all of them constantly emit a weak power without knowing it. Even if each individual one is weak, what might happen if a lot of them overlapped and combined into one meaning? See, think about the letters *B*, or *P*, in the alphabet. By themselves, they don't do anything, right? You put them together into words like *select* and *start*, and that's when they take on meaning. What if that's fundamentally what Miss Hyouka Kazakiri is? In my view, Hyouka Kazakiri is like programming code, made up of countless letters that form commands. Every student in the city is typing in one letter at a time. Those letters form commands, and all those commands come together to create a program," she explained.

She had said that it was like Hyouka Kazakiri had disappeared into thin air.

But that wasn't it.

What if there was never a person named Hyouka Kazakiri from the start?

What if the process was backward?

What if one didn't feel body heat because a person was there—what if one only *thought* a person was there because he measured body temperature?

Pyrokinetic espers create body heat, telekinetic espers create feelings on skin, and audiokinetic espers create sounds of voices.

All different sorts of involuntary diffusion fields were like innumerable letters of the alphabet. They combined to create commands, and those were then combined to create a program—what if that was it? What if it was creating a perfect being?

"Wa...wait a minute! That's crazy talk! You keep mentioning humanlike data points, but you just said yourself that there's, like, a million kinds!"

"I did! There *are* 2.3 million espers living in Academy City, right? For example, the body heat is provided by pyrokinetic espers and the bioelectricity by electro-espers, all without them realizing it. They're all creating one big computer application called Hyouka Kazakiri."

Her confident, unhesitating voice took Kamijou aback.

The blood drained from his fingertips.

He felt that he might even forget that he was deep in enemy territory right now.

Sure, if you used telekinesis to push on a finger, you might be able to feel the elasticity of human skin where none was. If you manipulated the vibrations in the air, you could hear its voice, and if you manipulated light refraction, you could even get somebody to *see* them.

"According to Himegami, there've been stories of sightings of *an incomplete Hyouka Kazakiri* for a long time. I think that back then, she was a vague, indistinct being—like a ghost. Going along with the programming code analogy, it's like the commands were missing certain letters, and there weren't enough of them. So she couldn't function properly, and you couldn't sense her with sight, or smell, or any of your five senses. Though even if you couldn't *physically* sense her, you might have been able to *sense* her presence. The Hyouka Kazakiri research lab said to be at Kirigaoka—perhaps it was specifically for investigating such vague, ghostly beings as closely as possible. Or maybe it was designed for researching involuntary diffusion fields?"

A vague, ghostly being.

He shuddered, the image of Kazakiri's head cavity coming to mind, but at the same time, he remembered something.

"But Kazakiri herself didn't seem to realize any of this. She's just a normal person, so she didn't know about how strange she really was. When she found out, she got scared and ran away. It wouldn't make sense if she was something so inhuman ever since she was born, would it?"

"What wouldn't make sense?"

"What? What do you mean, what…?"

"**If she thought she was human ever since she was born,** then she wouldn't have any doubts as to her own existence, would she?"

"Wha…"

What the hell…? he thought, nonplussed.

According to Miss Komoe, Hyouka Kazakiri was an existence created from the involuntary diffusion fields of the 2.3 million espers who lived in Academy City…apparently, anyway.

In other words, nothing was the way it was because she wanted it to be like that.

Even her very own emotions she felt—they were all just created by outside sources.

"Skipping to the conclusion, Miss Hyouka Kazakiri isn't human. She's a type of physical phenomenon, created from involuntary diffusion fields."

Kamijou felt his body go cold at her words.

"Shit...That's...that's insane. How cruel can this get?"

"Cruel...? Kami, you seem to have the wrong idea."

"...? What's that supposed to mean? Are you telling me that empathizing with a simple *natural phenomenon* is a stupid thing to do? Is that it, Miss Komoe?"

"You have it backward, Kami. If you keep on talking like that, then I will have to seriously lecture you!" For some reason, she seemed angry. "Listen to me, Kami. If my hypothesis is correct, then Hyouka Kazakiri isn't human. Even if she has assembled all the necessary pieces of a human, she is certainly not one. It doesn't matter how much she struggles or how hard she works. She's a fleeting illusion—one who, if we knew her essence, would just disappear. However..."

Miss Komoe paused.

"Is it such a problem that she isn't *a human?"* she asked, clearly and without hesitation. "I have never talked to Miss Hyouka Kazakiri, so I cannot say, but what was she like in your eyes? Did she look like she was just an illusion with no life or heart? Did she look like a cardboard cutout just standing around?"

"..."

No. She didn't. He thought back. When she was with Index, she seemed like she was having fun. She got scared at every word that came out of Kamijou's mouth, too. She was definitely thinking for herself and acting under her own volition.

"Was she somebody so inconsequential that you wouldn't care about losing her? Would it be okay to alienate her for an absurd reason like whether or not she's human or whether or not she's fake?"

"..."

No. Of course not. He could say it for sure—she was suffering. She had suddenly learned of her true identity, and she couldn't accept it. She didn't know what to do. All she *could* do was run away into the dark.

He bared his teeth in anger.

There was no reason that would ever convince him it would be okay to let her be killed.

Even if she was no more than an illusion that would disappear if he touched her with his right hand...

It wasn't right for her to just disappear. Not by a long shot.

"Tee-hee-hee! Excellent. I do so love when my little lambs grow up so nicely!"

Kamijou was relieved to hear her laugh, but soon other misgivings arose.

Miss Komoe had been looking into involuntary diffusion fields for her college friend, hadn't she?

"Miss Komoe, I just have a question. Was your friend investigating Kazakiri's true identity?"

"I wonder. Investigating the effects of multiple fields was definitely the idea, but who knows if it ever got this far. At the very least, I never heard anything about her when we discussed it. My hypothesis is purely my own, based on my friend's data."

"..."

"Hmm? What's wrong? You got quiet. Oh, it's all right! I won't tell my friend about any of this. She won't need this information to complete her thesis."

"I don't know how much it's worth, but isn't this, er, a huge scientific discovery or something? Should you really keep quiet about her to your friend...?"

"Ah-ha-ha. You're right—if I'm correct, then it would revolutionize the entire involuntary diffusion field...well, field! The one who discovered it would go down in history. In exchange, Miss Hyouka Kazakiri would get locked away forever in a cold room. Kami, are you really implying that your teacher would want such a thing?"

"Well..."

"If you were, then I would seriously get depressed! What kind of person do you think I am, Kami? Listen—I am a teacher. That fact may sound stupid and simple, but it's the strongest thing I've got that's supporting my heart. Selling out my students' precious friends to gain fame isn't part of my job description!"

Precious friends. That's what she said.

Kamijou knew just how much those words implied.

"Hee-hee! Please try your best not to make her cry, okay? I'll talk to you soon," she finished, then hung up.

"…"

He looked down at his cell phone for a few moments, but finally flipped it closed and shoved it into his pocket.

He knew what he had to do.

He knew where he needed to go.

"But…"

He gritted his teeth.

The statue. He knew he couldn't take that thing on alone. He couldn't even stand in the ring with it. The huge tremors from its foot stomping were all it took for him to end up prone on the ground.

Think. Calm down. Find the answer, and fast! Damn it, Kazakiri might pay the price for my screwup!

He was well aware that this wasn't something he'd be able to solve easily. In the meantime, he just didn't want to stop thinking. He searched every nook and cranny of his mind, examining every possibility.

A sneak attack.

That won't work. The shock waves from its stomp go out in all directions. I can't dodge it just by getting behind it!

Weapons.

That's no good, either. What weapon would I even need to bring down that huge hunk of junk? It must weigh in the tons. Knives or bats aren't gonna cut it! Anti-Skill officers might have rocket launchers or something, but high school students can't use stuff like that!

He scratched his head madly, beginning to panic. If he had to pull out every hair on his head to think of a solution, then he'd gladly do it. Every second that passed, his nervous sweat worsened, and he felt more and more like roaring like a beast. Suddenly, he noticed somebody reflected in the glass window behind him.

"?!"

Kamijou turned around so fast there might have been a gust of wind.

There was…

"Hah…"

A smile crossed his face. His pent-up sigh turned into a laugh. His expression had made its way onto his face without his permission.

For a few moments, he looked at the reflection in disbelief. Finally, he constructed a smile of his own.

"That's right…"

He grinned.

"…How stupid of me. The whole world would look at me and call me stupid. Right, Touma Kamijou?"

He grinned fearlessly and made up his mind.

The ultimate trump card against that giant statue was standing right in front of him.

4

Hyouka Kazakiri, at long last, began to feel a scathing pain.

"Ugh, guhh…?!"

Half her face, her left arm, and her left side. Each of them throbbed with the burning pain of molten steel. She couldn't even stand, much less run, and she fell to the cold, hard floor. Then she began to flail her legs and roll around to try and distract herself from the pain.

The pain signals were enough to make a normal person die outright, but she was not even allowed to escape into death. It was truly a living hell.

However, it didn't last long.

"Ah…?"

A terrible change occurred.

There was a *squish* like jelly, and her wound began to close up. It was happening at a pace impossible for humans—like she was watching a videotape being fast-forwarded. Within moments, the cavity had repaired itself.

The madness-inducing, intense pain suddenly withdrew like a fever breaking.

It had clearly been a fatal wound.

It would be far stranger if she lived through it.

It wasn't only her skin, either. The glasses that had been blown off her. The fragments of torn clothing. Each began to slowly but surely return to its original position.

"Ah, ahh…!"

As the pain faded, her mind was now free to think again—and her memories unfolded before her eyes.

Her body was empty.

She thought she was normal, but she was as far from "normal" as you could get.

Now that the lid on her memories had popped open, they all started to flood into her mind's eye.

"Agah…gh! Gah, guh…uhhggghh!! Geh…gh…kah…gh…gh…! Hih, gah, ghggkkuh…igh! I…ugh…gah…aaaahhh!!"

She lacked the composure to form words, but the vast pressure crushing her very soul forced screams from her lips.

Then, as if attracted by her despair, another reason to despair appeared.

Grishhh!! A tremor shook the entire underground mall.

Kazakiri flew into the air like a rider thrown off her horse, but she still tried to look into the darkness.

There she saw a twisted monster, made of iron and concrete.

Behind it was somebody even more worthy of fear—the blond-haired woman.

She was smiling.

As if to remind Kazakiri that humans could look more twisted than monsters.

"Hee…ah…!"

She remembered the pain of being crushed by the monster's log-like arm and reflexively tried to run. However, her overload of terror and panic prevented her from moving her legs.

The woman said nothing.

She silently waved her chalklike white oil pastel, and the stone statue let loose with a fist at Kazakiri's back.

She immediately tried to get down.

However, her long hair fluttered a second behind the rest of her, and it got caught in the stone fist. She felt extreme pain, like her head was being completely torn apart, and her body went flying like a cannonball.

"Geuh...?!"

Clonk!! A dreadful noise sounded from within her. As she slid along the floor at a terrifying speed, she felt more pain, like her entire body was being shaved down with a giant file.

"Ah, agh, agh...!"

She left a meters-long trail of torn skin fragments and long strands of hair behind her on the floor.

She heard a strange *gzzt* noise coming from her face.

She brought her hand up to her face to find that its surface was billowing strangely. The part of her face that had been torn off and dragged across the floor was trying to return to normal.

"What exactly is that, I wonder?"

Finally, the blond-haired woman spoke. Her odd smile implied that the scene before her was just too strange.

"I had wondered what the key to the *i*th School District looked like, but this is ridiculous! Ah-ha, ah-ha-ha! These *science* people cherish something like *this*? Hah, you're all insane!!"

Kazakiri's body restored itself as the woman continued to cackle. The wet, sloppy sounds ceased before even ten seconds had passed, and her face was back to normal.

"H-hee?!"

She felt dread and hate at her own body. Then, Sherry declared in amusement,

"Heh-heh. Killing you seems like it would be a pain. Oh, then let's try something, shall we? Let's see if you can still go back to normal after I've crushed you into ground meat!"

"Wh...wh...why...?"

"Eh?"

"Why...why are you...This...this is terrible...!"

"Hmm? Oh, I don't really have a reason."

Kazakiri had nothing to say at those incredible words.

"There's no particular reason it has to be *you*. It doesn't have to be you! But you seemed like the easiest to deal with, that's all. See? Simple, right?"

Before Kazakiri could ask what she meant by that, the woman brandished her oil pastel, and the stone statue, Ellis, lunged at the downed Kazakiri with another fist. She managed to roll to the side, but Ellis's fist hit the floor, and the tiles it shattered struck her all over her body. The impact launched her into the air. There was an incredible sound, and somewhere in her body twisted up. Her mind went entirely blank from the intense pain. But even as she tumbled across the floor, she began to recover extremely quickly. She had been launched all the way to the far-off intersection, and yet she was still breathing.

Once again, she had failed to die.

And the woman's expression, despite failing at killing her, didn't change a bit.

It was like she didn't care at all whether she lived or died.

The humiliation at her life being treated as if it were nothing caused tears to form in her eyes. The fact that she could do nothing to stop this situation, despite how mortifying it was, made her even more upset.

The woman saw this, and she seemed to have lost some interest.

"Hey, wait. What are you making that face for, hmm? What? You're not gonna start saying that you're scared to die, now, are you?"

"Eh...?"

"Hey, hey, wait, wait! Don't look at me like that'd be the obvious thing to do. Would you just realize this already? Look how much I've crushed you, and yet you're still alive and kicking! You're not a normal human, damn it!"

"..."

"Oh, don't get all blue in the face. Now you want to call for help, is that it? Not gonna happen. You think this world would lose anything if someone like you disappeared? For example..."

The blond-haired woman tapped her index finger to the side of the oil pastel she held.

A moment later, the stone statue swung its fist to the side. It went straight into the wall, and its arm burst apart from the inside.

"*This is all I'm doing to you, isn't it?*"

"Ah…"

"All I did was crush a monster's limb. Of course it's not gonna start crying! You understand? What on earth are they projecting feelings into an object for? Creating a puppet, a mere personification, and making it able to cry? It's disgusting. I'm not some kind of pervert who gets excited when she undresses a *puppet*."

"Agh…uah…!!"

The stone statue's destroyed arm began to regenerate once again before her hopeless gaze. It returned to normal with fragments of glass and building materials nearby—it was, curiously, just like her.

This was Hyouka Kazakiri's true form.

Her ugly, horrid true self, underneath her skin.

"You understand now, right? You're a monster, just like Ellis. You can't run away from that. Where would you even run? You think anywhere would accept a monster like you? You get it, right? Come on, work with me here. Why don't you understand this? *You don't have anywhere to go!*"

The oil pastel in her hands wobbled from side to side. The stone statue began its slow approach.

Hyouka Kazakiri could do nothing but look at it, dazed, still fallen in the middle of the intersection.

She couldn't move.

There wasn't any damage to her physical self. Her wounds had long since healed.

There wasn't any fear seizing her mental self, either. Her mind was screaming for her to run right now.

But…

Where should she even run *to*?

She thought back.

—This was the first day she'd gone to school.

So she figured that she was a transfer student.

—This was the first day she'd eaten a school lunch.

So she said that she wanted to eat at a school lunch restaurant.

—This was the first day she'd talked to a man.

So she thought that boy had been hard to deal with.

—This was the first day she'd bought juice from a vending machine, too.

She knew how to buy the juice, but she had never actually experienced drinking it. What logic had allowed her to put these strange situations to the side for this long?

The first time. The first time. The first time. The first time. The first time. Every single thing, top to bottom, A to Z, *everything* was the first time.

Why hadn't she noticed it? What on earth had she been doing before then? It was almost as if she didn't have a past at all. It was like she was nothing more than an illusion, a shadow, that had suddenly just appeared from the mists.

There was no meaning in looking away from it.

Pain wouldn't go away just by looking away from a wound.

And now that she had realized this, it was too late. There was nowhere for her to run to. Nowhere for her to hide. There was no paradise in this world that would welcome her horrid self with open arms when she didn't even know who she was.

In her skirt pocket were the photo stickers she'd taken with a certain girl in white.

Index may have been smiling in them, but she didn't know.

She didn't know that Hyouka Kazakiri was actually a monster.

She...

If she knew what lay under but one layer of skin...

She wouldn't be smiling anymore. She might even think back to how she smiled at Kazakiri, ignorant of her true nature, and hate herself for it. The smiling Hyouka Kazakiri displayed in those photographs wasn't around anymore. All that was here, if you removed her human shell, was a monster.

Tears welled up in her eyes.

She wanted to be in a warm, kind world. She wanted to smile with others. Just for one minute. Even for just one second. If she could spend a tiny bit of time peacefully, then she would cling to anything with her life.

But in the end…

There was nothing she could cling to.

"Stop crying, you monster."

The blond-haired woman said mockingly, waving her oil pastel into the air.

"It seriously grosses me out."

The stone statue's arm, which seemed to be able to break even large trees, closed in slowly.

Aahh…, Hyouka Kazakiri thought hopelessly.

She didn't want to die—that wasn't it.

But above that, if she was just going to be treated as a monster everyone would throw stones at as soon as they saw her, and she wasn't useful to anybody ever again…she thought that dying might be the better way.

She closed her eyes tight.

She braced herself for the hellish pain to come…

…but she never felt an impact.

She never heard a noise, either.

But the eerie silence came over her gently, like a blanket. It was almost like she had stepped back into a warm, indoor room after having been caught in a terrible storm.

"…?"

She opened her eyes in trepidation.

She thought she knew somebody standing there, but her eyes were filled with tears, and she could only make out a blurry image of the stone statue.

The somebody looked like a boy.

Kazakiri was in the middle of the intersection. The young man had walked between her and the statue from a nearby passage. She could vaguely make out the boy's profile.

The stone statue's movements stopped.

The boy had casually stuck out his right hand and grabbed the statue's giant arm. The fist had such immense power that it could bat away a tank as easily as a fly, and yet he was holding it back with the palm of his hand.

That's all it took for the statue to stop moving—and not only that. There was a *crick-crack* as fissures began to shoot through it.

"Ellis?"

From somewhere far away, she heard the woman's voice.

"Ellis. Answer me, Ellis! Shit, what's going on here?"

The young man didn't turn to look at the woman, despite her uncharacteristic panic.

He simply stared straight at Hyouka Kazakiri.

"Looks like I made you wait."

Her shoulders twitched at his voice. She couldn't make him out because of the tears, but she knew that voice. She only knew so many people, after all.

His voice was strong.

His voice was warm.

His voice was trustworthy.

And above all…

His voice was kind.

He went on.

"But everything's gonna be all right now. Would you give it a rest, okay? Quit crying over the small stuff."

Hyouka Kazakiri rubbed at her eyelids like a child.

The curtain of tears cleared.

And beyond them was *him*.

Touma Kamijou stood there.

He smiled at her like she was the most important friend he'd ever had.

Behind him, the statue's body began to crack apart and rattle and collapse.

As if the insurmountable wall of despair were breaking.

"Ellis…Are you kidding me?!"

Her enraged shout trembled.

Her hand tightened around the white oil pastel so firmly it seemed sure to break. Then, with the speed of a master drawing his sword

from its sheath, she began to scrawl something on the wall. At the same time, she began to rattle on very quickly and without pause.

The concrete wall crumbled like dried mud. It assumed a form, as if invisible hands were kneading it, and within mere seconds, she had completed a stone statue whose head butted up against the wall.

Her face had been tinged with panic, but she still hadn't lost her calm.

This was her trump card—however many times it was destroyed, she could create another one. This was her greatest strength. She could use it as anything—a shield, a decoy, a suicide attack.

Touma Kamijou turned around.

He stood there before the distorted statue, as if to protect the cornered girl.

Kazakiri was surprised at the sight, and the blond-haired woman's grin split her face in two.

"Kuh…ha-ha. Bwa-ha-ha! Where do you get such funny stories from? Who brought you up, anyway? They must have been feeding you garbage! Ha-ha! Be happy, you monster. This world hasn't given you up just yet. There's one moron like this in it, after all!"

Kazakiri's shoulders trembled at her rusty voice.

Yes, she was happy that this young man came along. But she couldn't stand him getting in the middle of a fight between monsters. Those warm, fluffy days Hyouka Kazakiri wished for, and the young man who created them—she wouldn't be defeated by them here.

But beside the horrified Kazakiri, the young man didn't move an inch, even before the giant stone statue.

"There's not just one," he said.

"Huh?" the woman said stupidly, and at that moment—

Crash!! A brilliant light fell onto her.

"?!"

Kazakiri had to shield her eyes from the blinding pool of white light with both hands.

She was sitting in the middle of the intersection. Light was being directed at the blond-haired woman from all three of the other passages. Her eyes stung from the intense light, but she managed to squint and look around.

First, the lights, as stark as car headlights.

Those looked like flashlights with mirrors attached to them. Not just one or two, either. There had to be at least thirty or forty people here.

Anti-Skill.

Not a single one of them was unharmed. They stood with their bodies and heads wrapped in bandages, dragging their arms and legs behind them. All of them seemed a better fit for a hospital bed than to be standing at all.

But they did not hesitate.

They didn't take notice of their own plight. They didn't utter a single word of complaint about their pain. They had run here, without skipping a beat, to what was nothing less than the jaws of death. They were not only the strong, brawny men seen as the heroes of action films—there was a woman, too. She brandished a transparent shield and was smiling an intrepid grin, despite her own injuries. Her eyes were saying that everything was going to be okay.

"Wh...why...?" asked Hyouka Kazakiri, truly baffled.

They didn't know who she really was. But they should have at least figured out that she wasn't an ordinary person. They should have witnessed her face being broken by the ricocheted bullet. They should have seen her abruptly getting up after being punched by that statue.

So she couldn't help but ask *why*.

Why?

She deserved to be pelted with bullets just the same as that terrorist did. Why had they stepped out to defend her? She didn't understand any of it.

"You're an idiot. We don't need a reason," answered the boy, however, without missing a beat.

Kazakiri knew she was a monster, but Kamijou didn't look away from her for a second.

He wore the same expression he had when they talked at the arcade.

Bathed in light, he spoke.

He spoke normally, casually. His voice was like a cloudless sky.

"There's nothing special about any of this, you know. I just told them something."

Within the overflowing light, he spoke.

"I told them, *please help my friend.*"

For a moment, Hyouka Kazakiri didn't understand what he meant.

After all, she wasn't human. She was a monster. Her body was empty on the inside. There was nothing there if you peeled away one layer of skin. She could survive a gunshot and a punch from a stone statue. Doctors and scholars would look at her body and be astonished.

Would they not care? Would they abandon her? Somehow she hoped they would.

If she had been in their position, she would abandon this hopeless Identity Unknown body.

Perhaps that's just how this city was. Eighty percent of it was students, and every single one had awakened to some kind of ability. Every single person knew they were a bit different. Maybe that's the only reason they could accept Hyouka Kazakiri, who was *different from others.*

Was it really okay for her to stay here?

Would they accept her existence with a smile?

She was still dazed as the boy continued.

"Wipe your tears and look ahead. Stick out your chest, too. Everyone here would rather not let you die."

Kazakiri looked up.

The world of darkness she had been looking at this whole time was no longer anywhere to be seen.

"We'll show you that we can still save this world you live in!"

She knew.

This underground mall might have been plunged into darkness by the blond-haired woman's tempest of cruelty.

But he stood up to that darkness with the light.

He was reaching his hand out to grab someone drowning in the darkness.

Finally, he said, "And I'll show you! That illusion of yours—the place where you belong—isn't something that can be broken so easily!!"

5

"Ellis..."

Hidden in the shadow of the stone statue, Sherry's voice trembled with anger.

"...Kill them all! Leave not a single one alive! I'll use their flesh as part of your body!!"

As she screamed, her oil pastel ripped through the air. Dozens of overlapping lines became strings to control the statue.

"Not so fast!! Position B! Top priority is the civilians' security!"

With that one yell, fire erupted from every gun at once.

The Anti-Skill officers were set up with a front line wielding the transparent, polycarbonate shields and a back line firing their rifles from behind them. The shields were not meant for Ellis's attacks, but rather to block ricocheting bullets.

As the ear-splitting gunfire rang out, the female Anti-Skill pulled the nearby Kamijou and Kazakiri down to the ground. She held the shield up to defend the two of them.

Chak-chakka-chak-chik-chik!! rang the shield.

Kamijou, surprised, stared ahead. Simple ricocheting bullets coming off of Ellis's body were enough to do all this. Kazakiri shook like a dog during a thunderstorm, perhaps because she'd been hit by a bouncing bullet herself once.

He looked at the stone statue in front of them.

The gunfire was focused on Ellis's leg like a magnifying glass focusing sunlight, and the golem had stopped. It seemed to be desperately trying to walk against a raging vortex, against gales blowing at it. Because its body was spread like a wall, it almost looked like it was being tossed around by strong winds like the sails of a yacht. Pieces of concrete and glass that made up its body tore off and fell, one after the other, but it immediately regenerated itself using the nearby floor, walls, and even the bullets being fired at it.

"Shit!!"

He heard Sherry shout from behind the curtain of gunshots.

"Likeness of God, Michael! Healing of God, Raphael! Power of God, Gabriel! Fire of God, Uriel! Symbols of the four heavens representing the four planes—guide us with your righteous power, in a righteous direction, in a righteous position!!"

Distorted crosses appeared from the oil pastel and began to scribble themselves all over the air nearby.

Ellis's body made a loud *creak*.

It was crying out.

It was a cry of pain from every joint of the stone statue, which had no mouth to create words. The command forced these dangerous creaks from the stone statue's giant body, like cogs jammed with a cloth beginning to move again anyway.

And still, Ellis moved.

As it created those eerie noises, it took one step forward.

Thud. The heavy sound shook the floor just a little.

Sherry, pleased by what she saw, accelerated her frantic waving of the oil pastel.

"Ah...ah...We can't...," muttered Kazakiri without thinking, in the midst of the roar of gunfire.

"It's all gone according to plan so far. I don't like the fact that we went straight for the worst case...It would have been better if we could push it back or at least hold it in place, but I guess we're not that lucky."

His words made her doubt her ears.

Then, the Anti-Skill woman holding the transparent shield spoke up.

"Young man, are you sure you want to do this? No one will blame you for chickening out at this point, you know."

"It's not about me wanting to, it's about it needing to be done. You saw what happened before, didn't you? When I crushed the entire pile of garbage just from a touch of my right hand? That's the kind of ability it has."

"Well, yeah, Tsukuyomi has told me about that before, but…"

Kazakiri felt the energy steadily draining from her fingertips.

What is this? she thought. *It feels like something crazy was decided without my knowing it…*

"Whatever you choose, that thing's gonna get here soon. And even if it didn't, you don't have infinite bullets, right? Even your arms won't be able to hold out for very long."

"You've only got one shot at this. If you fail, we can't come back for you. We'll have to begin firing again, and when we do, you'll get shot along with that statue, you know."

Kazakiri was flabbergasted at her words. "…Wait, just…wait a… wait a minute…umm…What are you—?"

"That's obvious," Kamijou interrupted. "I'm gonna go stop that monster now."

The statue brought down another dull footstep.

It was stronger than the last one. Sherry and Ellis would adapt to the firing very soon.

"You…you can't…! It's…it's too dangerous…!!"

"Yeah, but I need to touch it with my right hand for my power to work. I mean, sure, it would be way more convenient if it were a long-range attack like a certain Railgun…"

Slam! The ground shook again.

The stone statue trudged its way forward like a traveler fighting against a northerly wind.

It was less than ten meters away now.

"I'll give the order. One last time—you sure about this?"

"…Yeah."

He'd known what he needed to do before coming here.

So he only needed to give one word in reply. That way there would be no regrets.

"You're really pushing it, kid—how cool can one student be? Jeez, why does *she* get all the good students?"

The Anti-Skill chuckled, taking out her small transceiver.

"All right, I'll go along with this! But make sure it works, no matter what—and come back alive. We'll do as much as we can for you."

Kamijou smiled in spite of himself when he heard that.

At last, Kazakiri realized that he was desperately holding himself back from shivering.

"Preparations!…Count down from three!"

She gave a command through the transceiver.

Kazakiri was stunned. Was he actually going to leap out from behind this shield and make a run for the stone statue? Into this storm of pinballing bullets that not even the shooters could predict the trajectories of?

He'd die if he got hit even once.

He should be too scared to breathe.

"…Two!"

Kamijou, who had been lying on the floor until now, raised his upper body ever so slightly.

"Wait…you…you can't!…You'll…you'll never be rescued…like this…! I don't…I don't want that! I…!"

"Don't stop me, Kazakiri."

For some reason, Kazakiri was on the verge of going crazy, and Kamijou was the one to speak in a calm voice, despite being in the most dangerous situation here.

"I think my right hand is why you've been avoiding me. It erases every strange power out there, whether or not it's good or evil. You're probably not an exception to that."

So don't reach out with your hand and touch me without thinking.

Kazakiri caught her breath as if she'd been punched in the gut.

"…One!"

Sherry, perhaps having realized something was coming up, began to wave her oil pastel with even more frenzy. Ellis, taking the brunt of the bullet rain, stepped forward with more strength.

But in that exact moment, Kamijou wasn't even thinking about Sherry.

He just looked at the girl in front of him.

How surprised she looked, now that she knew Kamijou's power and the reason she'd been avoiding him.

"Don't worry so much about it. We can still be friends even if we can't touch each other, right? Also, don't kill me off like that, got it? I'm coming back alive for sure. Got it?"

"...Ah. You'll...you'll come back...?"

"You got it. And then I wanna go out and do something with you and Index afterward,"

He said simply, giving a single smile.

Then, he directed his gaze ahead.

As if cutting the final binding thread between Kamijou and her, the Anti-Skill officer announced,

"...Zero!"

In that moment...

The Anti-Skill officers pouring all of their rounds into Ellis—*all of them stopped at once.*

Sherry probably hadn't expected anything like this.

After all, those bullets were the final barrier keeping Ellis at bay. They'd be dead meat as soon as they stopped shooting. However she looked at it, it seemed to be the very definition of suicide.

But it *did* have an effect.

Ellis's slow, stolid body suddenly began to fall forward.

It was like the raging winds it had been putting all its effort into walking against had suddenly stopped. Its own power had been used against it, and it lost its sense of balance.

Kamijou leaped over the clear shield like a hurdle and made a mad dash toward it.

It was about seven meters away.

"Damn. Get him, Ellis!!"

Sherry hurriedly swung her oil pastel again when she saw Kamijou approaching like an arrow.

Ellis loyally obeyed her command and balled its hand into a fist. However, it still couldn't stand up straight. It was about to topple over—if it were forced to throw a punch, it would end up sprawled out on the floor. And then, Kamijou wouldn't even need to bring down his hand. Sherry would lose her own shield and wouldn't be able to escape the gunfire. He'd just have to get back down on the ground so that no bouncing bullets hit him.

And yet, Ellis still swung its fist.

As expected, this completely destroyed what little balance it had left, and it fell toward the floor. The statue was a little more than four meters tall. Given the seven meters he started from, Kamijou wouldn't get buried under it.

He aimed for where Ellis would fall, tightened his fist, and...

Thud! Ellis delivered its punch.

It did so even while it was falling. *It had ignored Kamijou and gone for the ground under them.*

"Wha...?!"

Fissures spiked out of the floor for eight meters around Ellis like a spiderweb. The ground undulated like a trampoline, tossing Kamijou's body up into the air. The walls, ceiling, and support beams all began to creak and squeal uncannily, echoing throughout the underground mall.

And now, Kamijou, on the ground, saw.

The golem, Ellis, had used the reaction from its fist to spring back up to its feet.

Sherry's right hand flashed to the side.

Its giant fist swung around and down, once again, to crush the bug crawling around beneath it.

"Damn it...!!"

Kamijou heard faint, metallic sounds. The Anti-Skill officers must have taken up their rifles again. But they didn't shoot. If they began firing another shower of bullets, they would deflect and hit him for sure.

Argh, this is bullshit! Think! Think...!!

Ellis was towering over him at the moment, bringing down its fist. Even if he used his right hand to stop its descent and destroyed it with the Imagine Breaker, he would still be hit by a multiton avalanche of debris.

He would only be able to take a single step if he tried to run. But Ellis, more than four meters tall, had an arm bigger than him. Jumping or rolling to one side or the other wouldn't get him out of range.

Damn it, shit! Isn't there something I can do? Anything?!

Ellis's fist, with all its weight behind it, came down straight onto Kamijou's head. At the very least, he knew that stopping it with his right hand would be tantamount to suicide. He brought up his legs, using all of his mental strength, and leaped, praying.

Not to the right, not to the left, and not behind—he leaped forward.

Ellis's body was more than four meters tall.

That meant it had a lot more weak spots to close in on than humans did, and there was a gap of almost two meters between its feet. Still, it would, under normal circumstances, immediately deliver a kick as he tried to get under its legs.

However, in the moment that it let loose with its punch...

Just for that one moment, its body was unstable. It wouldn't be able to kick its feet around without compromising its balance. Kamijou knew how this worked—he was used to city brawls by now. An overswing might look strong and flashy, but it was weak in that it was simple to counter. Its center of gravity ended up right in the middle of the attack, so any sort of evasion is impossible.

Ellis couldn't move its feet before it finished its swing.

The fact that it was forced to try and maintain its balance like a human was its failing.

Kamijou crouched and, so low he could lick the floor, sprang forward. He went as fast as an arrow and dove straight through Ellis's legs!!

Right after that...

Bang-bang-bang-bang-bang-bang!! Sparks began to fly from Ellis's body. The rifle-wielding Anti-Skill soldiers had opened fire.

Ellis's movements were once again restricted.

And funnily enough, none of them hit Kamijou, who now stood behind it.

He stood up slowly and was about to touch his hand to Ellis's back, but he thought about it for a moment and decided not to. He took his eyes off of the statue and turned around.

There was Sherry Cromwell.

"Eh? Ellis...,"

She said, her voice tinged with panic and fear. But she probably understood as well. If she were careless in moving Ellis, they both might end up on the wrong end of the Anti-Skills' bullets. And she also couldn't get out of the tiny little boxing ring in Ellis's shadow.

The oil pastel in her hand swam clumsily through the air. The act had none of her previous resolve behind it. She didn't know what to have Ellis do at this point.

There was no one she could ask for help now.

Her ultimate weapon was right there in front of her, but not only could she not move it, it was even shielding Kamijou from the bullets.

"All righty then," he said.

He swung around his right arm, testing out his shoulder.

"Hah..."

Despite herself, Sherry bared a pained smile at this hopeless situation. "Ha-ha. What's this? I can't run away like this!"

"You don't need to run."

Kamijou shut one eye within the resounding gunfire.

"You just need to shut up and go to sleep."

He punched Sherry Cromwell across the room, showing not a scrap of mercy.

Her slender body rolled across the floor like paper trash blown by the wind.

6

The guns still hadn't quieted.

Ellis had stopped moving because Sherry had been taken down, but he hadn't dealt the finishing blow to Ellis. It was only natural that the Anti-Skill officers weren't letting up. Kamijou took his eyes from Sherry, collapsed five meters away, and turned back to face Ellis.

But if I break this too suddenly...Man, I'd better not get hit by any stray bullets.

Slowly and carefully, he reached his right hand out to Ellis...

"Heh. Heh-heh-heh."

Then, he heard the woman's laughter and whipped back around to look at Sherry.

Did I not hit hard enough? Wait, was she *the one who jumped back...?!*

She was grinning. She was laughing down there on the floor. But her hand still gripped the white oil pastel.

Bsh-wshh! She swung it almost as fast as a fencing master, frenetically scrawling some sort of characters or symbols he didn't understand onto the floor.

"Wha...Shit! Making a second one, are we?!"

Kamijou was about to rush over there to stop her, but before that, she said,

"Heh-heh. Heh-heh. Eh-heh-heh-heh. No, I can't do that. If Ellis is out like this, I won't be able to control another at the same time. Besides, if I could make more than one at a time, I would have brought an entire Ellis army with me. When I try to force a second one into existence, I just can't maintain its shape. It gets all squishy like rotten mud and collapses. But—"

She gave a ferocious grin.

"By applying it well, *I can do this, too*!!"

A moment later, the entire floor beneath her collapsed, with the characters she wrote at its center, stretching out about two meters in every direction. She was caught up in the collapsing ground and disappeared as if it had swallowed her.

"Damn it!!"

Kamijou rushed over, but only an empty hole remained. It was deep—he couldn't tell how far down it went. However, he could feel air flowing from within it.

She got away. There's a subway line right under here...

Kamijou cursed his luck, and at the same time, the unmoving Ellis broke up into a lot of pieces and noisily rattled down to the ground. Since she couldn't make two at once, she had probably broken the old one to make room for a new one. As the old Ellis fell apart, the vortex of gunfire ceased abruptly.

But that's strange...

Kamijou had a sudden doubt as he peered into the dark hole.

Sherry Cromwell didn't seem to have any real attachment to any one target. She was clearly different from the sorcerers he'd met before. None of *them* would have ever run away so easily with Hyouka Kazakiri (and, well, Kamijou as well) right before their eyes.

Think back. What's wrong with this?

Scraps of Sherry's words floated across his mind. He looked down, his face deep in thought, but after a few moments he looked up abruptly.

"Oh dear, I see the key to Imaginary Number District isn't with you. Hmm...What was she called again? Kaze, or wait, Kaza... something-or-other. Damn, why are Japanese names so complicated?"

Now that he thought about it, she never seemed to have much interest in Hyouka Kazakiri from the start.

"I'm starting a war, and I need a trigger for it. I need as many people as possible to know that I'm a pawn of the English Puritan Church... right, Ellis?"

What if Sherry had some other objective, and Kazakiri was just one of the options she could have chosen?

"It doesn't matter! Nothing matters. I don't absolutely need *to kill that brat. No, not that one."*

What if she could substitute others for Kazakiri instead?

"Hee. Hee-hee. Hee-hee-hee-hee. The Index of Forbidden Books, and Imagine Breaker, and the key to the Imaginary Number District...Which one should I choose? Can I have any of them? Tee-hee-hee. I don't know! So many options to choose from!"

What if she hadn't fled...

...she'd just decided upon a different target?

And...

She had three targets. Right now, Kamijou and Kazakiri were being guarded by Anti-Skill here.

The only one who wasn't here, who wasn't being protected by Anti-Skill, was...

"Damn...She's going for Index?!!"

INTERLUDE TWO

Footsteps echoed through the dark subway passage.

They weren't the kind of sounds a human could make. They were the footfalls of the golem, Ellis, made of concrete and rail tracks, boasting a height of four meters.

Sherry sat in Ellis's arm, motioning with her oil pastel to control both of Ellis's legs. She knew where she needed to go. Before she made the second Ellis, she had released dozens more mud eyeballs and located her target. They would have gotten in the way of creating a second golem, however, so she'd already destroyed them.

She felt her cheek sting from the punch. Normally, her feet, hidden beneath her long skirt, didn't touch the ground—they floated a few centimeters above it in order to avoid Ellis's earthquakes. Unfortunately, when that boy had punched her, the impact had ruined her levitation spell. Thus, Ellis was carrying her at the moment.

She looked around, then whispered.

"How wretched."

This concrete underground maze was wretched. This foul stench was wretched. This filthy, dusty air was wretched. The one who created all this was wretched. The very ability to create this was simply *wretched*.

She hated this city.

She hated this city's water. Its wind. Its earth. Its fire. She hated all of it. She wished she could rip it off the map. Out of history. Out of peoples' memories. Out of the world itself.

The cheek the esper had punched flushed redder with heat.

Sherry cursed. It was all because of this city. Nothing was right.

"Ellis...," she said.

Ellis was not the name originally given to this type of golem.

It was the name of an esper who had died twenty years ago.

CHAPTER 4
Full Stop
Beast_Body, Human_Heart.

1

Unlike the dark underground, on the surface, the sunlight was dazzling.

Index and Mikoto Misaka had been left in the streets by themselves. Kuroko Shirai was still carrying the trapped students out of the underground.

Kamijou and the others hadn't come back safely yet, so it would be heartless to go home right now. But they didn't have anything to talk about, either. A singular silence fell over the two of them under the blue skies pelting them with brilliant sunlight.

Ah, jeez, Kuroko…

She cursed her absent underclassman under her breath. She could just blow up the underground mall partition with her Railgun, but then the terrorist might get out. She couldn't risk anything so dramatic.

The cat in Index's arms flailed around, not appreciating the heat.

Finally, she said, "…It's so hot."

"Yeah." Mikoto nodded. "But what are those clothes, anyway? Why are you wearing long sleeves in this crazy heat…? Oh, do you get sunburned easily? I think I heard on TV that if you don't have much pigment, the sun fries you pretty easily."

"It's never bothered me. There's a nice draft in them right now."

"Hah?...Wow, now that I look at it, there're safety pins all over the fabric! Why is it all messed up like that?"

"Ugh...I don't want to reopen any old scars, so I'd rather not talk about why..."

Index cut off the conversation there, so they stopped talking again. But now that they *had* spoken, Mikoto got impatient with their newfound silence pretty quickly.

"They sure are late."

"...Yeah. I wonder what I should do. That sorcerer kinda seemed like she had her eyes on Hyouka. Her spells were just like London's, too. I hope I'm just thinking about it too hard..."

"?" Mikoto was confused. She wasn't used to hearing the words *sorcerer* and *spells* being tossed around.

When Index was brought out of the underground by Kuroko Shirai, she didn't thank her; in fact, she made a fuss, demanding to know why she'd escaped first and insisting she take her back there immediately. Mikoto thought she remembered the girl using the word *sorcerer* then, too, kind of like a joke.

She thought about it for a few moments, but then decided it wasn't worth the effort. From her clothing, she looked like she was involved with a church. For someone without any scientific knowledge, espers must all look like they're using magic.

"'Hyouka'—that's the name of the girl who was with you, right?"

"Yep. Oh, Touma didn't drag her along this time, though! I met her *first*."

"...'This time,' huh? I see."

Mikoto averted her eyes and grinned darkly, but the innocent Index didn't notice. She started to sway left and right, with the cat still in her arms.

"Urk. I'm kinda worried. Leaving a girl behind in a place like that is one thing, but leaving her and Touma alone in the dark is another thing entirely!"

"...Hmm. For some reason, it's only at times like *this* that I think we could be friends." Mikoto paused. "Not like I care or anything, but you're not worried about *him* at all?"

For just a moment, Index stopped moving.

"Huh, Touma? I'm not worried about him. He always comes home, no matter what happens," she answered, though it was already contradictory. If she really weren't worried, then she wouldn't feel the need to wait patiently under the blazing hot sun.

I guess it wouldn't do any good to tell her not to worry in this situation, She thought, reflecting on how their conversation had ended once again. On the other hand,

Hmm. "Comes home," huh?

Comes home *to whom*—that didn't even need to be said. The silver-haired girl probably didn't mean anything special by it, but that only made the damage worse. That meant for them, it was just life as usual, and not something they paid attention to. It had permeated into their common sense.

Mikoto fiddled with her bangs.

But, so what? Why am I so shocked by that? She frowned at how she felt about this.

Then, with a high-pitched *meow*, the calico in Index's arms suddenly escaped.

"Ah!"

Index cried. Mikoto redirected her attention away from herself just as the cat slipped out of Index's arms and hit the ground. As if saying, "I'm not sticking around until it gets even hotter," it ran away.

Index immediately began to run after the tiny deserter, but stopped. Unsure of herself, she glanced between the fleeing cat and Mikoto. It seemed like she wanted to go after it, but she also wasn't sure about leaving this place.

"It's fine. I'll stay here, so go get that cat and bring it back. I couldn't chase it anyway. Cats don't really like me."

"Sorry! I'll do that, thanks…Hey, get back here, Sphinx!!"

Index bowed her head quickly. She chased the cat into the shade behind a convenience store and disappeared. *Its name is Sphinx?* Mikoto thought. *What absolutely terrible taste in names. I don't even know what to say.*

Suddenly, she noticed the manhole cover at her feet rattling.

"What?"

She wondered, but then the cover on the change return of the vending machine across the street started to flap back and forth. The leaves on the trees lining the street began to sway to and fro, even though there wasn't any wind.

It didn't quite feel like an earthquake. The odd tremors felt more like a big sea monster was stomping around somewhere far away.

Maybe that cat used its animal senses to detect the tremors and ran away because of it, she thought.

2

Hyouka Kazakiri sat flopped down on the ground of the dark underground mall.

Neither the blinding flood of lights nor the piercing storm of gunfire remained. The Anti-Skill officers were busy shouting orders over their wireless communicators in an attempt to prevent Sherry from escaping to the surface.

Suddenly, she heard people arguing. She looked over and saw Kamijou and the female Anti-Skill deep in conversation—well, actually, Kamijou was so heated that he was almost grabbing her.

"I said that thing's not in the underground mall anymore! Why the hell can't you open up the mall again?!"

"I've told you this a dozen times—the ones controlling the mall are under different jurisdiction than us, 'kay? We're in contact with them, but there's a distinct chain of command. It'll take a bit longer to lift the seals!"

"Shit!"

Kamijou cursed, kicking the wall. Kazakiri twitched in surprise, but she realized that he was acting strangely. The immediate threat, Sherry, was no longer here. What was he so flustered about?

The Anti-Skill who Kamijou was discussing something with looked like she was getting a message over her radio. She left him and began to argue over it using a lot of specialized vocabulary, or abbreviations, or something.

Kazakiri floated over to Kamijou like a fish floating downstream. He was coming off as a little scary, but he also had this air about him that she couldn't leave alone, like a child about to start bawling.

"...U-umm...Thank you for...for before."

"Hmm? It wasn't really anything you need to thank me for. Anyway, are you all right?"

"Ah, yes...I think...I think I'm fine, but...Umm, well...Is...is something going on...?"

Kamijou didn't say anything for a few moments. He looked like he was wrestling with whether or not to tell her. Finally, he began. He spoke slowly—not like he was carefully choosing his words, but like things that were pent up inside were dribbling out little by little.

"Sherry Cromwell...That grimy goth lolita woman didn't run away. She's just going after her next target—Index."

"Eh...?"

"Apparently she didn't come here to kill you or me. Under the right conditions, she can go after anyone she wants. And one of those people is Index."

Kazakiri caught her breath. She *did* remember that blond-haired woman saying something along those lines. Kazakiri and Kamijou were under the protection of a crowd of Anti-Skill officers, but Index was totally defenseless. If she could go after anyone, then obviously she'd go for the easier choice.

"I was haggling with the one Anti-Skill, but she says they can't open up the underground mall yet. We can't get out if they don't raise those thick shutters!"

"...B-but...Speaking of them...There's plenty of Anti-Skill officers on the surface, too...You could just get them to go defend her..."

"We can't." Kazakiri thought her suggestion was sensible, but Kamijou denied it without thinking.

"What...Why?"

"Index doesn't live in this city. If Anti-Skill finds her, she could be arrested. It's not a sure thing...but she *could* be."

Kamijou lowered his voice. "She's got a guest ID, but who knows if that'll help now that we're in an emergency and under Code Red?

It's possible they'll ask her to show them other identification, like a license or a credit card." He gave a *tsk*. "That would be bad. Bottom line, she has no identity. Bank cards, insurance, proof of residence—she doesn't even know her age, blood type, or birthday. And 'Index' is clearly a fake name. You think people on the lookout for a suspicious outsider would let a blank sheet of paper go?"

With that, Kazakiri finally understood why Kamijou was in such a state of panic. Compared to Hyouka Kazakiri, Index had far fewer allies, even though there were so many people in this city.

"But...but I...I don't actually live here, either..."

"Your case is a little different. Your ID isn't registered with the city, but that's it. You might be a little different from normal, but *that doesn't mean you're dangerous.* But Index is different. She basically belongs to an organization separate from Academy City. And because she does, she could be judged as *extremely* dangerous."

Finished, Kamijou began to walk away by himself. Kazakiri hurried back up to him.

He was headed for the edge of the big hole in the floor the blond-haired woman used to escape.

"I guess we gotta go through here. Damn it. The partitions are right over there. I could beat her there no sweat if they opened them up. Why do I have to tail her like this?!"

Kazakiri peered into the hole.

Without light, it was pitch black. She couldn't see the bottom. Would he be okay if he jumped down there? Who knew how far down it went? He wouldn't even be able to judge when he hit the ground so he could soften the impact. And besides...

"W-wait...Are you...are you really going alone?"

Kazakiri believed that they should notify Anti-Skill, even if it was a risk. She knew how scary that blond-haired woman was. She had destroyed Kazakiri's body numerous times.

She could say for sure that she wasn't an opponent a high school student could go up against without thinking.

Kamijou probably knew that as well. The only reason he survived was because of the sheer number of Anti-Skill members forcing the situation. Not even a tank could beat that thing one-on-one. It was nothing less than a *monster*, in every sense of the word.

But even knowing all that, he didn't waver.

She knew the reason without having to ask. He was harboring an enemy of Academy City. He wanted to protect her no matter what happened.

Kazakiri understood the feeling well. Index was an important friend, and the first she'd ever made. To lose that—to even think about her being hurt—made her hair stand on end.

But...

It wasn't a good enough reason for *him* to be hurt.

If Kamijou felt that strongly about losing Index, then she firmly wished that they wouldn't lose their bond with each other.

They had to protect Index from that monster.

She couldn't let Touma Kamijou fight that monster.

What would fulfill both of those conditions? Kazakiri froze when she thought of it.

There was a way.

"...It's...it's okay. There's a way to...to save her...without you having to go."

Kamijou frowned and eyed her suspiciously.

"To fight...a monster...just...just use another monster."

Kamijou caught his breath, and Kazakiri smiled softly.

"I...I don't know if I can win against that monster...but I can at least be...a decoy...I can let her flee...while I'm getting punched. Because...because I'm a monster. That's...that's all I can do, but..."

Kamijou didn't know what to say to that.

But then, his expression changed from surprise to fury.

"Are you still going on about that?! Listen to me! You don't seem to understand, so I'll spell this out for you. You are not a monster! Who the hell do you think we all ran in here to protect?! Why don't you get that? Why aren't you even trying to understand?!"

Touma Kamijou's words were straightforward and without lies.

When she saw how angry he was at her masochistic words, her chest got tight.

"You think I'd be *happy* if we do that?! Do you think Index would just turn her back on you as that monster beat you to a pulp?! Bullshit! Even if you abandon us, we wouldn't leave you to die! We would never do that!!"

However, he realized it, too.

The thing that Kamijou and the members of Anti-Skill had stood up to in order to protect Hyouka Kazakiri was **still a monster, the same as her.** That monster had been shot with guns, collapsed to the ground, and its remains were scattered all over the place.

And even when they looked at the monster's remains...nobody thought anything of them.

In the end, that's what it meant to be *inhuman*.

"...But it's okay. I'm fine...with being a monster...,"

Declared Kazakiri, without looking away from Kamijou's eyes.

"I'm...a monster...No matter how many times that statue punched me, I didn't die. I'm...I'm a monster...which means I can stand up to it..."

So she just said one thing, to mark the end of the conversation.

"I...I can defend someone important to me...with my power. So I...I'm happy to be a monster."

She smiled, and then jumped over the edge of the hole Sherry had left. Kamijou shouted out and reached out with his hand, but he stopped halfway through. His dominant hand had reacted because he didn't have time to think...but it was his right hand.

That hand with absolute power, that would wipe out any monsters it touched.

He, too, must have known it deep down.

Gravity took Kazakiri's body down into the hole. She smiled quietly. Kamijou was blaming himself for stopping his hand like that, but her smile told him he wasn't at fault.

The monster fell into the dark.

From this place at the ends of the Earth, where she had finally been accepted, down to even deeper depths.

3

As soon as she landed at the bottom of the dark hole, her ankles made a harsh noise.

She was on the grounds of a subway. The hole had been deeper than she'd thought, and because of the uneven ground due to the tracks, it wasn't easy to break her fall. In fact, if she'd been a regular human, the bones in her ankles would have broken into a hundred pieces, and she'd be writhing in pain right now.

Yes, *if* she were a regular human.

She certainly heard her ankles cracking and felt a dull pain. However, it receded in less than five seconds. She tapped her toes to the ground a couple times, as if adjusting her shoes, but there were no further issues. A strange power coursed through her veins, as if isolated gears had finally clicked together. Were they the names of her own identity?

She ran through the dark premises.

This place wasn't designed for humans to pass through—it was even darker and dirtier than the underground mall was. A line of concrete pillars separated the passage in two, with tracks on either side going in opposite directions. She made her way deeper and deeper in, relying on the occasional blinking of the barely functional lights. She knew exactly where she was going. There were clear footsteps in the concrete ground like snow. They were likely made by that super-heavy statue running through.

She ran through the stagnant air like a knife.

Every time she saw the lights blinking on and off in the darkness, another broken fragment of her memories flooded back to her.

She was not human.

One day, ten years ago...

When Hyouka Kazakiri came to, she was standing in the middle of the city.

The city was not Academy City. However, it lay in exactly the same location. It was an invisible mirage city, created by the involuntary diffusion fields given off by Academy City's 2.3 million espers. In this mirage city, there were no shadows, no weight, no movement of the air. It barely even seemed to exist at all. The buildings, the trees, and the people would sway sometimes, like a candle flame being blown by the wind, and there would be a gray noise. They looked like insects that had mistaken protective colors for dangerous ones.

If there were someone who could properly see involuntary diffusion fields, they would realize that this mirage city overlapped precisely with Academy City.

Hyouka Kazakiri wasn't the only thing that had been created by these fields—they included buildings, roads, trees, cars, and the crowds of people, as well. She was a person made from those fields, living in a city made from those fields.

—Her memories came back little by little like crumbling shards.
—She felt the unseen chains binding her coming off one after another.

Even now, she didn't understand how she had come to be in the mirage city.

It had been like she'd awoken from a daydream at some point. The next thing she realized, she was in the middle of a road. From her possessions, she learned her name, address, phone number, and other information.

She had no other way of knowing what was happening.

The people passing by her wouldn't tell her anything.

And they were strange in the first place. They would essentially change forms depending on where they were. She would see one cleaning the windows of a shop, and a moment later, the employee would morph into a janitor wearing overalls. Then, when he was finished wiping down the window, he would change from a janitor into a child. He would take an ice-cream cone up to the register, and then he would transform into the child's mother and reach for her purse.

＊　　＊　　＊

—She began to think of herself not as a "human," but once again as a "monster."

—And she felt power flow into every nerve of her body, like internal limiters were being released— No, like she now had full access to the powers she always possessed.

All of the denizens of the city were like that. Everything from their physical appearance to their personality and memories would change according to where they were. When she tried to talk to a passing postman, he would immediately transform into a police officer on city guide duty. Office workers and female high school students, too—everyone just changed into the same middle-age police officer when she addressed them. And all the words they spoke were empty, without meaning.

They would all change their shapes to fit their role of answering Hyouka Kazakiri's questions. Eventually, she grew scared of them. She felt like her actions were in control of their bodies and minds.

—*Thud!* The concrete ground rumbled heavily with every step she took.

—Humans weren't heavy enough to create these shakes, nor could human muscles achieve such force. It exceeded human capabilities in both meanings.

At first, she didn't understand why she was the only one not to undergo that kind of change. However, slowly but surely, she formulated a hypothesis. The people in this city changed according to their role—meaning that as long as they were not given a role, they would not move at all, and the city would come to a halt.

She was like a coiled spring. If she were to go into a store to buy some juice, the employees there would begin moving, the juice distributors would begin to work, the power plant that supplied electricity to the refrigerators would power up, the factory that made the juice would begin to work, and the recyclables collectors would start to move. The people of this city were cogs. All of them had been affected little by little by Kazakiri, the spring, until at last, it breathed life into the giant machine called *society*. She was not the master of the system—she was only one part of it. Only the spring.

She was scared.

They were not lifeless puppets—they were all humans with real lives.

She realized that she would greatly affect the lives of others whether she walked forward or backward. She found herself unable to take another step. Her own role felt far too heavy for her.

—*Slam!!* She crashed into one of the pillars head-on with energy to spare.

—But there wasn't a single scratch on her. In fact, the pillar made of concrete shattered and collapsed around her instead.

She was scared of this mirage-like city. She wanted to run away from it.

But if she wasn't careful, she'd get others mixed up in it. So all she could do was stand there like a ghost and watch—the other city, which she couldn't touch despite it being right there. The *outside*—Academy City.

Nobody in Academy City noticed she was there. She could stand right in front of students, and they wouldn't see her. When she held out her arm, it would pass through them. She was surrounded by smiles but would never be allowed into their circle.

Even though she understood that, she never stopped trying to communicate with them. She thought that she wouldn't need to interfere with others to escape to the "outside" at the same location—to Academy City. She wanted to try everything she could, even if it was pointless or would never work.

Even if she was ignored. Even if she wasn't noticed.

Even though she knew it would hurt somebody one day.

Imagine her surprise when she was able to touch the shoulder of that nun wearing white at that school.

*　　*　　*

—Something unable to be seen was overflowing within her sup-
posedly empty body.

—She felt like she would be able to overtake a train as she was now.

Unseen coincidences had occurred one after the other, and they
had resulted in her enjoying being with others at last.

Those others were precious treasures to her. What had probably
happened was that she'd sealed away her memories of being a monster in order to protect them.

But now, Hyouka Kazakiri had decided to let go of those
treasures...

...so that she could protect something even more important.
Something that couldn't afford to be lost.

"...!"

She shot like a bullet through the tunnel.

She went so fast that an onlooker would spit out their drink in
surprise.

She was scared of fighting that monster, of course. Not logically,
but physically. The pain of her limbs being torn off and the agony of
her body being flattened like a cloth...and the humiliation of crawling around on the filthy ground, unable to die even though it would
mean less suffering.

But above all that...

She was much more scared that her friend, Index, would be scared
of *her* when she saw her true identity as a monster.

But I still...

There was no stopping her. She looked straight ahead.

Her first and last outing after school with Kamijou and Index was
fun. She was so happy she could have cried. She wanted to stay in
that world forever if she could. Just thinking about never being able
to walk with them again stole the heat from her fingertips. She had
finally gotten out of that mirage city, and now it would be pointless.

...I...

But…

She was scared of losing it—and that's why she wanted to protect what was important to her.

Even if she would never be on the receiving end of their smiles again…

…she wanted to protect this world of theirs.

I…I will…!

She ran through the darkness as a monster, having abandoned her humanity. She could feel something welling up within her empty body.

She vowed to see this through to the end.

To protect her precious friends.

4

The calico ran away. Index chased it.

The cat had darted behind a convenience store; when it saw Index coming after it like a bull, it panicked and ran away. It dove under a parked car, leaped over a wire fence, and sprinted from alley to alley. Finally, as it tried to jump into what looked like an abandoned concrete building…

"Get over here!!"

…Index scooped it up by the neck.

Now in the grip of an infuriated, heavily breathing girl, its animal instincts caused it to start struggling around in an attempt to get out of her arms. Though, in the first place, if she hadn't been chasing it around while screaming so loudly, it probably wouldn't have kept running.

As Index held the cat, meowing unhappily as if to say, "Please, no more, it's just too hot out," she looked around.

It did indeed seem to be an abandoned building.

This place was essentially a back alley surrounded by tall, tightly packed buildings, but it seemed like all of those buildings were set to be knocked down soon. Their signs had been taken down, the glass windowpanes had been removed, and the entrances were without doors, hanging wide open. The inside was unfurnished as well, and she could clearly see the concrete support pillars. It seemed like they were going to knock down all of the buildings nearby and build some sort of new establishment here.

The cat swung around its tiny legs, incorrigibly trying to dive into the abandoned building, but Index puffed out one cheek in anger.

"Mgh! Don't get testy with me, or you'll be in a lot of trouble, mister!"

She blew in the cat's ear, and it meowed instinctively and cringed, then began to tremble. For a moment, it extended the claws on its short front legs out of reflex, but then pulled them back in. Perhaps it had decided not to be *that* mean.

"Okay, we're going back to where the short-haired one is. Understand?"

The cat meowed reluctantly.

But just then…

Its head jerked back up. Then, it began flailing around, once again trying to slip out of Index's arms. It was struggling with more power than before, and Index started to worry that she was holding the cat too hard. She tried a few things to calm it down, but all were in vain.

Something came rattling down onto Index's head.

"?" Index put a hand to the top of her head, and it came back with concrete powder. She looked up to see dust falling from the walls of the towering abandoned building.

The manhole cover at her feet began clattering around.

"…The ground is shaking?" Index wondered, confused. It didn't take her long to realize it, though. That sorcerer who seemed like she was using London's techniques was underground—meaning she was under her.

She felt the ground beneath her feet begin to writhe and wriggle like a living creature for a moment.

"?!"

Index immediately leaped backward, and the ground she'd been standing on exploded. The stony hand of a monster reached out from the center of the impact. It was almost two meters tall. The arm's fist blocked her passage, like a long-necked dinosaur staring down at her.

Pieces of the road flew everywhere.

A clump of asphalt bigger than Index's head flew right by her face. Having lost her cool, she crouched, tucking the cat into her belly. Immediately after, like a swarm of angry bees, a vast number of the fragments flew straight over her head in a line.

The rain of asphalt collided with the building behind her, making a strange *crick-crack* noise.

She didn't turn to look. She kept her gaze fixed ahead of her. Slowly, she saw a giant statue of stone coming out of the ground, like a dead body crawling out of a grave. She couldn't spot anyone around who would have cast this spell—it was possible they were controlling it from afar.

Index silently narrowed her eyes and thought.

Knowledge surfaced in her mind from the vast stores of it she possessed as the archive of forbidden books belonging to the 0th parish of English Puritanism—Necessarius, the Church of Necessary Evils. This information assembled and organized itself in less time than it took her to blink, and the identity of this enemy appeared in her mind's eye like an embossed image.

Base theory is from Kabbalah...main use is for defense and the elimination of enemies...witnessed during the sixteenth century...and according to Gershom Scholem, its essence is formless and unstable.

Many, when faced with the word *golem*, would immediately think of a dumb, lumbering monster made of stone and earth, but they were actually different.

In the teachings of Kabbalah, God created man from the earth. The imperfect being created by man, however, using the same method, is called a golem. In other words, golems are failed human reproductions. They were essentially more like Pinocchio than anything else.

Has applicability. The original has been mixed with English Puritan techniques. The language family has been changed from Hebrew to English. Body parts correspond with crosses. Its construction is closer to an angel than a human copy.

This golem was, however, different from a simple humanoid one.

It was on a higher level of existence—it seemed the sorcerer was attempting to construct a humanlike angel. The head, right hand, left hand, and legs were each like the end of a cross, and the power of the Four Archangels was distributed throughout its body. The sorcerer must have wanted to create a more combat-oriented angel even out of mud and dirt.

If there was one bright side for Index, it was that humans' ability to control them was limited. Human hands cannot create perfect angels. It wasn't as if, for example, somebody could assemble the Archangel of Water itself.

That didn't change the fact that even something imperfect could present an enormous threat, though.

There was a *thud* and the earth trembled as the statue took a step.

"…!"

Still holding on to the cat, Index took a step back.

She didn't have a chance of winning if she made a frontal attack. Normally, this sort of golem had a kind of safety on it called a *shem* for if it went berserk—if you simply stroked it with one finger, it would completely shut down. However, her enemy was a professional as well. She probably wouldn't have placed such a thing in a spot where someone else could touch it. The *shem*, its core, was most likely buried deep within its stone armor.

Index could neither use magic nor supernatural abilities. She had no connection whatsoever with such strange and mysterious powers, and she was physically weaker than most. She had only her vast troves of knowledge at her disposal, and the giant statue was swinging its arm down mercilessly at her.

Roar!! The statue's attack seemed to crush the air—maybe even space itself. Before such a strike, she inhaled a bit and shouted one thing:

"TTTL! (Twist to the left!)"

The golem's fist was traveling straight for her, but a moment later, it suddenly veered away to the left, like a snake. Shooting a contemptuous glare at the statue, swatting at empty air, Index took a step forward and stood next to it.

The statue, still facing away, swung its fist down and around.

"CAU! (Change angle upward!)"

However, that attack, too, wiggled out of its path and passed over her head. The golem tried to throw yet another punch, but before it could, Index continued,

"PFBTLL! (Pull foot behind the left leg!)"

Ignoring its own balance, the golem jerked its foot behind it. Having lost its center of gravity in the middle of its swing, the golem came crashing down on its face.

Tap-tap. Index took three steps backward.

She was using a method called Notarikon. It was a way to speak quickly. By chanting only the first letter of each word, she could both encode them and speak them more quickly.

Index was unable to temper magic despite having an immense knowledge of it, so she couldn't actually use magic. However, anyone who saw what was happening would have thought she was a bona fide sorcerer.

The statue stood up. It backed away from Index as if setting up a running approach, then unleashed another fist like a cannonball. She uttered something to herself. Just from that, the golem's fist strayed in an unnatural direction and caught only unrelated air.

It looked as though Index's words were interfering with the golem's movements. As if she were interrupting the spell caster's commands and hijacking its control.

It was called *spell interception.*

It was a simple concept. Magical commands are constructed within the mind of the caster. If one is able to confuse the caster's mind, they can impede that control. It's similar to messing up someone trying to count by whispering random numbers in their ear.

Index couldn't use magic.

However, she *could* force the enemy sorcerer to self-destruct.

The caster manipulating this statue wasn't present, but just from how the spell had been put together, Index knew that it wasn't autonomous; it was being controlled from afar. That meant the caster was observing Index in detail via the golem's five senses—and that's where she found her opening.

"CR. (Change right.) CBF. (Cross both feet.) TTNATWITOD! (Turn the neck and the waist in the other direction!)"

The statue threw its punches one by one, and Index rattled off her shouts in rapid succession. The golem's fist flew all over the place, like a blindfolded drunkard swinging his arms around in the dark.

I can't just...stay on the defensive!

Index pulled out all the safety pins in her habit skirt. The act exposed most of her leg like a cheongsam, but she didn't have the time to care about it.

She readied the safety pins and stared down the golem.

They were weak, superbly ineffective weapons against a gigantic stone statue.

Reverse calculating self-healing technique. Occurs approximately every three seconds. If I want to use that against it, it has to be...now!!

Without hesitating, she hurled the safety pins at the golem's foot. They arced through the air slowly, unable to damage human skin, much less rock-hard armor. However, when they bounced off its foot, they got sucked back inside it like they were attracted by a magnet.

And then, a moment later.

Criiick. They obstructed the golem's right foot as if she'd driven a wedge into the joint.

This had a similar mechanism to spell interception. This stone statue built and regenerated its own body automatically by using objects in the area. This meant that she was able to turn it against the golem by throwing in something it didn't need—indeed, something that was actually *harmful*. It was as though a broken bone had been left alone and solidified into a strange shape.

103,000 grimoires slept within her.

But simply storing all of that knowledge was pointless. The important thing was how well she could apply it to come to the most suitable solution in the least amount of time.

I think I can do this, she thought, shuffling backward. There were exceptions that her spell interception wouldn't work on, such as the alchemist's Ars Magna, which was an entirely unknown spell to her, as well as Ouma Yamisaka's azusa bow, which emphasized the tool rather than the incantation. However, this golem didn't have any particular problems. She was definitely interrupting the golem's control, and she had dealt damage by utilizing her safety pins. *If I keep on hampering its movements, then I might be able to get the spell to fail and crush the golem,* she considered.

Thud!! Suddenly, the golem stomped on the ground.

"Kyaah...?!"
The massive tremor caught Index's foot and made her trip up. She clicked her tongue in disappointment. However much she interrupted her opponent's attacks, she couldn't avoid the entire ground shaking.

The statue approached the prone Index slowly, dragging its right leg behind it.

"! CR—" she tried to shout, but before she could, the golem punched its fists together.

Slam!! The shock wave pounded on her ears and cut off the words she had been putting together. The cat cradled in her arms let out a cry at the earsplitting roar.

The golem raised its fists into the sky.

Index rolled onto the ground, still holding the calico, and tried to distance herself as much as she could, as she called out,

"MBFPADCOG! (Move both feet parallel and destroy center of gravity!)"

However, the golem shook its head once and seemed to flip a switch and decide not to listen to Index's command.

This...isn't good! She changed it from long-range control to fully autonomous—!!

If the caster wasn't here, Index's spell interception wouldn't do anything. Her words could only trick humans, not a mindless, inorganic substance.

The golem swung its fist around into the air, ready to strike. Index could no longer stop its attacks by herself…

There was a *splat*.

It was a dull sound, like flesh slamming into concrete, that echoed through the area.

5

Kamijou at last dropped down the big hole into the subway tunnel.

It had taken a while for him to find something to use as a rope, then to find somewhere to tie it. He let go of the thick fire-fighting hose he had utilized and began to run down the dark path.

Damn! I'm so sick and tired of everyone just going off and doing whatever the hell they want and causing trouble! This situation is already a mess! Why'd you have to go and add another hurdle?!

Ellis's footprints were sunken into the concrete ground at fixed points. He couldn't see Hyouka Kazakiri anywhere down the tunnel, nor could he hear any footsteps.

He tightened his right hand into a fist as he remembered how she had smiled before disappearing like that.

His ultimate hand.

A transient, illusory girl who would be destroyed if he touched her. *I won't let it come to such a shitty ending. I'm not letting it happen!*

Kazakiri had called herself a monster, but she was wrong. She may not have been human, but nobody could call her a *monster*.

So what if she wasn't human—did that mean she wasn't allowed to ask for help?

Did that mean she needed to hold in her tears and endure it silently?

Of…of course not!!

He bit down and proceeded ahead.

There were rectangular concrete pillars placed at regular intervals down the center of the subway tunnel, separating the inbound line from the outbound one. It was wearing on him, too. No matter how far he ran, his view didn't change a bit.

But suddenly, a pillar next to him began to fall over.

It was clearly unnatural. It was like a huge, invisible hand knocking down a pile of building blocks.

"Shit...?!"

Kamijou panicked and jumped to sidestep the pillar falling toward him. With a massive *thump*, it scattered concrete dust into the air.

"Yes, I see it won't be easy to take *you* down..."

A voice addressed him from the darkness. Coughing, he looked over. Sherry Cromwell was standing there, her slightly dirty dress hanging off of her like she was dragging it.

She was a little more than ten meters away.

He scowled. Ellis, that symbol of cruelty, wasn't here.

"Hu. Uhu-hu. Uhu-hu-uhu. Ellis? I sent her up ahead. She's probably already reached her target. Or maybe she already pounded her into a lump of meat?"

"Y-you...!!"

Kamijou dropped his weight and made a fist. She had a way to control Ellis without using her pastel. Having two experiences relayed to her mind must have been putting a strain on it.

Sherry stared at him and smiled, satisfied. "That's fine. Yes, that's just fine. I'll have you keep me company in the meantime. I won't let you through to Ellis."

It was at this moment when he finally realized what she had up her sleeve. Kamijou could destroy Ellis with one hit, so whatever the cost, she had to stop him right here.

Hyouka Kazakiri would have already passed through this area, but he couldn't find her anywhere.

Sherry had probably let her go on purpose. Despite Kazakiri being one of her main targets, she didn't seem to care—she was already completely focused on Index.

And...

The sorcerer had discarded Kazakiri, as if to say she had no time for unnecessary opponents—as though she was content with only Kamijou.

He thought back to what Sherry had told him before.

"I'm starting a war, and I need a trigger for it. I need as many people as possible to know that I'm a pawn of the English Puritan Church... right, Ellis?"

Sherry was trying to start something with Academy City, so he didn't need to ask what part of the English Puritan Church was trying to start the war.

But was this really the opinion of the entire English Church?

At the very least, he didn't think that Stiyl, Kanzaki, or Tsuchimikado would ever think this way.

"...What the hell are you trying to do? I don't have a clue about what's going on behind the scenes here, but science and magic are still in balance right now, aren't they? So why are you trying to disrupt that?! What the hell would that do?!"

Sherry simply grinned at him.

She smiled and said, "When an esper uses magic, their body is destroyed. Did you know that?"

"What?"

That wasn't the question he'd asked at all. He frowned.

"Haven't you ever thought it odd? **How do we know that in the first place?**"

Her words tried to worm their way into Kamijou's heart.

"They tested it out. Like, twenty years ago. At some point, English Puritanism and Academy City wanted to try and join magic and science, and they created a department with us in it. We brought our respective tech and knowledge into one institution and attempted to create a caster with both abilities and magic. As for the result..."

Kamijou could guess what was coming next, even without hearing her out.

When espers use magic, their body bursts. He knew that well from the students at Misawa and Motoharu Tsuchimikado.

"That institution...what happened to it?"

"Well, it went under. Or maybe someone *made* it go under. When word got out they were in contact with the science side, they were hunted down and killed by members of the very same English

Puritan Church. Tech and intel were leaking to the other side—that's more than a valid reason to attack like that."

Kamijou kept silent.

It wasn't about scientists and sorcerers joining hands. It wasn't about how it was stopped. It wasn't about how they tried to hurt others.

"Ellis was my friend," said Sherry simply. "She was one of the espers brought there by a faction in Academy City."

Kamijou frowned. Ellis was the name she'd given to the golem. He thought about the feelings that went into her giving it that name, though he knew that she was the only one who could ever understand them.

"Ellis was covered in blood because of the spell I taught her. When the Knights came to crush the institution, she took a mace to the head and died to let me escape."

A church-like silence settled upon the dark subway tunnel.

Slowly, she continued. "We're supposed to be separate. And we shouldn't just be quarreling—we should be baring our fangs at the very *thought* of trying to understand each other. Unless sorcerers and scientists keep to themselves and to their own work, we'll keep repeating the same mistakes over and over again."

Hence the war.

"Shit. You're not even making sense. A war in order to protect both its sides? No, I don't think you actually *want* a war. Your objective is just to make people think that we *could* have gone to war, or that it was right before our eyes, even if it didn't actually happen. That would be enough, wouldn't it?"

"Don't overestimate me, you stupid brat. I have no need for your pitying stares!"

Kamijou, however, was sure that his suggestion was correct. She wanted to avoid a decisive clash between sorcerers and scientists—that contradictory desire meant they should be far apart, but also that the idea of trying to understand each other wouldn't even come to mind.

Parties that have absolutely no connections to each other wouldn't harbor either hate or goodwill toward each other, after all.

19

She didn't want them to oppose each other.

She wanted to prevent the friction that came with attempting to cooperate.

"..."

Sherry's claim that sorcerers and scientists should live far away from each other did have merit. Against that, any arguments Kamijou could make might be construed as selfishness. But there was one big reason he wouldn't be persuaded by her opinion.

He and Index might not be able to see each other anymore.

Actually, if she were used as Sherry's "trigger," then she might be killed outright. The reason was an absurdly personal one.

But he felt that he wouldn't be able to deny it, no matter what.

Not ever.

Sherry Cromwell brought a white oil pastel out from her ragged dress sleeve. He kept his eyes on her fingers, though he was taken aback by this. If everything she said was true, then she couldn't create two golems at once. And given that he'd punched the shit out of her after locking Ellis up one-on-one, she didn't seem to have anything more powerful to throw at him.

Sherry grinned, her unruly hair waving.

"Damn. I didn't expect you to not notice. All this darkness is really doing the job, I suppose."

"What?"

Returned Kamijou. Sherry gently waved the oil pastel in her hand. Unable to create a golem, her scribbling symbols on the floor or walls would only be able to bring debris down on them.

"Oh, my. You never felt anything wrong with this? Why am I showing myself out in the open when it's so dark in here? Normally, I'd just wait, hidden in the shadows, until you passed by, and then attack you. It'd be way more effective, yeah?"

Kamijou was dubious. All she could do right now was break the walls nearby. She shouldn't be able to do much at a distance of ten meters.

"Yes, and this particular place—why did I choose it? There's only one way through here, so you would have to come this way. Why did I wait in this one particular place, hmm?"

But if that was the case...

Why had that nearby pillar fallen on him just before?

"Let's compare answers...It's like this! Grit your teeth!!"

Sherry swung her oil pastel through the air with a *wshh*.

The next moment, the entire subway tunnel began to glow faintly.

What the...?!

Kamijou was dumbfounded. There were patterns drawn by her oil pastel all over the walls and ceiling. Even behind him and past Sherry—as far as he could see. It probably didn't cover the entire underground subway line, but the scrawls were at least one hundred meters from one end to the other.

On the floor were magic circles drawn at points, like raindrops falling from the ceiling.

Shit...Are these magic circles for Ellis...?!

Kamijou trembled. The magic circles, upon closer inspection, were all the same pattern and were laid next to one another like tiles.

According to Sherry, she couldn't make two golems simultaneously. If that was true, then he wouldn't have to deal with another Ellis here.

But what the hell had she *done* after she fled into this tunnel from the underground mall?

When the golem's magic circle failed, the floor got destroyed. She'd inscribed those magic circles all over the inside of the tunnel, which meant...

Damn...She's gonna drop the whole tunnel?!

When buildings are blown up for deconstruction, they apparently use many smaller bombs to cover the entire place rather than use one giant bomb. These magic circles could have been serving the same function.

How many of them were there? If one had a diameter of a meter, then one line of them would contain one hundred. And they were covering the walls and ceiling, too. How many times that would it be? If they were each a separate magic, then he couldn't just touch one or two and erase them all.

Sherry had stayed here to set all this up. Just by arranging everything beforehand, she could bring the entire place down at a word, without even needing to get close to him.

"The earth is my ally. Thus, dark pits enclosed in earth are my territory," she announced.

There were magic circles drawn near her, too, so she would be caught in the landslide as well—but she probably had a way out, of course. Perhaps she set it up so that she could make a dome around her that would deflect the debris, or maybe she had calculated where it would fall and was standing where she would be able to escape to the surface.

"Shit...!!"

Kamijou cursed. He wouldn't make it to Sherry or get far enough away in time. He was caught in her trap. There was no way out of it.

She gave him a relaxed look, as if she'd even calculated his impatience.

"Destroy it all, like a mud puppet!!"

In answer to her scream, his surroundings lit up brighter than before. Then, the entire tunnel writhed as though they'd been inside the belly of a giant snake the entire time.

Damn it, what do I do...?!

He couldn't just blindly run away from this. He also couldn't just erase the hundreds of magic circles with just his one hand. Besides, he clearly couldn't even reach the ceiling in the first place, and those were the most dangerous ones—he could nullify all the floor and wall circles he wanted, but if he couldn't block the ones on the ceiling, he'd be buried alive.

Suddenly, he froze.

The magic circles on the floor?

"Swallow the fool! Knead him into the dirt! With that I will construct your flesh!"

Shouted Sherry, as if flipping the final switch.

Massive fissures ran through the walls and ceiling, and the inside of them ballooned inward. No—the ceiling had lost its durability and was buckling under the weight of the soil above.

"Khh...?!"

Under the ceiling about to burst like a soap bubble, Kamijou bolted off like a bullet. He had one aim—to go forward. The location that the caster, Sherry, was standing in was probably the only safe zone that wouldn't get buried by the rubble. But his legs would never be able to take him all the way there. It would be impossible.

But that's not where I'm going!

He balled his right hand into a fist and lowered his stance as he ran, his head nearly low enough to lick the ground. He had but one target—not Sherry Cromwell, but the magic circle on the floor in front of her.

Index's angry yelling in the cafeteria came back to him.

"Okay, then, Touma, you know this, right? About how when you're casting a spell in a sanctuary to create an idol and fill it with Telesma from an English cross? You know how the time and cardinal directions are related to the caster's position, right?! You know about defensive magic circles to protect yourself from the main spell's aftereffects, and how you have to put it in a very precise location! And how if you're even a little bit off, the main spell will eat up the defense and it won't work properly! This is a golden rule, but you knew that already, didn't you? Come on, it's just common sense!"

That one magic circle doesn't mean anything.

The magic circles on the walls and ceiling were probably to destroy the tunnel and bury Kamijou alive. He knew that much. But that would mean circles on the floor weren't necessary. Destroying the floor wouldn't help bury him.

That means...that one circle means something else!

Sherry Cromwell's face blanched with surprise when she realized where he was headed. She hastily swung her oil pastel and delivered commands to the nearby walls and pillars, but she was too slow. Kamijou evaded the crumbling walls and slipped past the falling pillars, thrust his hand toward the magic circle on the floor...

...and brought it down without a moment's delay.

The magic circle shattered like a frozen raindrop.

That was the *second* spell Sherry had needed.

If it was to create a safe zone to protect her from the landslide...

Now that she had lost her protection, she could no longer be careless with the landslide.

"Damn!!"

She whipped the oil pastel around. The ceiling, creaking as if it were about to burst like a dam break, stabilized once again.

Bam!! came the sound of a grand footstep.

Surprised, she looked away from the ceiling back in front of her. Kamijou had shot off the floor like a skipping stone and was right up next to her.

She instantly tried to swing the pastel again…

…but his fist easily went around it and landed straight in her face.

Her hair and dress went everywhere as her body was blown through the subway tunnel. She flew for several meters before finally coming to a stop. Intense panic and fear were plastered on her face, as if she couldn't believe that her carefully laid plan of attack had been evaded.

"…Shit, damn it!" she cursed hatefully, wobbling back one or two steps. The oil pastel in her hands quivered as well, appearing as though her fingers were squeezing it so hard it would snap in the middle.

"I need to create the trigger for a war. Don't stop me! Why don't you understand that the current situation is incredibly dangerous?! Academy City seems to be loosening its guard. Even the English Puritan Church is getting lax—they're lending that *index* to someone else. It's just like the time with Ellis. And when that happened to us, it ended up in such tragedy. If this blows up to all of the city and the Church…! It's so simple to consider what would happen if we tread on enemy territory without thinking!"

Sherry's voice echoed several times in the dark underground, and Kamijou wiggled to catch it all.

Her impetus was the death of a friend.

Sherry believed that scientists and sorcerers getting too close to each other would cause tragedy. It wouldn't just be from fighting with each other—even thinking about getting along would backfire. From her point of view, in order to prevent warring between science and sorcerers, they needed to clearly define where they each lived and controlled, and trade back every single person who didn't belong in their area.

And to do that, she was trying to create the trigger for a war.

She didn't want them to harbor feelings of mutual understanding. She knew those feelings, though positive, would always backfire in the end and cause a tragedy.

She didn't actually want to start a war. As long as the fact was that she *created the trigger for it*, her goal would be accomplished.

Kamijou sighed in irritation after thinking that far.

"What a load of crap. That doesn't justify a damn thing! Tell me, what did Kazakiri do? What did Index ever do to you?! You're up on your high horse preaching that war is bad, but who do you think you're trying to kill for it?!!" he yelled, venting everything from his chest.

Because there was something he just couldn't accept.

"Fine! Get angry! Get sad! I don't care; I won't stop you. But you're pointing your sword at the wrong person! You shouldn't even be pointing it at anyone! I know it's painful. I know that I could never understand any of this! But if you point your sword at someone, then *you're* the one starting a goddamn war!!"

Ellis died because a group of scientists and sorcerers tried to get together, and the English Puritans saw it as dangerous.

What had Sherry felt like when she found out about all that?

Did she vow revenge for killing her friend?

Did she make an oath never to let such a tragedy happen again?

"...I don't get it."

Sherry Cromwell bit down on her back teeth.

"Damn it, of course I hate them! Everyone who killed Ellis should go to hell! I want to take all those sorcerers and scientists and tear them limb from limb! But that's not all! I really don't ever want sorcerers and espers to fight again! My mind has been a complete wreck ever since the beginning!"

Her contradictory return shout reverberated in the dark tunnel.

She sounded like she was being torn apart by her own voice, as though she realized it as well.

"I don't have just one opinion! I suffer because a lot of different viewpoints can convince me! I don't live by one rule! I can't live as a wind-up puppet! If you want to laugh, then laugh all you want. I've got as many beliefs as stars in the sky! It wouldn't hurt a bit if one or two of them disappeared!!"

Touma Kamijou said one thing in response.

"Why haven't you realized this yet?"

"...What was that?"

"I mean, yeah, your words make no sense. You're directly opposed to what you're trying to say, because you can understand other people's opinions. That's why your own beliefs are so hard to hold on to...That's how you're thinking about it, isn't it? You know, that's wrong. You've only ever had one belief this entire time."

Then, he said it...

...the one answer that she never even realized.

"You just didn't want to have to lose an important friend, right?"

Yes.

Sherry Cromwell may have had countless different beliefs, and some of them clashed directly with each other—but the very first root of them all never changed. All of her beliefs started with the incident with her friend and were no more than branches and derivations coming out of it.

Even if her beliefs were as numerous as the stars in the sky...

...the feelings she had for her friend never changed.

"Take that first and think about it. Think about everything, all over again! You were watching us with those mud eyeballs, weren't you? What did you see when you saw us? Did Index and I look anything like people who had to stay far away from each other so that a war wouldn't happen?!" he shouted. "You have as many beliefs as there are stars, right? Think about what they all have in common! Did Index or I do anything to you?! Did it look like I was forcing Index to come along with me against her will? No, it didn't, did it?! We don't need to stay away from each other! We can be with each other without having to do that!!"

He didn't suggest that his relationship with Index was what Sherry herself really wanted. He couldn't tell her not to break apart this ideal situation. Sherry had one wish that would never be granted and that couldn't be replaced by something else. If someone had told Kamijou to take someone else instead, he'd throw a punch right at that person's face without a second thought.

So he didn't say that.

The only thing he said was this:

"I don't want your help, so please, don't take someone important away from me!"

He saw Sherry Cromwell's shoulders jolt in surprise.

Even if her wish could never be granted, she should remember how important it was to her. She would know well the pain of having that taken away from her.

Sherry's face twisted up like she was trying to endure suffering.

Kamijou's words were so simple. They weren't hard to understand. However childish they may have been, they *had* to have gotten through to her—because she would have yelled the same things at one point.

"—My entire being for my lost friend—Intimus115!"

However, she shouted it down and rejected it.

She had given her magic name.

She probably understood Kamijou's feelings so well that it hurt.

But on the other hand…

Sherry Cromwell didn't have just one belief. She could probably even understand what it was like *not* to understand that. No—maybe it was *because* she was convinced by his feelings. She wanted to drop him, who had something she no longer had, into the pit of hell—that was probably one of those innumerable beliefs she held.

Bshwshh!! Her oil pastel flashed through the air.

A moment after a pattern appeared on the wall beside her, it came apart like papier-mâché. The clouds of dust that whipped up immediately obstructed their vision.

Kamijou saw the gray curtain of roiling mist coming toward him and, without thinking, tried to jump backward.

But just then, Sherry cut through the dust right in front of him. She was diving straight for him like a bullet, oil pastel in hand.

His heart jumped into his mouth. Anything that oil pastel drew on, whether it was iron or concrete, would be made into Ellis's body. Maybe human flesh wasn't an exception.

"Die, esper!!"

Her monstrous roar came from a face that looked about to cry like a baby.

Oh, I see.

He reflexively balled his right hand into a fist as he came to a realization.

This wasn't her trump card. If doing this could stop Kamijou for sure, she would have used it at the beginning. Anti-Skill may have stopped Ellis from moving, but the golem couldn't be taken down very easily, and she wouldn't have needed to set this elaborate trap in the subway tunnel.

Sherry Cromwell said she had as many beliefs as the stars in the sky.

She yelled that she suffered because she could be convinced by anyone's ideas.

Then...

"...Then you can understand feeling like you want somebody to stop you."

Wham!! Kamijou's fist shattered the soft oil pastel to pieces.

His fist still had power in it; he curved it around and struck Sherry Cromwell straight in the face.

Slam!! With an incredible noise, her body bounced across the ground of the tunnel.

She came to a stop up against a pillar. Kamijou slowly approached her. She seemed to be out like a light.

And Ellis...Did this stop it?

He wasn't too confident about that. He thought about giving Sherry a wake-up slap and asking her, but she might not answer him truthfully. His unease about it wouldn't disappear whether she said yes or no.

Damn it. Guess I have to go and see for myself!

Just to be safe, he picked up the abandoned cord he had dropped and tied up her limbs. After making sure her wrists were tight behind her back, he once again ran deeper into the tunnel.

As he did, low, dull rumblings crawled through the floor toward him, growing little by little in intensity.

He wouldn't need to ask where Ellis was.

"…"

Ten seconds later, Sherry Cromwell opened her eyes slightly.

She'd been conscious the whole time.

She wondered why he hadn't just killed her. She wouldn't be able to take issue with it—that was one of the feelings she understood, so she had launched a reckless, suicidal attack.

That was indeed praiseworthy, but she held countless beliefs, and she didn't know which of them would come to the surface after this. She might just undo her bindings and go after him again to kill him.

In the same way, she understood his words. She could feel a desire *not* to kill him sprouting within her. But on the other hand, she thought exactly the opposite, too.

Her hands still tied behind her back, she wiggled around and got an oil pastel out of her clothes.

What…about…Ellis…?

When she had taken the fallen oil pastel into her hand, she suddenly realized that Ellis was no longer under her command—she was acting autonomously. She wouldn't listen to a simple "destroy yourself" command. Someone would either have to destroy the *shem*, her fail-safe, or blow away 90 percent of her body within a span of two seconds. Those were the only ways to stop her.

She viciously crushed her last remaining oil pastel in her hand.

It was impossible for her to create two Ellises at the same time. As long as the current one wasn't destroyed, she couldn't make a new golem. In other words, she couldn't break out of her current situation—lying on the ground with her hands tied behind her back.

Ellis...

Sherry Cromwell, movements entirely restricted, sent an order to Ellis that wouldn't reach.

Was it a command to destroy her target? Or was it a directive to stop everything?

She could understand having done either of them.

6

The head of the golem snapped up.

Index's spell interception wasn't working anymore.

The behemoth swung its fist up in a wide arc...

...and an awful noise of flesh being crushed rose in the gaps between the abandoned buildings.

However, it was not the sound of Index's body being smashed. The cat didn't have a scratch on it, either. At the same time, it wasn't the kind of noise a golem could make—it was made out of stone, after all.

Hyouka Kazakiri.

She had jumped over her head from behind and delivered a flying kick to the statue's stomach. Both her speed and power were anything but ordinary. It was more like a meteorite striking it.

Gdumm!! came a deafening noise.

The golem's body launched back, much like an iron ball with momentum slamming into an iron ball without it. It spun lengthwise three times in midair and landed on its face. The assault had sent the juggernaut almost seven meters back. In contrast, Kazakiri, having transferred all of her kinetic energy into it, hung in the air for a moment.

Then, with the grace of a feather falling, she set foot back on the ground.

Boomm!! There was a low rumble.

The moment she touched down with her opposite foot from the

one she used to kick, the ground began to crack apart in a two-meter radius like it had been pounded with a gargantuan hammer. It looked almost like the force of gravity applied tenfold to Kazakiri.

"Hyou...ka...?"

Index tried to call out to her from behind, but she caught her breath.

Kazakiri's right leg, which had performed the kick, had been blown to smithereens from the thigh down. The attack she'd carried out had been strong enough to knock over a mammoth weighing in the tons. No human body could withstand that sort of recoil.

Or, so she thought.

But inside her severed leg was nothing but emptiness. The wound itself looked completely unnatural, as though the paint had been torn off a see-through pillar.

...Wh-what is that?

Index, still holding the cat to her breast, thought.

Tiaoshi magic. Necromancy. The Hand of Glory. Vetala sorcery. Elixirs. She had mountains of magical knowledge, and some of that magic could affect even the dead. Horrifyingly, there were even techniques where one would rig something inside a corpse to gain total control over it.

However...

Even she found herself unable to explain the sight before her eyes. Could a human even *be* changed to such an extent? *Should* one be?

Swishh! She heard a sound like a flag flapping in the wind, and a moment later, Hyouka Kazakiri's destroyed leg returned to normal without leaving a trace. It happened at such an incredible speed that it seemed to leap out of her severed leg like a powerful spring.

"Please, run."

She didn't turn around.

She simply spoke behind her.

"Please, get away from here...It's still...dangerous, so..."

Her voice was that of the girl Index knew well, and because of that, she hesitated to say anything in reply. She didn't know whether she should be on her guard or not—or whether she was the real Hyouka Kazakiri or an identical fake.

A creaking noise split through the air. It was from the stone statue that had fallen on its face.

It seemed to be trying to get up, but Kazakiri's hit must have damaged the stone structure itself. It shook its joints and made cracking sounds, like it was a human trapped under something covering its waist...

Then there was the *snap* of a bone breaking, loud and clear.

Its attempt to move its body anyway had caused the interior of its constructed body to be destroyed.

Gigigigigagagagaga!! the stone monster cried out. It had no vocal chords to do so—it was the cacophonous sound of all the joints in its body being moved by force. It couldn't stand back up. As it crawled on the ground, it raised its head toward the sky as if to howl.

Roar!! came a gust of wind.

Heavy winds like a tornado blew forth with the screaming golem at its center. It was like a gigantic clump of wind that wanted to swallow the entire abandoned building district whole. It was **not** the sort of violent winds that would lift up everything in the area and blow it away in every direction. It was more like a whirlpool, pulling in nearby boats, trying to drag them down to the seafloor.

The wind wasn't directed outward—it was slicing inward.

Rocks, empty cans, bicycles that had been left here and forgotten, window frames without the glass—everything but the kitchen sink drew in toward the golem. An unseen force crushed them and turned them into part of its body.

That's...not good...The golem's regeneration functions might be going crazy from that attack!

While holding tight to the cat, who was liable to come flying straight out of her hands, Index shuddered with fear. "Hyouka Kazakiri's" attack had probably dealt fatal damage to the statue. Even down to the *shem*, its core, its safety device hidden inside its body. And now that it had tried to heal its irreparable wounds anyway, it was repeating its reconstruction command to its body, haphazardly collecting anything it could find.

Its wound wouldn't be healed, no matter what it did.

Thus, it would relay its command to continue repairing itself until the wound was healed, forever and ever and ever. The part it was trying to repair would stay as it was, and the golem's body would continue to absorb unnecessary things one after the other, expanding like a snowman. Its body had been close to four meters tall, but in a span of less than thirty seconds, it had already ballooned to twice that size, both across and high. Since it was in a crawling posture, it looked like a roof covering up Index and Kazakiri.

The buildings nearby began to squeal.

Index blanched when she heard the gigantic architectural structures emitting an eerie sound like trees being blown around in a tempest. At this rate, the storm would rip down all of the buildings around them. There'd be no saving them if they were caught in the collapse. Unfortunately, if the tornado grew so powerful it could break the building, all of Index's greatest efforts wouldn't prevent her feet from leaving the ground and being swallowed up into the golem's body.

We have to get away, she thought.

Now that it was active without a caster, under its own power, her spell interception wouldn't affect it. Now that its regeneration was malfunctioning and it was doing this while knowing it would be destroyed, she couldn't hamper its movement using a mere safety pin or two. She hated it. She was frustrated. She didn't have the ability to produce mana, and all of her immense knowledge was for naught.

Index couldn't hold that golem back. As far as she knew, the only one who could get this situation under control was the boy with that one-and-only right hand.

"Hyouka, let's get out of here!" she shouted. She still hadn't confirmed that the Hyouka Kazakiri before her was the same one she had been with after school that day, though.

Right then, the outer wall of one of the abandoned buildings separated.

It was caught up in the whirlwind—a clump of stone dancing through the air like the hammer of a giant. Index quickly crouched down, still cradling the cat. A lump of concrete rocketed over her head and crashed into the asphalt. The scattered shards of the ground, too, were caught by the wind and sucked into the golem.

She was far from running away. If she even held her head up without thinking, she could be slammed by flying debris.

Despite the hopeless situation, Hyouka Kazakiri maintained her stance, unmoving.

A huge piece of debris bigger than her body shot right by her face, but she didn't flinch. She looked like an old man looking out at a storm on the ocean. She didn't move a muscle.

Without turning around, she said quietly, "You should…get out of here."

"What do you mean? What about you?!" asked Index, holding fast to the cat, which seemed about to be taken away by the wind.

"I'll…" After thinking a moment, she continued. "I must…stop that monster."

As if to answer her declaration, the crawling stone statue brought its right arm into the air. It did so slowly due to its increased weight—or perhaps because it was waiting for the right moment to let all its pent-up energy loose, like a dam on the verge of breaking.

If it let that punch loose, the vicious attack would crush both the buildings nearby and the girls into fine grains of dust. There was no doubt about it. You couldn't protect yourself from it—it would be beyond human endurance.

"You can't! Hyouka, we have to run away! Humans can't face this thing! It may be down on the ground, but you can't go around behind it with a plan! You don't need to fight like this, Hyouka!"

Kazakiri didn't turn around at her words.

The stone fist stopped abruptly, as if taking precise aim at its target.

"Hyouka, that's not a human! Please, you can't fight a monster like that! If you do, then there won't be any way to save you!" she shouted, and at last, Hyouka Kazakiri slowly turned around.

Despite a cannon-like fist staring her in the face, she turned around, not looking at it.

"…It's all right," she said.

She smiled, still looking about to cry.

"I'm...not human either."

Index caught her breath in spite of herself.

Smiling that ragged, painful smile, Hyouka Kazakiri told her one last thing.

"I'm sorry...for lying to you this whole time."

Behind her, the stone fist shot toward her.

Roar!! went the air as it was crushed. The attack was nothing short of a meteor crashing down. Index curled her body up out of reflex and called Kazakiri's name.

She would no longer answer.

She turned her whole body back to the golem. She spread her frail arms to the left and right and stood as a wall to protect Index.

She watched the rocky fist approach.

The enormous incoming strike was more like a wall than a bullet or a cannonball. There was absolutely no balance between their respective strengths. It was like a landslide crushing a thin branch.

Ger-slam!!

Hyouka Kazakiri's slender hands caught the golem Ellis's fist.

Her hands, feet, chest, stomach, back, and neck all took the brunt of the immense impact, and she was overcome with a pain that felt like all her joints were coming apart. Her arms' length shrank five centimeters. Because of her arms' compression, her girlish, vibrant skin was pushed up in a creepy, bumpy fashion. It came with a raw feel, like ribs being pushed up against one's skin.

"Agh...ah...?"

Hyouka Kazakiri heard her flabbergasted voice behind her.

She couldn't turn around to reassure her.

She couldn't even say everything would be all right.

Her entire body cracked and creaked as she was racked with agonizing pain from within. It felt like an iron file were shaving down her teeth, except over all of her.

She didn't feel that she was stopping the fist.

The immense, hopeless power, like that of a landslide tumbling down a mountain slope, just kept coming. Her fingers holding back the garbage-assembled iron fist of the golem snapped. Her feet on the ground were pushed backward into the asphalt. Her calves couldn't withstand the pressure and bent and warped out of shape with a smashing sound, like tree branches losing to the weight of snow atop them. Pain exploded inside her body. It felt as though someone had slammed a hammer into her shins at full force.

The golem must have decided it would crush the pitiful resistance with brute force, and like tightening a vise, it directed more power into its fist.

"Ah, aaaaaaaahhhhhgh!!"

Kazakiri screamed and strained against it. Her limbs expanded vigorously. She wasn't straining her muscles. Like blowing air into a balloon, her limbs that were being crushed with sheer force expanded and forcibly regained their original form.

Her vision blinked in and out at the pain, which felt like a nearly closed wound had been torn back open.

The stone monster gave even more pressure to its fist.

Her body was caught between the force trying to crush her from without and the force trying to return her to normal from within. It gave awful creaks and groans like old floorboards.

Kazakiri bit back against the intense pain, but she still didn't let go of the golem's fist.

There was no way she was ever letting go.

A girl she needed to protect was behind her. The girl in white wasn't a monster like Kazakiri was. She didn't have the strength to stop the fist of a behemoth.

Monsters…

…must be the ones to fight other monsters.

But…

But however much she struggled, there would be no saving Hyouka Kazakiri.

Even if she saved Index, she would be defeated by the golem in return. She'd never tested the limits of her body before. And she couldn't even imagine what would happen to "Hyouka Kazakiri" if **her own flesh were assimilated into the golem** like pillars or bicycles. Even if she somehow managed to avoid it and miraculously returned alive...well, Index already knew that she wasn't human.

But still...

Times like when she met them in that school cafeteria...

Days like the one she'd spent after school in the underground mall...

She'd never return to them.

But still...I cannot abandon her...!!

Hyouka Kazakiri channeled all her strength and strained her legs. All of her—her hands, feet, waist, back—continued its cycle of being crushed from without and expanding back out from within. The terrible noises shooting through her body resounded through the area like nails on a chalkboard.

"Hee...ah...?!"

She could hear the girl in white behind her gasping.

"Bgyahh! Shaa!!"

She could hear the cat behind her growling threats.

She wondered how she looked to the two of them. She had been just walking around with her casually not an hour ago. How did she look to her?

But, as if to gouge open her wounds yet again, she channeled strength into her body.

Because they were friends.

The girl in white, having seen her like this, probably wouldn't feel the same way, but Hyouka wanted to stay friends with her from start to finish!!

Crack.

The golem's body squealed.

Amid the flood of pain tearing her insides apart, she saw it—the golem, having lost its temper, swinging its other fist into the air.

Both of her hands were already tied up holding back the golem's right fist.

Guh...!!

She gritted her teeth. If that was how it was going to be, then she made up her mind and made her final choice—she would buy enough time for that girl to escape.

The golem's arm stopped in midair at a point, as if taking aim.

Kazakiri reflexively shut her eyes at the destruction that was sure to come a second later, when...

"Ka...za...Kazakiriiiiiiiiiiiiiiiiiiiiiiiiiiiiiiiiiiiiiiiiiiiiiiiiiiiiiiiiiiiiii iiiiii!!"

...she heard the voice of a boy she knew well.

It came from behind her. After the shriek, she heard footsteps in an all-out dash. She didn't have the luxury of turning to look, but she knew. She knew without seeing. She knew what his expression was. What he felt. How quickly he had run here.

He...

Even after seeing her fully transformed into a monster, he still called her *Kazakiri*.

Not *monster*—but *Kazakiri*.

As she stood in blank amazement, the black shadow flew by her like a javelin.

That was when the golem chose to launch its other fist.

He didn't hesitate. He didn't give it a second thought. And he was not afraid. His right fist was their only trump card, and he tightened it into a fist as strong as a boulder.

Glonk!! The two fists collided.

Vivid red blood spurted from the boy's fist.

But it wasn't because of the golem's strength. He had just wailed on the surface of a craggy rock with all his might. Its cannon-like attack lost all its strength the moment his fist touched it. More accurately—when it touched some kind of invisible magnetic field, perhaps, that shrouded the golem's fist.

The pressure about to crush Kazakiri like a suspended ceiling vanished.

At the same time, the bloated golem began to crack apart and crumble down to the ground. Gray dust soared into the air—much more and much grander than the scene from the underground mall—and obscured the vision of everyone present.

It's over...

Hyouka Kazakiri smiled to herself, lonely, within her closed-off area within the gray curtain.

That's...all for this nice, gentle illusion...

Her limbs, which had been crushed, expanded and returned to normal once again with a sound like bending plastic back into shape.

Feeling truly, truly lonely, but smiling, she decided to leave this place before the dust settled.

The crisis had been averted.

There was no longer a place for Kazakiri. She was like a weapon left over after a war ended. If she stayed in a peaceful world with such power, she would only be feared. And she couldn't bear to face the girl in white she had wanted to protect.

She was glad that they couldn't see each other.

She didn't have the courage to see what sort of expression Index, behind her, was wearing.

7

Kamijou stood by himself in a corner of the ruins.

When the gray dust cleared, Hyouka Kazakiri was nowhere in sight. Only two or three drops of water fell to the ground, even though it wasn't raining.

Having overheard the commotion, Mikoto and Shirai arrived quickly. *Anti-Skill and Judgment aren't far off, so we should get out of here before we get in big trouble.* Those were their words, not his.

And the two of them pulled along Index, who was trying to stay with Kamijou, and used teleportation to leave the area. Shirai's ability had a limit on how far it could go, so they were probably leap-frogging a hundred meters or so at a time. Kamijou, as usual, would nullify her powers, so he was left to run away by himself.

As for Sherry, Anti-Skill would deal with her, but considering what had transpired, he didn't think he'd be seeing her name in the newspaper anytime soon.

"Gee…trouble all over, huh?" Kamijou sighed. There was still something he needed to deal with before Anti-Skill or Judgment arrived on the scene. He looked overhead to confirm something, then entered one of the abandoned buildings.

The windows and interior of the building had already been stripped away, exposing the gray concrete beneath. There were letters, like directions, scrawled on the floor and walls in red chalk using technical terms. Maybe it was their procedure for knocking the whole place down. The red sunset shone in through the paneless windows and cut through the dust in the air like a laser.

The railings had been removed from the staircase; Kamijou ran up it.

He went up, and up, and up, and up, and up, and up, all the way to the top floor.

The door to the roof had also already been removed.

He set foot onto a roof dyed in vermilion. The place looked like it was used for a sky garden. The soil spread over the flower beds had dried out and was cracking apart. The remains of flowerlike plants had rotted into a brown color and were swaying in the wind.

In the very far corner of that paradisiacal graveyard…

Hyouka Kazakiri was sitting with her back to one of the emergency metal handrails. Her head was down; he couldn't see her face.

Her crushed limbs had already expanded back to their normal size. There were no wounds to be seen on her.

But she didn't have a word of happiness to give, and she hid her face.

He let down his eyelids a little.

If Hyouka Kazakiri had disappeared to flee from Index—or from people in general—then she would have had to come here. She just wanted to get away from Index, but there was nowhere to run, so she had to hole up inside one of the abandoned buildings.

The girl was all alone and didn't say a word to Kamijou, even though he had come onto the roof.

Tip-tap. He heard the sound of water drops falling.

Her head was down and she was holding the photo stickers in her hands. Clear droplets were falling onto it.

"I...I'm happy...That's all, okay?"

Kazakiri had noticed his gaze. She finally looked up slowly and smiled faintly.

"Because...I used all of my strength...and I protected an...an important friend. I did it...No one else did...*I* protected her. S-so I...I'm happy. I'm so happy...I'm crying...That's the reason..."

"..."

"Why...why are you making that face?...Please smile. Praise me a little...And if you say you're jealous, that would be great...I-I... I stole your place as the knight right...right out from under you... Ha-ha, what am I even saying...?"

Hyouka Kazakiri was smiling, but Touma Kamijou wasn't.

He couldn't.

He couldn't look at her completely ragged, forced smile and smile himself.

"Hic..." Kazakiri bit her lip, and her smile disappeared without a sound.

"I...I knew...from the start...,"

She said suddenly.

"...It was...so obvious. Anyone...anyone could understand... what would happen if...people knew I was a monster...I might have been able to...to do something about it, if I kept hiding it...but I stupidly...I knew what would happen if I revealed it myself. I didn't want to...Nobody wanted me to show myself like this!"

Kazakiri's words got caught up after that.

Her voice let out a sob.

"...But...what was I supposed to do?"

Her lips trembled and worked desperately.

"She was the first person…who said I was her friend, ever since I was born…I wanted to protect her, so…what else was I supposed to do…?"

She had probably been prepared for this all along.

This ending, where she would lose something important to her in exchange for revealing her identity as a monster. And because those terrible visions were so vivid in her mind, she wished, somewhere in her heart…

…that her prediction would be wrong.

She never thought about how low the probability was—she was just clinging to the hope of a miracle.

And the result…

"Why…why do I need to lose things?"

Slowly, she pulled her back from the railing and wobbled to her feet.

"Why…do I need to be so afraid?!"

Crying, she buried her face in Kamijou's chest.

She released all of her pent-up lamentation at zero range.

"I-I…I…! I just…I couldn't bear to watch…an important friend be hurt…That's the only reason I stood up for her!…I had the power to protect someone important…I just couldn't let her be like that! That's all! And yet…"

Her slender hands beat on Kamijou's breast.

He heard her muffled voice.

"It's…cruel! It's…it's frustrating! It hurts…! Why…why do I have to feel like this?! Did I…did I do something wrong?! Is it so wrong to just want to protect someone…?!"

The wailing of her torn heart pounded on his eardrums.

Though she knew yelling wouldn't change anything, she couldn't help it.

"I…I wanted to always be with her! I wanted…to be friends! I thought we would get along! But this…Why is this happening?! I risked my life…You can't understand what it felt like when I heard her gasp!…I can't even understand it, even though they're my own feelings!!"

She continued to shout, unable to organize her thoughts.

No—she was backed so far into a corner that she could no longer endure silence.

"Is it so bad...for a m-monster to protect someone?! If I were human...none of this would have happened, would it?!...Of course I couldn't do it! Even if she's scared of me or hates me, I could never just let her die...!!"

"..." Kamijou silently listened to what she had to say.

Despite her shaking and crying right next to him, he couldn't even stroke her head.

This illusion was so fleeting, so transient, that if he touched it, it would break.

The Imagine Breaker.

The boy called that couldn't even embrace her.

So instead, he asked,

"Does it hurt?"

"...Mmm..."

"Are you sad?"

"Mgh...!"

She stopped banging on his chest and grabbed his shirt like a child as her sobs she'd failed to fight leaked from her drawn lips.

"If you feel that way, then you're not a monster. It may be a totally stale, clichéd thing to say, but you're *human*. I can vouch for that. And also..."

He paused for a moment.

"This story of yours isn't over just yet."

"Huh?" Hyouka Kazakiri looked up to him, confused.

Clack. They heard footsteps from behind Kamijou.

Figured she'd be here soon, he thought, grinning.

Mikoto Misaka had said that getting caught by Anti-Skill or Judgment would be a huge pain, so she would take a certain girl and leave the area. And Kamijou knew she didn't want to leave until the very end—she wanted to stay with Kamijou.

Perhaps she'd guessed where Hyouka Kazakiri had gone all along.

Maybe she just couldn't run here quickly enough because Mikoto and Shirai forced her away.

And perhaps she had been worrying about Kazakiri this whole time.

*   *   *

All that led to one conclusion—she would definitely come here.

"Wha...what?"

Kazakiri lifted her face from Kamijou's chest and looked at the person behind him, at a loss.

He turned around slowly.

Far away, at the entrance to the roof with no door, stood a girl in a pure white habit. The safety pin in her skirt was taken out, and it looked like a cheongsam. Her breathing was ragged, and she was drenched in sweat. She must have run here without stopping to take a break.

That girl...Index...

After confirming that Kazakiri was there, she ran up without a second thought. Without any fear or hatred—with the face of a mother who had found her lost child at a playground.

Hyouka Kazakiri couldn't even blink as she watched.

"But...why? This is...this is strange."

Her body shook. It trembled as though it were cold.

"I mean...it's...weird. I-I'm not...a human! I told her...that I was a monster...so why is her face like that...? Why is she...Why is she looking at me like...a friend?"

Kamijou sighed in response.

"Well, yeah, you may be put together a little differently than other people, and you can do things that others can't."

His tone suggested that she was foolish to ask such an obvious question.

"But it doesn't change the fact that you're her friend, does it?"

At those words, Hyouka Kazakiri fell to her knees in tears.

Index dove at her and the two of them fell over onto the roof.

Kazakiri carefully brought her hands to Index's back and embraced her.

Touma Kamijou looked at the two of them and gave a little smile.

EPILOGUE

In Back of Front Stage

"See? Check this out! I didn't have to get hospitalized or anything this time. Wow, man, I'm great. It's like I evolved into my next form! Don't you think so?" said Kamijou in delight in the hospital ward to the frog-faced doctor. Komoe Tsukuyomi and Aisa Himegami both gave him a whack on the head, each from one side.

"Kami! You caused us so much trouble! So much worry! And you're not even caring about it, are you?! I can't believe you'd put Anti-Skill through all that...grumble grumble. My word! I'll hear a full report later and then give you another lecture!"

"That's why I told you. To be careful of Hyouka Kazakiri. I went through all the trouble to warn you. You are indiscriminate when it comes to women. Maybe your personality needs to be completely reformed."

"...Excuse me, these people are really scary, so, uh, can I get you to hospitalize me anyway? And put a sign up on the door that says *absolutely no visitors*...I request asylum until this dynamic duo cools off, at least," pleaded Kamijou to the frog-faced doctor. The two girls began to hit him on the head at a high speed.

The sun had already set, and clinic hours had long since ended. Despite looking fit as a fiddle, Kamijou was still an emergency patient. He'd gotten caught up in a firefight and attacked by landslides underground. Getting checked out despite having no injuries was really the obvious thing to do.

Index and Kazakiri, meanwhile, were in the waiting room. Kuroko Shirai would be up all night cleaning up after the incident, apparently.

The frog-faced doctor gave him a look like he was fed up with the after-hours work he was doing.

"What I don't understand is how you can be smiling in a situation like this, hmm? Perhaps you're under the effects of a runner's high due to over-exhaustion. If you had made a wrong move, your fist could have sustained a compound fracture, yes?"

"...What?"

"Your pupils are contracting, hmm? It certainly wouldn't be an unnatural thing, you know. Human fists are capable of many precise movements, and it has many joints to let that happen, meaning it's weak to impacts, right? If we're talking about simple blunt attacks, it would have been safer to use your forehead."

Kamijou realized his right hand had, in fact, been stinging a bit. He shuddered. The ladies behind him may have been angry, but this doctor had an entirely different level of destructive power.

After he'd subtly threatened his patient, the frog-faced doctor began to quickly wrap Kamijou's hand in bandages.

Now that Kamijou had stopped talking, Miss Komoe and Himegami began to quiet down.

Miss Komoe looked at Kamijou's bandaged right hand, then finally said,

"There are many things we don't understand."

"What do you mean?"

"Well! We don't know what we don't know, so we don't really need to talk about it...but I'm going to say it anyway, since I would feel bad keeping it to myself."

Miss Komoe smiled vaguely and held up her index finger.

"Firstly! Why did this Miss Hyouka Kazakiri appear near you, Kami? Academy City should be filled to the brim with involuntary diffusion fields. She could have appeared anywhere in the city. But she didn't—she consistently showed up close to Kami. Why? I mean, if it were a coincidence, then that settles it, but still."

Then, she held up her middle finger.

"Secondly. Sherry said that Hyouka Kazakiri held the key to the *i*th School District, the Five Elements Society, but in the end, what did that mean? This was told to her by a Kirigaoka teacher, so if it were just baseless speculation, then that settles it, but still."

Finally, she stuck up her ring finger.

"Thirdly and lastly. Why did our terrorist, who just appeared today, decide to go straight for Miss Hyouka Kazakiri? Not even the residents of Academy City knew she existed, so her information must have come from some pretty deep parts of the city. Although, if that ends up being a coincidence, too, then everything is pretty much settled, but still."

She opened the rest of her fingers and brought them to her face with a *slap*.

"But that would just be too many coincidences, wouldn't it? That's the strangest thing about all this."

Silence settled upon the hospital room.

They didn't have any of the required resources to make a judgment call on any of these things.

The frog-faced doctor casually looked away from them and out the window.

He couldn't see it from here, but there was a windowless building in that direction.

"Are you happy now?" spat Motoharu Tsuchimikado, taking his eyes off the image floating before his eyes, in a room of a building with no doors, windows, hallways, staircases, elevators, or even air vents.

Aleister, who was floating upside down in the giant glass cylinder before his eyes, smiled lightly.

There was no response. The unnerving silence made Tsuchimikado force his words as if it bothered him.

"And so by manipulating your human pawns, you're closer again to the completion of the key to bring the Five Elements Society under your grasp. Honestly? You look like a monster to me."

The Five Elements Society—also known as the *i*th School District.

"Who would have thought that its identity was actually the involuntary diffusion fields **themselves**? That the naturally occurring powers of the 2.3 million students who live here are creating the thing."

The Five Elements Society, constructed with involuntary diffusion fields, was something that would appear wherever espers were present, such as in this city.

Nobody even knew if it was harmful or benign.

It wasn't an enormous power source like nuclear power. If something like that flooded the streets, everyone would notice it. The Five Elements Society was purely involuntary diffusion fields. It was so slight that you wouldn't know it was there without measuring it with machines.

However, it was an unstable existence, like water kept at zero degrees Celsius through decompression.

Decompression—in other words, extremely low pressures—will reduce the freezing point of water and allow it to be brought to zero degrees without freezing. However, as soon as you disturb the water, like with a stick, the low-pressure water immediately freezes over.

The concept here was the same. The power was so tiny that only machines could detect it, but given some kind of impulse, its power would explode. The strength Hyouka Kazakiri had displayed at the end was only a glimpse of the power that either the golem's attack or some other source had given it.

The issue was that they didn't know just how strong the impulse needed to be. Just sticking a finger into it carelessly could cause an explosion, or it may not be anything to worry about.

And despite saying that the energy could explode, it was nothing more than a prediction. They didn't know how it would manifest or how wide its effects would be. It could wipe Academy City off the map or it may not be anything to be scared over.

They didn't know how deep to tread or what would happen. Thus,

Academy City couldn't destroy the Five Elements Society impru-
dently, either.

Hence the need for a method to control it without destroying it.

And for that, they needed a key...

"So it's Hyouka Kazakiri, is that it? Damn. She might be a part of
the *i*th School District, but planting an artificial ego into her and aid-
ing in her materialization? You must be out of your mind."

There was a boy with a right hand called Imagine Breaker.

It could be said to be the one menace to the *i*th School District.

And that threat created a *self.*

In the same way as the desire to eat or sleep, the needs created by
the instincts of biological organisms are created as signals to keep
on living and to avoid death. Someone without knowledge of life or
death wouldn't have sprouted instincts or a sense of self from the
start.

So what about the other way around?

If it were taught *death* by Imagine Breaker, a mindless illusion
would come to acquire a self.

Then, Aleister's mouth opened, though it had been silent until now.

"This, too, is a means of controlling the *i*th School District. Its
movements become easier to predict when we've given it the ability
to think rather than a mindless being that doesn't know what to do.
And if we play our cards right, we can even negotiate or threaten it."

"Sure, that would be fine if it created a good person like you predicted. What would you have done if it had turned out to be completely evil?"

"Evil is much easier to control than good. The differences between
them simply lie in what cards you use to make deals with them."

This bastard, Tsuchimikado cursed to himself. In the first place,
Aleister's idea of how to treat humans was far removed from how
normal people thought.

"Is there a point to going so far to wrangle the *i*th School District?"
he finally asked.

"Yeah, the *i*th School District is a threat to Academy City. But we've
got other threats to worry about on the outside, too. You were the

212 A CERTAIN MAGICAL INDEX

one who tolerated this incident, and now the world is slowly beginning to go mad. Whatever the reason was, you took down an official member of the English Puritan Church with the help of Anti-Skill. The people at St. George's Cathedral aren't just gonna sit back and allow it. You can't possibly think that this one city could defeat all the world's sorcerers, do you?"

Aleister maintained a smile despite Tsuchimikado's threatening voice.

"Sorcerers would be insignificant if we only took control of *it*."

"It?" Tsuchimikado frowned.

The *i*th School District, the Five Elements Society, was certainly an unearthly existence. They didn't know where in Academy City was safe and where was dangerous. But that was still just limited to within Academy City. Involuntary diffusion fields only developed around espers.

When he thought that far, he suddenly felt a chill run down his spine.

Wait...just a minute...

Once again, he thought about the Five Elements Society—that conglomeration of involuntary diffusion fields.

Like infrared or high-frequency waves, it was right there, but you couldn't observe it...

A life-form created from the aggregate of a certain kind of power, existing in a different phase from humans.

Motoharu Tsuchimikado knew it.

He knew exactly the word used for this concept in sorcery.

No...An angel?

No, that couldn't be it. If the residents of the *i*th School District—Hyouka Kazakiri, for example—could be expressed as an angel, then the city that she lived in...that meant it was...

"Aleister...You can't be trying to construct an artificial heaven, can you?!"

"Well."

Aleister answered with one word, in a bored tone.

Creating an artificial heaven...No. If you could create one using only scientific ability, you couldn't use existing words like *heaven* or *netherworld* for it. It would be an entirely new world, a *plane*, for which nothing—not Kabbalah, not Buddhism, not Crossism, not Shinto, not Hindu—had a name for.

And the construction of this *plane* would mean the annihilation of magic.

Suppose, for example, that the fundamental values of buoyancy and lift changed greatly.

Under such conditions, amateurs could create an airplane from a blueprint drawn on paper, but it wouldn't ever fly. But if you got a professional—perhaps a sorcerer—to create a proper airplane based off a blueprint...it still wouldn't fly. And if it did just keep running along the runway and manage to get into the air, it would immediately flop over and be destroyed.

That's what would happen to a magical environment if a new world appeared. If sorcerers tried to use magic, their bodies would explode. The temples and cathedrals supported with magic would lose their pillars and collapse in on themselves.

This would apply to *every* religion.

Think about it—every religion and form of sorcery follows rules. The rules, of course, aren't the same. Buddhism has its own rules and Crossism its own. The world is like an enormous canvas with paints of many colors overlapping one another.

Every religion operated under some type of rules. That didn't change.

And if a new plane were to appear in the midst of those rules, which were already set in stone, what would happen? The formerly stable rules would be messed up, and sorcerers would find themselves engulfed in their own accidents.

No matter how wonderful a violinist is, if the instrument itself is badly tuned, she won't be able to perform well at all. That's what it meant to mess up these rules.

The key to the *i*th School District seemed to be incomplete for the moment, but when it was, sorcerers would no longer be able to use magic within Academy City.

Academy City was like a microcosm of the world.

Its ability development would expand to a global scale, and once everyone in the world had awakened to supernatural abilities, the entire world would be covered with involuntary diffusion fields. The ith School District, too, would blanket the whole world, having been limited to only Academy City.

No...

Preparations for *that* had long since been completed.

The ten thousand man-made espers, the Sisters, that Kamijou had saved...They had been sent to establishments cooperating with Academy City all over the world to recover. Tsuchimikado had already doubted the need for sending them all outside the city for physical adjustments—and here was his answer.

That insane experiment that had used Accelerator hadn't been a plan to Shift him into Level Six at all. It was to mass-produce espers and place them throughout the world. In order to send them outside in the most natural way possible, the Radio Noise project was destroyed, and even the project that used that as a front, the Level Six Shift experiment, was crushed. With those two incidents as a front, the Sisters had been spread across the planet.

The scheme had clearly been successful. In reality, the various Church factions, not least of all the English Puritans, had not noticed that the Sisters had been distributed outside the city walls. And even if they had, they wouldn't be able to grasp its importance. They wouldn't think of it as anything more than the cleanup for one of the city's private problems.

Espers had been placed throughout the entire world like antennae for the ith School District.

Now, if they could completely control the incomplete ith School District and bring forth a new plane...

The appearance of this plane would cause every sorcerer to self-destruct by his own hand...

And espers wouldn't be affected in the slightest by the involuntary diffusion fields.

If it came to that, the result of any wars between the worlds of science and magic was clear. Actually, it wouldn't even get to that point in the first place. It was like shooting the heads of enemies who had raised their hands one at a time.

No...

After thinking that far, he shook his head.

Is this really Aleister's final goal? Maybe, maybe not. I get the feeling that he would smile and say that was all just preparations for something bigger. And it's possible he's not thinking about any of this.

I don't know.

Aleister—who appeared both male and female, both old and young, both holy and sinful—connoted all human possibilities. Thus, he couldn't predict how the person thought. It wouldn't be an exaggeration to say that he held every opinion humanity could possibly conceive.

He shuddered, then grumbled like he had been the one to be defeated.

"Hmph. If the English Puritans knew about this, they'd open fire immediately. At this point, I can sympathize a bit with Sherry Cromwell. Having gotten a taste of your words and actions, I realize she wasn't purely the bad guy here. She was respectable—another person who stood up to protect the world she lived in."

"Do not inflate such absurd delusions. Not a hair on my head wishes to make an enemy of the Church. And to create an artificial heaven, like you are thinking, would require knowledge of the original kingdom first. That is the territory of the occult, of course. For me, a scientist, it is out of my expertise."

"Nonsense. Nobody on this planet knows more than you. Right...?"

Tsuchimikado's lips twisted.

"...Aleister Crowley, the sorcerer?"

Long ago, in the twentieth century, lived the greatest sorcerer known to man.

He was called both the most talented sorcerer in the world and the one who held it in the highest contempt.

And his greatest insult to sorcery in the long history of the world, which no sorcerer had ever done…

…was to abandon mastery of magic and attempt to master science.

No one knew why Aleister, the man who had stood at the pinnacle of sorcery, had abandoned everything. However, it was the greatest humiliation to the world of magic that had ever occurred. The most superior sorcerer in both name and reality had abandoned magic and tried to rely on science. In other words, Aleister had named himself representative of the culture of magic and, without anyone's permission, had raised the white flag to the culture of science.

In so doing, Aleister Crowley turned the entire world's sorcerers against him. Not only the witch-hunting English Puritans, but every single person who knew the least bit about magic, without exception.

There was a reason Stiyl hadn't seen through Aleister's facade when they met face-to-face. The English Puritan Church had been basing its pursuit of Aleister Crowley on information they'd gathered over many long years—but this information was all planted by Aleister. Since their information source was nonsensical, it would do them no good to investigate him either magically or scientifically—nothing would add up. As a result, he was treated as someone who happened to have the same name or someone who was using it as an alias.

Tsuchimikado had to marvel at the skill and guts that brought him this far. Tsuchimikado would never have crossed such a dangerous bridge even if it *were* possible. That was just the extent of the gap between their strengths.

"This is gonna come off totally as my being a sore loser, but let me warn you about one thing, Aleister."

"Hmm. Let's hear it, then."

"Do you know the term *hard luck*?"

"It is another way to say *rotten luck*, correct?"

"It has another meaning behind it—the strong luck with which one will always overcome hellish misfortune, no matter how many times one encounters it." Tsuchimikado gave a little grin. "I don't know what you're thinking, and I probably wouldn't understand if you explained it. But if you're really set on making use of that Imagine Breaker, then you'd better be prepared. If you confront it with shallow conviction, that right hand will devour your world of illusions."

When he finished, the teleporter entered the room, as if timed.

Escorted by the girl, thirty centimeters shorter than him, Tsuchimikado left the building.

Now alone in the room, the man floating upside down said to himself,

"Hmm. The world I believed in has long since been destroyed."

Index and Hyouka Kazakiri sat next to each other on a couch in the hospital waiting room.

Hospitals generally don't allow pets, so the cat was waiting back in the student dorm. The sister in white swung her arms lazily like she was uncomfortable, maybe because the cat wasn't with her for once.

Kazakiri said to her in a withdrawn voice, "U-umm...Aren't you going to fix your skirt?"

"Huh?" Index looked at her legs. She had taken out the safety pin in it during the battle with the golem, so the skirt part was open on one side like a cheongsam.

"It's...It looks really b-bold and defenseless. It's kind of dangerous...you know?"

"But we got caught up in all those problems, so I figured I'd leave it for later. Hyouka, does it really look that weird?"

"I-I think so...It looks really weird. You were already suspicious... and now you look more so."

"Already?" Index lowered her eyelids. She got the gist of how she was feeling.

Then, something strange happened.

As she gave a vague, wry smile, Hyouka's outline blurred, like mist wavering in the wind. Index felt like the girl's body would disperse and melt into the air if she wasn't paying attention.

Kazakiri's contours blurred a lot, then a little, in front of the surprised Index. Not a second went by without her blurring like that.

"H-Hyouka, you're…"

"Umm…yeah…well, a lot happened, so…" She was smiling. "My body, it's really…like a big, rolled-up ball of supernatural abilities… I'll always be unstable like this, no matter what…since I won't exist forever…," said Kazakiri, but Index considered a different possibility.

The Imagine Breaker.

The ultimate right hand that could cancel any preternatural powers at a touch, whether good or evil.

"No, that isn't it," assured Kazakiri, judging her thoughts from her expression. "I didn't come into contact with his power…And if I had…I would have just disappeared without a trace right then. So it isn't his fault…," she said gently, though her voice was uneven.

"…It's all right. I may disappear, but it won't happen that soon… My body is…made of the power of 2.3 million people…So in terms of life span, I have many times longer than you all to live…"

She was smiling.

Index knew she should feel reassured, combining her knowledge with Kazakiri's words…

…but for some reason, a heavy unease settled in her chest.

Without making any noise, Kazakiri's outline continued to blur back and forth. The flickering somehow seemed to be getting larger, little by little, as if a thick fog were steadily lifting.

"Oh…right, I forgot…This might be…important to you, but… maybe not…"

"What is it?"

"About his power…I don't…know the details or anything, but…"

Hyouka Kazakiri stopped for a moment there, then finally told her…

…about how Touma Kamijou's right hand couldn't be explained by supernatural abilities.

"Huh?" Index froze in her seat.

"Wait. Wait a minute, Hyouka. That can't be. Because…because there's no hand like that in sorcery, either! I have the knowledge from 103,000 books in my head, but I don't know of any rule-breaking powers like that! If it's not a supernatural ability, then how do you explain it?"

"Sor…cery?…I don't know…what that is, but…" Kazakiri smiled faintly. "At the very least, it isn't an ability…I mean, my body is made up of…the powers of every esper in Academy City. If he were an esper…then that tiny little power would have gotten into my body, and I would have fallen apart in the blink of an eye…"

Now that she mentions it… Index thought back. It didn't seem like his power was something that Academy City had made. It wasn't artificial—it was completely natural, and he'd had it since birth.

Then…then just what is his power? she thought.

It wasn't sorcery, and it wasn't an ability. It was like a power from another dimension.

"Okay, well…I need to get going soon…," Kazakiri said, rising from the couch.

The thoughts swirling in Index's mind all blew away and her head bounced back up. Suddenly she didn't like this. Get going? **Where was she going back to?** Thinking normally, it was getting late, so one would think she was going home…but Index, for no reason, couldn't help but think that casual utterance held more meaning than she realized.

Kazakiri smiled gently to her. She looked like a child who had been left behind by her parents.

"You don't need…to worry. Even if my body disappears…I won't… die or anything. You just won't be able to see me…or feel me, that's all. Even if…you don't understand…I'll always be at your side…"

Why is she saying something like this now? Index wondered.

She was talking like they would never be able to meet again.

Index didn't know why.

Hyouka Kazakiri hadn't said anything that sounded like a clear farewell.

"Hyouka!!" Index shouted in spite of herself to Kazakiri's receding back.

She turned around slowly and asked,

"What is it?"

"Tomorrow...you'll come and play tomorrow, too, right?" asked Index, about to burst into tears.

Hyouka Kazakiri smiled.

She smiled and answered.

"Of course."

AFTERWORD

Good to meet you, those of you who decided on a whim to buy all six volumes at once.

And hello again to those of you who have been buying each volume as it comes out.

I'm Kazuma Kamachi.

So, this is volume six. The main character, heroines, enemies, the ending, and the backstage are depicted in a strangely different way from the series thus far. As for how exactly the ball is changing up on you, well, you'll just have to read the book.

The occult keyword this time around is *golem*.

A lot of people will think of a golem like a slime, in that they're relatively popular in video games, and thus aren't used as a final boss—but apparently actual (well, not *actual*, but you know what I mean) golems were really pretty fantastic. Especially the part about all of it being magic based on the mystique of God's creation of man, and how followers of Kabbalah were the only ones able to use it and master it.

It's kind of like alchemy's philosopher's stone, in that having it proves that you're number one. I mean, they even had safety mechanisms, so if you ever wanted to destroy it, you could easily reduce it back to dirt. It feels like the basis for giant robots frequently having a self-destruct button.

I'd like to give great thanks to my illustrator, Mr. Haimura, and the editor, Mr. Miki. Thank you both for not discarding my works despite being so extremely busy.

And a big thank-you to all of my readers who took the time out to pick up my books. It is, without a doubt, because of all of you that I am able to eat white rice.

Now then, as I give thanks for this book reaching your hands, and as I quietly hope that it won't ever leave them, today, at this moment, I lay down my pen.

In the end, the so-called *killer of illusions* actually protected hers, didn't he?

Kazuma Kamachi